# DYING MOON

## SHAWN OETZEL

# DYING MOON

*by*

**Shawn Oetzel**

2nd Edition 2018

1st Edition Trade Paperback 2014

All Rights Reserved

**Dark Recesses Press**

657 Craigen Road

Newburgh, Ontario

Canada K0K 2S0

Edited by Wayne Goodchild

Cover design by Bob Freeman

Library & Archives Canada ISBN

978-1-988837-10-9

# ALSO BY SHAWN OETZEL

*The Adventures of Captain Kitchen*

*The Agency*

*Scrunchies From Hell*

*Faith and a Hammer*

# DEDICATION

*For my children*
*- Connor, Alysh & Sheadon -*
*Dreams really can come true.*

# Acknowledgments

A special thanks goes out to friend and fellow writer, Donnie Light, who is always available for some advice or a quick word of encouragement. I look forward to working with you more in the future. Lunch is on me next time.

To fellow writers David Lee Summers and B.T. Robertson, thank you for always being there with a kind word, invaluable advice and support.

A special thanks needs to go out to my best friend and computer guru, Brad Clauson, who saved *Dying Moon* from the black hole of a crashed hard drive. Brad - thanks for saving my manuscript and in turn keeping my dream alive. The next few Crab-Fests are definitely on me!

Last, but certainly not least, my family. It is your love and support which makes this moment all the sweeter. Your patience and understanding of the eccentricities of having a writer for a husband and father helped ease the burden of working towards a life long dream. I share every ounce of success with you, because without having all of you in my life, none of this would have been possible or even worthwhile. I love you guys.

# TABLE OF CONTENTS

# —Chapter 1

Kalen Or'wain walked up the worn path that cut through the lush gardens and led up the hill to where the council chambers were located in the Keep of the Full Moon. Normally an evening stroll through the serene garden would have calmed him. Tonight though, the cool air brought in on the evening breeze left him chilled. At least he hoped it was the wind and not the nervous energy tingling deep down in his gut, warning him something was amiss causing his exposed skin to prickle.

He lowered his head, making an effort to concentrate on taking one step at a time. He noticed the beautiful violet lilies that lined the path he was walking. The flowers glistening in the moonlight were like a soothing balm, and he refocused his attention on the task at hand.

He had received word that the Elven Council had requested his presence via an official courier barely an hour before. He had no idea why he had been summoned, but with the lateness of hour, he was fairly certain whatever the council wanted with him, it was not going to be good news.

He had been at his home on Lake Alorien, having just come off duty, when he had been summoned. As the Captain of the Royal Guard, it was his job to maintain the Royal Family's security. It was a duty he took very seriously, and one he had performed flawlessly with honor since his promotion to captain two years before. He was on his deck, overlooking the beautiful and serene Lake Alorien and enjoying an evening glass of wine, when a knock on his door startled him from his musings.

The lake was beautiful, its surface calm and placid. He often sat on his deck staring across the water for hours. Legend had it the Moon Goddess Alorien would come down to bathe in the waters, hence the name, Lake Alorien. He was not a great believer in legends, but could not deny the calming effect the water had on him.

The moonlight was not reflected off the surface of the lake so much as it was absorbed. It was also well known that the waters from this very lake, when handled by a trained Magisiter, had uncanny healing powers. He was uninterested in all the old legends or the mysteries of the healing water; all he knew was when he stared out over the beauty of Lake Alorien, he felt more at peace than at any other time. He felt at home.

"Who could that be at this hour?" he had wondered.

He remembered taking a final glance out over the beauty of the lake as an odd sense of foreboding overtook him before he went back through his cottage to answer the knocking. When he opened the front door, he was startled to see the forest-green uniform of an official council page. The young Elf was doing his best to try and look dignified, but Kalen could tell by the way that he shifted his weight from one foot to the other every few seconds, he was quite nervous.

He had given the page a cursory glance, and though he noticed the young Elf's edginess, did not mention it or try to play it down for fear he would embarrass the young courier. The page stood at attention, or at least what he thought was attention, and handed over a sealed parchment. Kalen took the official letter without saying a word. He glanced at the seal, and was a bit confused when he saw the Elven Council's official mark. This was odd, because the council only met for the week of the full moon each month, and the council meeting had been over for hours. Kalen, being the cautious Elf he was, had taken this as a bad omen.

He gestured to the young Elf to enter while he read the letter. The page politely thanked the elder commander and waited just inside the cottage door while Kalen continued to inspect the official parchment.

He walked over to the fireplace in the large hearth set into the stone chimney at the back wall of the front room. The soft glow from the fire gave the cottage a very homey feel. This quickly changed as he stoked the fire to increase the light. The page stood quietly at attention.

Even though Kalen, as Captain of the Royal Guard, was one of the most celebrated heroes of the Elven people, this room of his home was sparsely furnished. There was a pair of swords crossed over the fireplace. They looked old, but even the most casual observer could easily tell they were well taken care of. There was a simple couch and one chair set out in front of the fireplace. A table that was worn and tarnished sat between them. Along the wall, to the right of the fireplace, was a portrait of a very distinguished looking Elf all decked out in a full ceremonial Royal Guard uniform. This was Kalen's Father, Duncan Or'wain.

Duncan Or'wain had been Captain of the Royal Guard for twenty years, and had died protecting the King from a would-be assassin. Some said Duncan's ghost still roamed the palace, carrying out his duty of protecting the Royal Family, honor bound even after death.

Kalen caught the page staring at the portrait of his father. He knew as a court page the young Elf had more than likely heard the rumors and tales of Duncan's ghost. The page seemed mesmerized by the eerily lifelike portrait. Even though Kalen was slightly unnerved by the parchment he had yet to read and still clutched in his hand, he decided to have a bit of fun at the page's expense.

"Do not look directly at the eyes, he might consider that a challenge," he said forcing down a chuckle.

The sound of Kalen's voice caught the page off guard, and he jumped, losing his balance causing him to stumble into the front door. This time Kalen could not hold back the laughter, and he tried to muffle the sounds of his chuckling behind his hand.

"I'm sorry. I did not mean to frighten you. Please come and sit," he said gesturing towards the only chair in the room.

The page, shaken and embarrassed, sat down and tried to apologize for his clumsiness, "I'm sorry sir. I... I was not paying attention. Please forgive my rude behavior."

"Think nothing of it. The hour is late, and I am sure you have had a long day already," he said soothingly, trying to put the young page at ease. "I will be finished with this letter in a moment, and then you can be on your way."

With that said, he turned back to the fire, and focused his attention on the ominous parchment. He snapped the official seal of the Elven Council with his fingers, unrolled the parchment, and read by the light of the fire. The message was short but direct. It read:

*The Elven Council of Ten requests your attendance to discuss a matter of great importance to the Elven people and those of the Human race. Tell no one of this meeting, and come at once.*

Grale Ash' lewn

Chief Counselor of the Elven Council

"The Human race?" he whispered confused.

The Elven people had not had dealings with the Humans in hundreds of years, so Kalen was immediately intrigued. What could be so important it would cause the Elven Council to reconvene at such a late hour, and then cause them to meddle in the affairs of Humans? His intrigue started to turn into worry. He turned to the page, who sensing a change in the captain's mood, stood up at attention.

"Return to the Council, and tell them that I will be at the council chambers within the hour," he ordered, his voice having a slight edge to it.

The page had heard that tone before. It was the voice Kalen used when commanding his men of the Royal Guard, and it left no room for questions.

"Yes sir," the young Elf answered quickly. The page swallowed hard and nodded briskly, seeming to sense that something important was about to take place.

The page showed himself out, and Kalen watched as the young courier disappeared into the night on his way back to the council.

He had stood still for a moment, pondering the message, which had been written on the parchment. He had heard the rumblings at the palace of a problem. He was a Royal Guard though, and did not have time for idle gossip. If it was information he was supposed to have, then his superiors would fill him in. Well, it seemed they might be about to.

He had waited a few minutes more before going to his bedroom to put on a fresh uniform. It would not do for him to appear before the council looking confused and disheveled, even though that was the way he felt. The message from the council had shaken him more than he would have liked to admit. He was disappointed in himself as he saw his hands tremble slightly while buttoning up his red Royal Guard uniform coat.

"Some captain I am. One mysterious parchment and I fall apart like some first year cadet. If the council could only see me now," he said to himself whimsically as he buckled the belt that held his sword around his waist.

He ran his hand through his long, blonde hair to smooth it down, and glanced at the mirror hanging above his dresser and was disappointed in seeing the image before him.

"I look as tired as I feel, but it will have to do, I guess. The council can revoke my rank if it likes. What do they expect on this short notice?"

That is how he came to be walking through the beautifully tended gardens of the council's keep. The moon roses were in full bloom that evening, and their roughly jasmine scent filled the cool night air. It was summer, but it had been unseasonably cool the last week or so and he shivered as a slight breeze blew through the garden. He was still unsure if this was a physical reaction to the coolness in the air, or the nervousness that was starting to overcome his sense. He hoped the shiver was not a portent of things to come.

He could see the great stone keep just ahead, sparkling in the moonlight. The place commanded respect by its very presence. The Keep of the Full Moon was the building where every major decision concerning the Elven Nation and its people was made. Even the beloved Elven King did not make a move or pass judgment without first consulting the Elven Council of Ten, and now that same council wanted to meet with him in private and after hours. This thought left him more than a little unnerved.

The actual keep did not look all that remarkable when seeing it from the outside. It was what took place on the inside that made the Keep of the Full Moon the focal point for the entire Elven Nation.

The keep was perfectly round, and made of steel gray stone. It was the oldest building in the Elven Nation as it had been constructed countless centuries before.

If one looked at the keep from up high, they would see the circular shape did indeed mirror that of a full moon. The shape of the keep, and the fact the Elven Council met here once a month during the full moon phase, gave the famed keep its name.

The inside was designed in a concentric circular fashion. The outer and largest circle held rooms for meetings with the various departments within the Elven government. The next circular hall was the living area for the pages and couriers of the Elven Council, with the following circle being the rooms for the actual members of the Elven Council of Ten. At the very center of the keep was the largest room. This was where the council deliberated, and landmark decisions concerning the Elven people were made. That very room was Kalen's destination.

He stood in the garden staring up at the keep. Having to cross the last few feet seemed like such a daunting task in that moment. The air seemed charged with expectancy, and he did not know if it was a premonition or not, but he definitely had a bad feeling about what he was about hear. It was with this last thought weighing heavily on his mind that he crossed the last few feet to the Keep of the Full Moon. Trepidation followed him with every step he took.

When he at last stood before the great wooden doors of the keep, he finally remembered to breathe. He had not been this nervous since he was a young private just starting out in the Royal Guard.

"Come on man, pull yourself together," he admonished under his breath, frustrated with himself for acting so skittish. "How bad can this be? If it was really important it would not just be me who was summoned. This is probably just another security check to see how fast the Royal Guard could mobilize. There is probably nothing to worry about."

He would look back on this moment some time later and he could not remember a time in his life when he had been so wrong.

Though the Keep of the Full Moon held some of the most important dignitaries of the Elven government, no guards were ever posted. This was a tradition among the council members, which dated far back to the time of the First Council. The Elven Council saw having guards at the keep as a sign of weakness. They felt if they were not safe within the very heart of the Elven Nation, then they were simply not doing their job. This was a point of view he had argued against many times, but always kept coming up short. It was against his nature as the Captain of the Royal Guard to be so trusting. He was cautious almost to a fault at times, but it was that caution which had kept him alive through many campaigns.

The doors to the Keep of the Full Moon were made from the wood of the great Ash trees from the forest the Elves called home. The wood was considered sacred, so naturally it had its place here at the keep. He grabbed the curved black iron handle, and with a final deep breath opened the door and walked in.

The entrance foyer was a well lit room with many cushioned chairs lining the walls. These were for visitors to relax in before they were granted an audience with the council. Kalen did not have the luxury of being able to relax at this moment though.

There were doors to his right and left. He knew from experience those doors led to the many conference rooms and offices of the Elven Council. It was the door that stood directly in front of him he was most interested in however, as this door was the one that would take him directly to the Council of Ten's main audience chamber. He also knew from experience this door only opened from the other side. This way no unwanted visitors could just walk in and disrupt an all-important council meeting. A person or visitor had to wait until they were summoned before they were allowed entrance to the central chamber. This was the reason he had sent the page ahead of him, so the council would be expecting him, and he could be summoned right away. He was not disappointed.

Immediately after closing the entrance door, he heard the unmistakable sound of hinges creaking with age. He turned his attention back to the council chamber door only to see the same young page who had brought him the original message from the council to his cottage earlier in the evening.

The young Elf bowed respectfully to Kalen before saying, "The council is expecting you. Please follow me, sir, and I will take you to them immediately."

The nervousness the page had had in his voice earlier this evening was still there, but there was also a hint of something else as well. If Kalen did not know any better he would have guessed it to be fear.

"Well then, let us not keep the council waiting," he said. He was anxious to get this meeting over with. That bad feeling he had had out in the garden still lingered in the back of his mind.

The page nodded his assent, and without another word, turned and led him down the hall. The corridor to the inner council chamber was lit by glowing torches, which ran along the wall on both sides every five feet. In between each torch were paintings of all the Elven council members who had served on the Council of Ten over the years. The artist's rendering of these portraits was astounding. They were so lifelike, he would not have been surprised if one of the painting's subjects would nod and wave in welcome as they walked by. This thought only added to his unease as he and the page made their way down the corridor.

The walk was shorter than he had remembered, but then again he had only been in the council chamber a handful of times, and not since he had been promoted to Captain of the Royal Guard two years before. When they reached the entrance of the council chamber, the page excused himself and went in ahead to announce him.

He was nervous, more nervous than he could ever remember being. He was sweating heavily under his dress uniform, and he was starting to feel a little queasy as he realized he was about to be addressed by the Elven Council of Ten in some sort of secret meeting. He was a steadfast and experienced soldier though, and if he could face a suicide charge by crazed assassins trying to get to the Royal Family, then he was sure he could handle hearing whatever it was the council needed to tell him.

The young page returned, and with a quick wave, motioned for Kalen to enter.

"The council is ready to see you now, sir," the young Elf said reverently. The tone in his voice was not lost on Kalen, as he too was feeling a bit unworthy to be meeting the much-heralded Elven Council.

He stepped through the doorway and entered the council chamber. All feelings of nervousness fled from him as his training took over and he became the dignified Captain of the Royal Guard.

The council chamber was round since it was the hub of the Keep of the Full Moon. It was not an overly large chamber, but the immensity of centuries of tradition made one think the room was larger than it actually was. The air seemed thick with the history of countless decisions that had been made and passed on to the Elven people by the famed Council of Ten. This chamber was the heart of the organism that made up the Elven Nation. The decisions made here were the heartbeat that pumped the all-important lifeblood into the Elven Society and their government. Kalen looked up, and prepared himself to face the council.

# —CHAPTER 2

Joseph Stanfield stood looking out his forty-third floor office suite window watching the humid summer night light up with the angry flashes of lightning as the storm released its fury on the unsuspecting populace of Los Angeles. He stood motionless like a stone gargoyle perched high atop an old Gothic structure as he watched evening stragglers scurrying about like ants trying to gain cover from the falling rain.

"Stupid little peons."

He walked over to the large mahogany bar, which made up one whole wall of his rather plush office and filled a glass with ice and Jack Daniels. He liked the potent whiskey; it was strong and powerful just like he was.

He took his drink and once again stood in front of the window to watch the fury of the storm. The rain was pouring down in sheets. It sounded like pellets as it bounced off the glass of his office window. A new wave of thunder rolled across the dark Los Angeles sky, when the intercom on his desk buzzed. He smiled with a predatory glint in his eye knowing it was his new secretary. She was pretty young, pretty dumb, and had a pretty nice body in his self-inflated opinion.

He ignored the buzzing, knowing this would force his secretary to come and speak with him in person. She would have to come into his lair where he was in complete control.

There was a tiny knock at the door, and when he turned, he saw his young secretary standing in the doorway to his office. He smiled the smile of a hunter knowing it has its prey cornered.

"Mr. Stanfield, I am leaving for the night. Is there anything I can get you before I go?"

*Oh, my dear, if you only knew,* he thought to himself, but to her he said, "No, that's fine. You go home. Try to stay dry out there. It's coming down pretty hard."

"I will. I'll see you tomorrow Mr. Stanfield," she replied.

"Oh by the way, I am starting a new project this week so be prepared to work some late nights," he said with just a hint of luridness. It was enough to put his secretary on guard, but so much the better. He liked to intimidate people, and that especially included women he planned on seducing.

"Sure Mr. Stanfield. I understand."

There was hesitation in her voice, but she turned, walked out of the office, and then down the hallway to catch the elevator. He watched lasciviously as her hips swayed back and forth. This brought yet another predatory grin to his face.

Once his pretty and soon-to-be plaything left, he returned to his inner thoughts as the storm raged on. He finished his drink and made another. He watched the lightning blast across the night sky and took a sip of his whiskey. The ice tinkled against his glass. He liked that sound. It reminded him of power.

After the drink, watching the storm, and still feeling good about the events of the last hour, he decided it was time to go home and get some rest. This upcoming week had the potential to be quite busy after all. He grabbed his briefcase and coat, and then headed down the hall.

Finding himself standing before the elevator he grumbled unintelligibly as his impatience grew. He pushed the down button again as if by hitting it multiple times he could will the elevator to arrive faster. When the doors finally opened, he stepped in, turned and hit the button that would send the elevator down to the parking garage where his Mercedes awaited him; God how he loved that car.

When the elevator finally reached the bottom level where the garage was located, and the doors opened, the first thing he noticed was that some of the lights were burned out, and the garage was blanketed in shadows.

"Worthless maintenance, I swear. Is everyone incompetent around here?"

The smell of stale air with an underlying hint of motor oil rolled over him like a heavily polluted ocean wave. He grimaced in disgust as if the whole idea of having to park his beloved Mercedes in something as mundane as an underground garage was beneath him. He hated anything associated with the common man. He was now a Senior Vice President after all, and the only thing he truly cared about was gaining more power.

His car was parked the farthest away from the elevator, but that would soon change with his promotion. The garage was not overly large, but the sheer inconvenience of having to walk the distance from the elevator to his Mercedes was enough to put him in a bad mood. The mere perception of having to have the farthest parking space was unacceptable. He laughed knowingly since after tonight, this would no longer be an issue.

He began making his way down the darkened aisle to his waiting sports car. As he passed the empty space reserved for the Senior Vice President he pumped his fist in a victorious salute. Starting tomorrow the coveted space would be his. He decided instead of going to his mansion he would stop by his favorite club and have another Jack Daniels.

His attention was so focused on the thought of another drink he did not notice a shadow separate itself from the darkness of the burned-out lights. He looked up ahead and glared in the general direction of his Mercedes seeing he still had a short distance to cover when he heard a loud whistling. The sound was quickly followed by a thud, and then a sharp piercing sensation in his right leg. He yelled out in pain and surprise.

Again he heard the whistling sound, and then the same thud followed by white-hot pain, this time in his left thigh. He toppled over like an aged oak tree that had been felled by a lumberjack. He watched as his briefcase went flying from his hand, scattering papers across the garage's concrete floor. The pain in his legs was excruciating. He looked down, and saw what appeared to be arrows sticking out of both his thighs.

"What the…?" was all he could think to say as he scrambled to try and get back to his feet.

Out of the shadow by his car he saw a figure appear as if it was detaching itself from the darkness. It was almost as if part of the shadow had come to life and taken a vaguely Human form.

He watched in shock as the dark figure raised its arms and pulled something back. He heard the whistling sound once again. It reminded him of the bottle rockets he would let off with his dad on the Fourth of July back home when he was a kid. That thought raced through his befuddled brain as the next thud hit him right in the chest and shoulder area. The impact was so hard he was actually thrown onto his back and he found himself lying near the now-closed elevator doors. At that moment, all he knew was pain. It was sharp and burning hot, almost tangible, like he could reach out and grab the pain and throw it away from him. He actually raised his arm to try.

The figure released the strange item that was in his hand, and it clattered loudly as it landed on the concrete of the garage floor. In the dim light, Stanfield could see it was a fairly ornate looking bow; what would probably be referred to as a long bow. His dad had been a hunter, and often took long trips with friends into remote regions to go big game hunting. On many of those excursions he would take his own bow though it did not look quite the same.

The arrow in his chest was buried almost to the fletching. He could see the feathers were black, but that seemed a moot point at the moment as an even bigger problem was approaching from the darkness. What was even more vital was the fact the pain in his legs was gone. The arrow had clipped his spine on its deadly path through his body, and he could not move or feel anything from the waist down. Realization he was in dire trouble finally set in, and he tried to yell out to the figure who was slowly approaching.

"Wh ...Wh ...Who are you? What do you want?"

The figure answered with silence. He heard a slight clanging sound as if metal was being drawn against another metal. He watched in horror as the figure pulled forth a long, slightly curved sword. It gleamed in what little light was left in the parking garage. The figure waved the sword in a complex maneuver. The blade, swishing through the stale garage air, made a noise he knew was meant to scare him. It worked. He began weeping and begging for his life.

"Please… I am a rich man… anything you want," he hated himself for being so weak, but at the moment he was out of options.

The living shadow was close enough now. Stanfield could see him smile. There was something odd about the assassin in the way he moved. It was with the grace of a dancer, and he made almost no sound as he stalked ever closer.

There was just enough light he could start to make out features as his attacker drew ever closer. He was tall – at least 6'5" and thin, but not skinny. There was a presence about the figure, an aura that gave off a sense of underlying power. His hair was a blonde Stanfield had never seen before. It certainly could not be natural, could it?

He smelled the unmistakable odor of urine, and realized that without control, his bladder had emptied. When he again raised his head, the figure was standing in front of him. He was dressed completely in black with a black suit and overcoat. He was wearing a matching black fedora as well.

Stanfield looked into the coldest blue-gray eyes he had ever seen. He was so scared he could not speak. The figure removed his hat, and that mesmerizing blonde hair fell down over the assassin's well dressed shoulders. What he saw was almost as shocking as the fact that he was lying in his own urine with arrows sticking out of his body. The man's ears were pointed! Stanfield's brain began to race to find the appropriate name; a word he had not heard since his childhood. A myth, a fairy tale figure … what was the word?

"Let me introduce myself," the figure spoke. His voice was soft, almost effeminate, but carried such an edge to it that it left no mistake as to who was in charge and what was about to happen. "I am your doom."

With that, the shadow man raised the finely crafted steel sword and slashed. So sharp was the blade's edge Stanfield never actually felt the sword slice through his abdomen spilling his intestines, but he screamed nevertheless. The figure slashed again and again in a frenzy of blood and gore. The blood flew from the blade in tiny crimson drops hitting the concrete floor in a steady pitter-patter cadence much like the rain still falling outside. A red mist surrounded the immediate area around Stanfield and his attacker. The smell of raw meat and bowel began permeating the garage.

Finally, the sword-wielding assassin stopped. He stood shaking and trying to regain his composure. From a hidden, smaller scabbard at his back, the black clad killer pulled forth a long jagged dagger. He leaned in close to stare into his victim's eyes as they slowly began to gloss over.

Amazingly, Stanfield was still alive. He stared back at the murderous stranger, and finally that word came to him. Just as the shadow assassin plunged the ornate dagger into his chest, one word rang out loudly inside his brain. His last thought before the darkness grabbed him and took hold. *Elf!*

The Elf, for that is what he truly was, looked down on the lump of flesh that was barely recognizable as Human and smiled. In his hand he held his prize. It was Stanfield's heart. Blood dripped from the now lifeless organ onto the black clad figure's hand. The Elf placed the heart in a bag he pulled from his waist. He walked back through the garage clutching his trophy tightly. He whispered some words and disappeared in a flash of light. A flash so quick and bright, it was as if someone had taken a picture. The carnage that was once Joseph Stanfield, a newly promoted Senior Vice President of ChemCo, the nation's third largest drug company, lay quietly on the cold concrete floor of the parking garage.

# CHAPTER 3

Amy Sommers opened the door to her one bedroom apartment, flushed and out of breath. She flipped the light switch on the wall located to her left, but did not wait for the electricity to take hold. She sprinted through her apartment, throwing her coat onto the couch as she tripped and stumbled through the living room on her way to the bathroom.

God she had to pee, and having to walk through the rain to get to her apartment had not helped. She struggled with the buckle of her belt momentarily as she danced around the small bathroom, and turned on its light as well. When she finally got the belt unbuckled, she slipped her pants down, and plopped down on the toilet seat so hard she almost slid off the other side. She grabbed hold of the sink, as it was the only thing within reach to steady herself, and let out a contented sigh as she was finally able to relieve the growing pressure on her bladder.

Even though she lived alone, she reached over with her right foot, and kicked the bathroom door closed. This was an old habit formed while growing up in a house with two older brothers. Privacy had been a precious commodity then, and it was something she never took lightly. When she finished, she washed up in the sink, and caught her reflection in the mirror hanging above.

She was thirty years old, but she still looked as if she had just walked off a college campus. She was someone who would never be described as beautiful, but she had a cute tomboy kind of quality she was always trying to live down. As the only female detective currently employed by Homicide Special Section I of the LAPD, being cute was definitely not an advantage.

Some would say that her eyes were a little too close together, or her mouth was just a bit too wide, and some would definitely say, her mother included, her hair was cut way too short. She had jet-black hair cut in a style similar to the old Dorothy Hamill haircut, which had been popular years before. Amy liked her hair short though. It was easy to take care of, and gave her a little more masculine look, which helped her fit in at the department. She was never going to be one of the guys, but she felt if she at least looked the part, she might gain some level of acceptance into the boys-only club.

She was also a little on the short side – only 5'3" – but she more than made up for her slight stature with a strength and determination that often made her male counterparts in the Robbery-Homicide Division more than a little uncomfortable.

Just as she finished washing her hands in the bathroom sink, the pager in her coat pocket began that incessant chirping she had grown to hate since joining the Homicide team. The pager had become a shackle, clipped to her waist instead of the more traditional shackles that fit around a suspect's wrists, which Amy had to take everywhere. She felt as if she could never get a moment's rest from its dire warning that her services were needed due to someone having died under suspicious circumstances. *This is Los Angeles, for Christ's sake, everything here is suspicious*, she thought. She always felt the people here were a little crazy, and they often times died in even crazier ways.

It took her a second to recall what happened to her coat. Then she remembered her harried sprint through her apartment on the way to salvation in the restroom. As she walked out of the bathroom feeling a bit apprehensive about checking the pager, she noticed her black suede coat balled up on the couch where she had tossed it.

"That's just great! I paid $300 dollars for that coat, and I toss it aside like a kitchen rag because I have to go pee," she said to herself, frustrated that the coat had already gotten wet from the rain, and now was thrown rather haphazardly on her living room couch.

She crossed the room, picked up the coat, and began searching through the pockets for her hated pager. She rifled through the front and side pockets with no luck. She checked the inside pocket as well, and still could not come up with the annoying little beeper.

"Well hell," she uttered in quiet frustration as she again began another search of the suede coat. "That damn thing is always around when I don't want anything to do with it, and now that I need it, it freaking disappears!"

She was a bit alarmed to hear herself swearing out loud. This was a habit she had picked up since joining the Los Angeles Police Department. She had been brought up in a strict Christian home, and that kind of language was just not tolerated. It was not until she attended the University of California that she had experimented with the more risqué use of the English language. Her friends would laugh, as she would inevitably use a less-than-acceptable word in the wrong situation. This had often been a source of slight embarrassment. Now that she was on the force though, she could swear with the best of them. What was the old phrase that her former lieutenant had used?

"Christ Amy, you swear like a drunken sailor," was what she remembered hearing from time to time.

While standing in her living room, feverishly searching her coat, and smiling at the quick memory flash of her old lieutenant, the pager again went off. The quick chirping sound was coming from somewhere near her feet. She looked down, and saw the little black box chirping away right by her foot.

The pager had fallen from the pocket as her coat had sailed through the air on its way to crash land on the couch. Shaking her head in exasperation, she bent over and scooped up the pager in her hand, and checked the number. It was just as she feared. The number code for the Robbery-Homicide Division shone brightly in the eerie greenish tint on the front of the beeper.

She debated whether or not she should even answer the page. She was off duty after all. Christ, she had put in a sixteen-hour day. What more could they want from her? She was not even on call tonight, Detective Hansen was. Couldn't anybody die in this town on somebody else's watch?

She silently reprimanded herself for being so callous. She was just tired from her long day, and from her adventure in the bathroom. The last thing she wanted right then was to have to restore the walls a homicide detective must keep in place in order to do their job objectively. All she wanted to do was grab a cold beer from her refrigerator, and pass out quietly in her bed. With the sound of the pager though, she knew that option was not going to be in her near future. Her long, tiring day was about to turn into an even longer, and more than likely, exhausting night.

She went to her kitchen, which was right off the living room, picked up her phone that was hanging on the wall, and dialed Robbery-Homicide's number so she could check in. She knew the number by heart what with having so much practice. The phone rang twice before someone on the other end answered.

"That was quick," Amy said, talking to herself.

"Hello LAPD, Robbery-Homicide Division," a tired male voice answered.

The gruff voice belonged to Sergeant Kelley. He was in charge of the desk during the night shift. A fifteen-year veteran of the LAPD, he had been shot in the line of duty eight years before. He had surprised a drug dealer on a routine traffic stop. The drug dealer, a seventeen-year old kid, pulled out a 9mm, and shot Officer Kelley twice in the chest. Luckily, Kelley had been wearing his body armor or he would have been dead before he hit the ground. Unfortunately, the second bullet from the kid's gun had grazed off Officer Kelley's Kevlar vest, and entered his left shoulder. The wound had not been life threatening, but the bullet had caused some nerve damage that left Officer Kelley with minimal use of his left arm. He had been in charge of the desk at the station ever since.

"Hey Kelley, this is Detective Sommers. I just got paged."

"Hey back, Sommers," Officer Kelley replied jovially. "I will transfer you over to Homicide Section I."

"Thanks, Sarge. The Dodgers winning tonight?" she asked knowing this would get a rise out of her fellow officer.

Officer Kelley was a lifelong frustrated Dodger's fan by his own account. He loved the team, but never had anything nice to say about them.

"Heck no! Those losers couldn't hit their way out of a wet paper bag. Hold on, and let me transfer you before I get really angry," he said in mock frustration.

Amy could hear Kelley push a button on the phone from his end, and her phone began ringing again. This time it was answered after only one ring.

"Wow, you guys are really on the ball tonight," she blurted out before the person on the other end could even say hello.

"Huh? Sommers? Is that you? Just where have you been? I have been paging you all night!" the loud, angry voice on the other end belonged to Detective Hansen, the on-call Homicide Detective for the evening.

Next to Amy, Detective Hansen was the youngest member of the Robbery-Homicide Division. He had been a patrol officer, who had worked his way into Robbery-Homicide. He was well respected by the other officers and readily accepted as one of their own. She was a little envious of the relationship he was able to develop with his fellow officers so quickly. It seemed no matter how hard she tried, she just did not fit in. She figured it had something to do with the fact that she had breasts. Though she and Hansen were not best friends, they did have a respect for each other. Hansen was about the only person on the homicide team she got along with, and Hansen was definitely the only other detective who treated her as an equal.

"Back off, Hansen," she retorted. Her blood began to boil at his gruff tone. "You only paged me twice, and it has only been ten minutes."

"Yeah, well it feels a heck of a lot longer than that," Hansen replied, his voice still rising in agitation.

"Look Hansen, either stop yelling at me for not being Little Miss Punctuality and tell me why you paged me or shut your mouth and let me get back to my beer."

Her response must have caught Detective Hansen off guard, and there was a momentary pause on the line before she could hear him take a deep breath to help regain his composure.

"Hey, I'm sorry, Sommers. It has been a crazy night," Hansen's voice had calmed considerably, but Amy thought she could detect a hint of apprehension. He cleared his throat, which added a nice dramatic pause. He then uttered the last words she wanted to hear, "There's been another one."

She closed her eyes and shook her head in resignation.

"Damn," she whispered under her breath. "When and where?" she asked. Her so-called Detective Mode was starting to kick in.

"A body was found about an hour ago, some big wig over at ChemCo," Hansen said as he dejectedly gave the information to her. "I thought you would want in."

"I'm on my way," she replied. She was about to hang up when she thought better, and in a quiet tone said, "Hey Hansen, thanks for the call."

"Yeah," he answered tiredly before hanging up the phone.

She hung her own phone back up on the kitchen wall as well, and calmly walked back to the living room to grab her already wet coat. Once she put it on, she gave her apartment one last longing look, wondering if she would be home anytime soon. After a deep breath, Detective Sommers turned her lights out, and prepared to walk back out through the pouring rain to get to her car.

"God I hate the sick ones," she said to herself as she pulled her coat up over her head, and made a similar mad dash to her car that just moments before she had made across her living room. It was going to be a long night after all.

# —CHAPTER 4

The first thing Kalen noticed as he faced the council was that out of the ten members, only three were present. This immediately put him on edge. He could only guess why the other members were not there. Either this meeting had been set up so quickly, the other members had not had time to get there or the matter at hand was so grave and secret these three members were the only ones who needed to be involved. He desperately hoped whatever he had been summoned for, it was not so serious or potentially upsetting to the Elven populace, that even council members needed to be kept in the dark.

The three members of the Elven Council of Ten he was facing right then were the three most prominent and arguably the most powerful. Grale Ash'lewn was in charge as always. Grale had been the Chief Councilor since before Kalen was born. Other than the King, Grale was the most respected Elf in all the Elven Nation. He oversaw much of the day-to-day operation of the Elven Government. The King was the actual face of the nation, but Grale was the soul. Not a decision was made concerning the Elven people that he did not have a say in.

To the Chief Councilor's right sat Luna Caer'run. She was the Chief Magister for the Elven Nation, which in turn made her the keeper of the magic. She was perhaps the most powerful Elf he had ever known. Her abilities far outshone any other when magic was concerned.

Luna had been nominated to the council during the previous year. She was the youngest councilor, but when she spoke most listened. Among her duties, she was the magical advisor to the King along with being the Headmistress of the Elven College of Magic. Although she was the youngest to ever hold these posts, none would argue against her qualifications. Many among the Elven people claimed Luna was the most gifted Magister the Elves had seen since before the Time of Separation.

Just to Grale's left sat the last of the three, General Braden Brandy'wine. He was the head of the standing Elven Army. If there was a more solidly built or put together Elf, then Kalen had not met him. Braden was as honorable and as loyal as they came. If he had a shortcoming, it was that he was too militaristic. Braden believed everything could be handled with a sword and brute force. This stand had more than once put him at odds with other members of the council, especially Grale, but it was not surprising to see the general here when such an apparently important event had transpired.

Kalen stood motionless and at attention with his head bowed in respect and reverence before the three council members. It was not until he heard Grale's voice that he looked up to meet the council members' gazes.

"Well met, Kalen Or'wain." Grale spoke with his usual tone of authority. "Your haste in making it to this somewhat unconventional meeting is greatly appreciated."

"Thank you Chief Councilor. I am always willing to come when the council calls," he answered, as he desperately tried to keep his voice from shaking. He was nervous, and the tension in the air of the council chamber was starting to grate on what was left of his already frayed nerves.

"Your loyalty has never been questioned, Kalen," Luna responded in her quiet singsong voice. "That is partly why you have been asked here this evening."

This only led to more questions in his mind. This quiet evening, which had already taken such an odd turn, was just getting stranger by the moment as far as he was concerned. He did not want to be disrespectful, but he felt that he deserved some answers and was not going to wait any longer to get them.

"If I may be so bold, why have I been summoned here, and where are the other members of the council?" He hoped his voice carried the appropriate amount of respect. It would not do him any good to come across as impertinent to the three powerful council members.

General Braden laughed loudly at his comment.

"You are Kalen the Bold aren't you?" General Braden asked, jokingly referring to the label the junior officers in the Royal Guard used to describe Kalen. "I can see that nickname is well earned and well deserved."

Kalen blushed somewhat from the general's joke. He was not sure if he was being mocked or not, but thought it better not to challenge the general's authority here and now when something so important was still hanging in the air. He simply replied in his best soldier's voice, "Yes, sir."

The Chief Councilor cleared his throat as if to signal the time for mirth was at an end. "I can see that you have many questions Kalen, and I will do my best to answer them for you if you just bear with me and my fellow council members a moment longer."

Kalen simply nodded in understanding. He was a soldier and the Captain of the Royal Guard. That was a position that came with great responsibility. He was used to giving orders, but he knew how to take them as well. He knew how to be patient, and he knew how to wait until his superior officers were ready for him. This was the position he now took. He stood at ease, and waited until Grale and the other council members were ready to tell him whatever it was he needed to know, even if that information was something he really did not want to be a part of. Unfortunately this was exactly what he feared was going to happen. After a few minutes of conversing with the other two council members, the Chief Councilor appeared to be ready to answer a few of his questions.

"I again thank you for your patience, Kalen," the Chief Councilor began apologetically. "It is imperative that the information I am about to relay to you does not leave this room. Under no circumstances are you to repeat anything you hear this evening. Is that understood?"

"Of course, sir," he responded hesitantly.

"Good. You have been summoned here this evening because we have received some rather disturbing news. Kalen, we have a rogue."

This last statement was the most confusing he had heard. *A rogue, is that all? Why would the council be in such an uproar over a simple problem of having a rogue? Yes, a rogue could be problematic but why all the secrecy?*

"I do not think that I understand."

Rogue was an Elven term used to describe an Elf who did not follow the Elves' traditional beliefs, and therefore would leave the forest. Those Elves would live alone or among the other races. It was rare an Elf would feel so strongly that the ways of the Elven people were wrong, but it did happen from time to time. That is only to be expected in a free society such as the Elves'. Occasionally these rogues would try to cause minor uprisings in the outlying villages, and the Elven security force would be called in to squelch the problem. As far as he knew however, this was as far as it ever got. This did not explain why the council members were so riled up and secretive.

"No Kalen, you do not fully understand. Not yet, anyway." This was from Luna. The grave look on her normally serene face sent shivers down the usually steadfast Elf's spine.

He remained standing at attention as he waited for the trio of council members to elaborate. So far though, this impromptu meeting had gone just as he feared. He was even more confused and worried now than he had been at any other time since he first received the notice earlier this evening.

He was deep in thought when Chief Councilor Grale interrupted. "This rogue has crossed over to the Human's realm."

Kalen was stunned. He actually had to take a step back to recapture his balance. He knew he was staring open-mouthed at the Chief Councilor, but he could not help it. This evening, which had been uncommonly strange already, had just taken a turn into the realm of the bizarre. He was beginning to understand the need for secrecy. He was also starting to feel the magnitude of the Chief Councilor's words as they settled on to his shoulders.

"How could this happen?" he asked when he was able to shake off the initial effect of the Chief Councilor's last statement, and find his voice.

"The Shadowed Arts," was the unnerving answer he received from Chief Magister Caer'run.

"There is more you need to know, Kalen," the Chief Councilor added before he could respond to Luna's answer.

His gaze shifted back to the Chief Councilor. What news could they possibly throw at him now? He felt as if he was a ball being tossed back and forth between two excited children, or better yet, a pawn being manipulated by two enthusiastic chess players. He was deeply shaken by what the council had already told him. He did not know what could possibly be said that would shake him more than he was at that moment, and was equally as unsure if he even wanted to know. Then General Brandy'wine dropped the biggest bomb yet.

"The rogue is Drè Fao'lain."

That was it. He felt himself beginning to swoon and the room began to spin. He needed to sit down or he was going to fall. Without asking the council for permission, he walked over to the table, pulled out a chair, and dropped down like a beaten man. Dedicated soldier that he was, his brief lapse of protocol was proof of how unnerved he had become. This was too much for his already overloaded mind to handle. Drè Fao'lain – that was a name he had never expected or, truth be told, wanted to hear again.

"Now you understand why we have convened so quickly without the other members of the council," Chief Councilor Grale noted. "You also should now understand the dire need for secrecy."

Kalen could only nod in answer. He was too astonished to trust himself to speak. That evening had just moved past bizarre and flown straight to nightmarish.

"Are you sure?" he asked, finally remembering how to speak.

"We are certain," General Brandy'wine said, in what for him was considered a hushed tone, yet his voice still rang out across the near empty council chamber.

Luna Caer'run chimed in, "I have been trying to follow Drè's use of magic for awhile. Four months ago he suddenly stopped and just disappeared."

"Through our contact in the Human realm, we learned of the crossover," Chief Councilor Grale added. "The news gets more disturbing from there."

The news had already been incredibly disturbing to Kalen. First of all, he had not even known or suspected the Elven Council had any contact with the Humans. As far as he, or any of the rest of the Elven populace, knew, contact with the Humans had ceased after the Time of Separation when the Elves had built the Great Barrier that now separated the Elven and Human realms. Even more shocking, the council told him that not only had a rogue crossed over to the Human realm, but that rogue was Drè Fao'lain, his oldest friend and mortal enemy. After all that, Chief Councilor Grale let it be known the news was to grow more disturbing! Kalen did not know if he could take much more.

Chief Magister Caer'run picked up where Grale had left off. "Once I knew Drè had crossed over, I was able to pick him up again. The magic he is using is incredibly strong. It reeks of the Shadowed Arts. From the news we have gathered from our contact, and through some spells of my own, I believe I have been able to ascertain what it is exactly Drè is doing."

Kalen was not sure if the Chief Magister's brief pause was for dramatic effect, but he did see Luna take a deep breath as if to steady herself before she could continue. If the usually sure and steady Chief Magister was this shaken, then he knew the news had to be incredibly bad. *Why not though,* he thought to himself, *the news I have been given so far had not exactly been uplifting.*

Luna Caer'run turned and briefly looked at Chief Councilor Ash'lewn for permission to continue. He simply nodded his approval. This simple gesture was not lost on Kalen. The grave look on the elder Elf's face was telling. Whatever was going on had clearly shaken the Chief Councilor to the core. The air in the council chamber had become so thick with anticipation of the impending news, he felt as if he would choke on it. It was stifling hot already in the council chamber and he was sweating profusely.

After gathering her thoughts, and getting permission to proceed from Grale, Chief Magister Caer'run continued. "I believe that Drè is attempting to perform the Ritual of the Dying Moon."

He gasped in horror. If he had been afraid before, he was downright petrified now. The Ritual of the Dying Moon was the most sinister use of the Shadowed Arts or any magic for that matter.

Only the strongest of Magisters would even think of attempting it. Not that any sane and rational Magister would want to. The Ritual had become nothing more than a legend, and it was often used as a bedtime story told to frighten children. Most Elves believed the Ritual of the Dying Moon to be just that, a story. There were others though who believed in its reality. Drè Fao'lain had been one of the true believers.

"There have been several murders in the Human's realm since Drè crossed over," General Brandy'wine informed him. "We just learned of another earlier this evening."

As shaken as Kalen was, he was beginning to wonder what all this had to do with him. Yes he had known Drè Fao'lain, but that had been a long time ago. He was the Captain of the Royal Guard, but his duty was mainly to serve as a protector of the Royal Family. It was not his duty to deal with rogues. He rarely, if ever, had any dealings with the Shadowed Arts.

He could understand the council's concern over these most distressing matters, but why would they feel the need to drag him into their inner circle? The hairs on the back of his neck began to rise in fear and suspicion. He was starting to develop a bad feeling of what his part in all of this was going to be.

"This news is most distressing," he started, "but what does this have to do with me? Why was it so imperative that I come before the council?"

The three council members turned to stare at each other. He could visibly see Chief Councilor Ash'lewn's shoulders slump. Chief Magister Caer'run hung her head and closed her eyes like she was in deep concentration. General Brandy'wine just stared out at him with an authoritative gaze. The news was indeed going to be grim.

"Those are fair questions, Kalen," Chief Councilor Grale replied in his gravelly voice. The wizened old Elf stared deep into his eyes before continuing. "We need to put a stop to Drè before he destroys everything the Elven people have worked so hard to maintain. After a careful deliberation, we feel that you, Kalen Or'wain, are our best hope of stopping Drè."

Kalen closed his eyes. He had known it. His soldier's intuition had been warning him ever since he walked into the council chamber.

"What do you want me to do?"

He was becoming the soldier again. He knew he was about to receive his orders. He also knew he was not going to like them, but as a soldier he was honor bound to do his duty, whatever that may be.

Luna Caer'run was the one who answered. "We want you to cross over to the Human realm, find Drè Fao'lain, and stop him by whatever means necessary."

A seemingly endless stream of questions began to run through his head. *Why me? How do I stop him?* and *What the hell are you Elves thinking?* were just a few. He was a soldier though, and having a choice in the matter was not really an option. He did not hesitate as he replied, "Very well."

"You are bold indeed, Kalen Or'wain," General Brandy'wine added respectfully. "Let no Elf say different in my presence."

"I knew that the Elven people could count on you, Kalen," Chief Councilor Ash'lewn said proudly. "We will need to prepare you for your journey. We shall reconvene in the gardens in one hour. At that time, Kalen, you will cross over. Bring nothing but what you have with you right now."

"Yes, sir," he replied. He was deep in his soldier mode right now. If he had not been, he knew he would have been running as fast as he could back to his cottage and the safety and comfort of Lake Alorien.

Kalen was too stunned by the events of the past few minutes to just get up and leave. The three council members had exited. Luna had said she needed time to prepare for the crossover. He had almost laughed to himself when he had heard this. He did not know how in all the realms he was going to prepare and with only an hour, anyway. He did not have anything to do except sit and gather his thoughts.

With the council members gone, he found himself alone in the circular council chamber. The only company he had right then was his memories of the past. His thoughts went immediately to Drè Fao'lain. Their friendship, their differences, and their eventual fight all flew back to him. He had always known that his path and Drè's would cross again, but he had held out hope his dealings with his former friend were over. However, with Drè's talent for unpredictability, he should have known better.

He remembered growing up side by side with Drè. His father, Duncan, had been Captain of the Royal Guard at the time. The same post he currently held. Drè's father had been a member of the Royal Guard serving under Duncan. The two families had been great friends. This of course led to him and Drè spending a lot of time with each other. They had developed a quick and strong bond, just like their fathers had.

Drè had always been exceptionally bright as a child, and had shown at an early age a strong aptitude for magic. This led to everyone around Drè coming to believe he would someday enter the College of Magic. Kalen had known right from the start he would follow in his father's footsteps and join the Royal Guard. This was the beginning of the rift between Drè and him; a rift which would only grow wider as the years slipped by.

Their philosophical differences had only grown as the two young Elves had matured into adulthood. They had remained friends but the differences between the two grew wider by the year. When Drè had come of age, he did what was expected of him, and enrolled at the College of Magic. He was on his way to becoming a powerful Magister for the Elven People. Kalen, on the other hand, followed his own dream, and joined the Royal Guard. The two Elves' fathers could not have been prouder.

During his first year at the College of Magic, Drè had discovered and began studying the Shadowed Arts. He did this in secret as the Shadowed Arts were a forbidden topic among the Magisters. Drè had become obsessed with the use of this kind of magic though, and unbeknownst to the faculty at the college, he was perfecting his use of a magic the Elves considered taboo. It was around this time Drè's father was killed protecting the King from an ill-advised assassination attempt against the Royal Family by a band of rogue Elves.

Throwing caution to the wind, Drè sought out retribution for his father's untimely death. Without regard for life or any of the principles the Elven people held dear, Drè left the college, and sought out the band of rogues who had killed his father. Through his use of the Shadowed Arts, he was able to locate the assassin's band quickly. He slaughtered them all without a second thought. The spells he let loose that night were so enriched by the Shadowed Arts that nothing grew on the site of the slaughter. The stench of death is said to still hang on the air, burned into the land for all eternity.

Once the Elven College of Magic had gotten wind of Drè's unspeakable act, he was expelled. There was even talk of banishment. Only a desperate plea made by Kalen's father, Duncan Or'wain, saved Drè. Kalen considered this to be one of his father's biggest mistakes.

In the year that followed, Drè would seclude himself for days at a time in the deep Ash Forest that made up the outskirts of the Elven community. There, in the deep dark woods, Drè continued his study of the Shadowed Arts in secret. The evil magic began to twist his mind and rot his very soul.

When Kalen would get a leave from the Royal Guard, he would speak with Drè, but the conversations always turned to his obsession with magic and revenge. Drè had spoken often of the Ritual of the Dying Moon. Though Kalen had never believed, Drè had taken this myth to heart and vowed to figure out the magic needed to pull this most evil of spells off.

It had become plain to him, Drè was slowly slipping into a declining state of mind. He brought this to the attention of his father. Duncan Or'wain, feeling a sense of responsibility for Drè, sought him out, and tried to bring him back into the college to receive help. Drè had vehemently refused. He had never forgiven the college for throwing him out and trying to get him banished.

Duncan went to the college and told the Head Magisters of the condition Drè had deteriorated into. They immediately set out to bring the now-demented Elf back to the college where he could receive help. Kalen, fearing the worst, had also attempted to help his one-time friend. It was at this last meeting that Drè had spoken of his plan to assassinate the King. He had begged him to join him in his endeavors. Kalen had left his friend alone with his madness vowing to help him anyway he could.

He relayed to his father what Drè had been planning. Duncan, who was then the Captain of the Royal Guard, took every threat to the Royal Family seriously. So with Drè's plans for revenge hanging in the air, the Magisters were sent along with the Elven Security Force to apprehend the now-dangerous Elf.

Drè killed the Head Magister, and wiped out most of the Security Force. Those who returned told tales of a wild magic they had never seen or heard of before. They said Drè was invincible and that he wielded the Shadowed Arts as if he were born to them. They said after Drè had finished toying with the Head Magister, he had promised to come after the King. He had then simply disappeared in a flash of light.

The Royal Guard was put on notice, and the Royal Family was sequestered within the palace. Kalen, who had only been with the Royal Guard for a little over two years, was stationed along the entrance. His job was to turn any would-be visitors away. He had been as alert as he had ever been in his life, but it was not enough. With his abilities in the Shadowed Arts having grown to new heights, Drè was able to enter the palace and get by the guards with ease – all the guards except Duncan Or'wain.

Kalen's father had stationed himself before the door to the Royal Family's private chambers. These doors held the strongest of protection spells the Elven Magisters could call upon. When Drè appeared, Duncan did not hesitate to act. He had loved Drè like a son, but his duty was to protect the Royal Family, and none would stand in his way of performing that duty, not even his late best friend's child.

Duncan pulled forth the same swords that now hung above Kalen's fireplace back at his cottage, and charged. Drè swept Duncan aside as if he were nothing more than an annoyance. He flung magic fire from his fingertips into Duncan's chest, throwing the Royal Guard Captain against the far wall; his chest was left smoking and ruined. Thinking Duncan dead, Drè turned his attention toward the heavily protected doors. Not taking Duncan's honor bound duty seriously cost Drè his revenge.

Duncan gathered what strength he had left, and flung himself at the obsessed monster Drè had become. The crazed Elf was caught completely off guard as his full attention was on the doors that served as the final barrier for his ultimate reprisal against the Elven people who had spurned him. Duncan grabbed Drè by the shoulder spinning him around so they could face each other. Staring straight into Drè's eyes, and seeing the madness that lived there, Duncan plunged his sword into his foe's stomach.

By this time, the other Royal Guards had come to the defense of the Royal Family. Knowing his plans had been thwarted, Drè pulled the sword from his body, and with a final curse, pulled his vanishing act once again. In a bright flash of light, he simply disappeared. The sword, which had mere moments before been used to stop his unconscionable attack on the Royal Family, clattered to the stone floor. Its master, Duncan Or'wain – Kalen's father – lay slumped against the wall, dead.

It had been believed the wound Drè had suffered at the hands of Duncan Or'wain had been fatal, but Kalen had known better. Drè's hatred and his abilities with the Shadowed Arts had grown so strong he was sure his former friend would survive. He also knew there would come a time when he would have to face Drè again. When that time came, he would be the one looking for revenge.

It was with this thought in mind that Kalen shook himself from his reverie. He had lost track of time sitting in the council chamber, being haunted by the ghosts of his past. His hour must surely be close to being up. With a deep breath to help settle his nerves and the queasiness settling down deep in his stomach, he gathered himself, and prepared to meet the council members out in the garden of the Keep of the Full Moon.

The night had grown cooler in the time he had spent inside in his meeting with the three council members. The garden was as beautiful and well kept as always. The Elven People shared a great affinity with the land. Their ability to plant and grow a variety of flora was unparalleled among the races. That ability was on display in the keep's garden.

At the center of the garden stood a great Ash Tree. These trees were held sacred by the Elves. The Elves did not so much live in the forest with the Ash Trees as much as they shared the forest. Their relationship could possibly be described as being symbiotic.

The Ash Tree in the center of the garden was believed to be one of the oldest in the forest. It was there the council members stood waiting for Kalen. Among the three council members was a fourth Elf. Kalen was amazed as he recognized the King, His Majesty Shander Stri'bier. Kalen walked the few remaining feet to the Ash Tree, and then dropped to one knee to genuflect before his Liege.

"Rise, Kalen Or'wain for it is I who should be kneeling before you for what you are about to do for the Elven People," the King's voice was soft, and it held a slight fatherly quality to it.

"Before you say anything, I already know that I am out here without the Royal Guards present. You are just like your father, overprotective," King Stri'bier finished this last statement with a wink aimed in Kalen's direction.

He found himself smiling and almost immediately at ease. This was a gift King Stri'bier had. Even at the most stressful of times, such as now, the King could alleviate the tension with a quick word or phrase and extend to his subjects a calmness that could permeate the thickest of tensions.

"I am honored by your presence here, your Majesty," he offered in reply to his King's kind words.

King Stri'bier smiled in response, and then turned his attention to Grale Ash'lewn. To the Chief Councilor, the King simply nodded his approval. Grale took his cue from the King and began addressing Kalen.

"As I mentioned earlier, there have been a series of grizzly murders among the Humans, and we now know these murders have been committed by Drè Fao'lain. From our contact within the Human's government we have learned of another murder that has taken place this very evening. It is imperative you cross over to the Human's realm and put a stop to Drè." The Chief Councilor's tone was grave as he explained the details.

Chief Magister Luna Caer'run picked up where Ash'lewn left off, "We know these murders are taking place in a Human city known as Los Angeles. We believe that is where Drè has made his headquarters and plans to launch the Ritual of the Dying Moon. We have arranged with the Humans for a guide to meet you once you cross over."

This news came as a surprise to him. He had been wondering how he was going to find his way around the Human realm. He had never seen a Human. No Elf alive had that he knew of. From the stories he had heard about the Humans from his childhood, they were a strange and untrustworthy people. They had no relationship with the land, and did not hold nature in anything close to the high regard that the Elven People did. This was just one more worry to add to his already over-burdened shoulders and overtaxed mind.

Luna Caer'run reached into her robe and pulled out a pendant. This movement caught his attention and brought him back to the moment at hand. "This pendant will allow you to speak the Human's language and understand it when it is spoken to you. Wear it always. The spell does not work if it is removed from around your neck."

He reached out and took the pendant. It was fairly unremarkable in appearance. It was a simple gold chain with an emblem that had the image of the Goddess Alorien etched into its surface on one side and a strange inscription on the other. He took the pendant nevertheless, trusting in the Chief Magister. He placed it around his neck as he had been instructed to do and felt a strange tingling throughout his body as the necklace settled into place.

General Brandy'wine stepped forward and handed Kalen his sword. "I would be honored, Kalen the Bold, if you would take my sword with you on your journey and use it to bring justice for the Elven and Human people."

"Thank you, General. I will do my best to see it gets returned to you."

His was surprised at the general's gesture, but he took the sword with the same respect with which it had been offered. After unbuckling his scabbard, and laying his own sword on the ground at the general's feet, he strapped the general's sword around his waist. The general nodded in appreciation of a fellow soldier's ability to stay calm.

"It will take me a few minutes to begin casting the spell that will allow you to cross over," Luna explained. "Once I finish, a door will open in the trunk of this great Ash Tree. All you need to do is step into it, and you will be transported through the Great Barrier and to the Human's realm."

It sounded so simple, yet it left him speechless and trembling with fear. What had he gotten himself into? How could he have agreed to such madness? But he knew the answer to those questions: Drè Fao'lain and the Ritual of the Dying Moon. So he once again just nodded that he understood.

"When you are ready to cross back over to our realm, return to the same tree on the other side, and read the inscription on the back of the pendant out loud. The door will open and you can step back through. If you lose the pendant, you will be stuck in the Human's realm," Luna explained to him in a desperate and pleading tone.

Chief Magister Luna Caer'run stepped back a bit, away from the others, and began to cast her spell. The other Elves watched in anticipation; few Elves had ever seen a crossing over before, and none of the Elves present at that moment had, not even Luna herself.

She began making the intricate gestures with her hands that were always the telltale signs of a spell being cast. He could see Luna chanting under her breath, but the words were unrecognizable to anyone other than another Magister. Luna's voice was rising and falling and the gestures she made with her hands grew faster as she fell deeper into the magic of the spell. After several long minutes of casting, she turned to stare at him.

"I am in the final stage of the incantation. With the saying of the last line of the spell, the door will open. Are you ready, Kalen Or'wain?" Luna asked with deep concentration. Her brow was furrowed and the sweat that was on her forehead glistened in the moonlight. Both were evidence of how hard she had had to work to call forth and control the powerful magic needed for this spell.

"Yes, I am ready," Kalen answered, though in fact he felt anything but. He took a deep breath and approached the Ash Tree. He stopped when he was within arm's reach of the trunk.

Luna resumed her chanting, and with a final flourish, she completed the spell. The moment she finished the last line, a crack showed in the trunk of the great elder Ash Tree. Blinding white light began pouring through, and after a few seconds, the crack began to grow. It took a square door shape and grew until it reached about six feet high, and five feet across.

With a final look out over the gardens of the Keep of the Full Moon, he silently prayed to Alorien to grant him strength and he stepped through the door. There was a loud whooshing sound as if a great wind was blowing. It was deafening. He looked back, but the door had already closed behind him. He found himself standing in what appeared to be a large room made of white light. When he turned his attention back to the front, he could see another opening beginning to appear much as it had done in the Ash Tree. The opening grew larger until he was able to step through.

He exited the dimensional doorway that had allowed him to cross over and stepped right into the middle of a rainstorm. A flicker of light and the quick smell of some kind of burning plant off to his right caught his attention. He turned to see a man leaning against a tree neighboring the one he had just stepped through smoking some kind of rolled tobacco. The man turned his attention and leveled his stare onto him.

"You Elves sure know how to make an entrance. I'll give ya that," the stranger remarked in surprise.

For what seemed like the one hundredth time that evening, Kalen was too stunned to reply.

# Chapter 5

The black-clad shadow assassin removed his trophy from the leather bag he had attached to his waist. The heart, which had once belonged to Joseph Stanfield until that evening, was now covered in dried blood. It looked almost as black as the gloved hand that held it there in the darkness. The murderous Elf held the lifeless organ aloft with a sense of reverence. He held the heart as if it was a piece of centuries' old fine China that would shatter if a wrong move was made.

A slight whisper could be heard in the silence of the abandoned warehouse as the Elf assassin began invoking a spell. Then, in a quick, bright flash the candles laid out along the floor flared to life. The dry air of the warehouse crackled with energy as the faint traces of the magic left over from the spell still permeated the air.

The Elf smiled as he crossed the warehouse with his treasure still in hand. The candles flickered as he passed. His shadow stretched out behind him, and seemingly danced with glee in the eerie candlelight.

This had been a big night for the Elf. He had moved one step closer to his goal. The spell he was planning to unleash required great patience. This was not a problem however, as he had been planning his ultimate revenge for years now. What were a few more months when compared to the satisfaction of setting loose the ultimate retribution? This thought brought another steely smile to the killer's face. His revenge was within his grasp. He could feel it as sure as he could feel the heart he now held in his hand. Finally, they would pay.

After crossing to the far end of the warehouse he had made his home, the Elf stood before his dark altar. At a first glance, the altar appeared to be a great oak tree, but on closer inspection, one would see several noticeable differences. The first thing that would cause an unsuspecting person to take notice was the pungent scent of rotting wood and decay. The great oak tree appeared to be dead, as it was black in color with no leaves. It was as if the Elf had somehow plucked a tree from some forest or park, and transported it right here into the warehouse where it now waited, dying. In actuality, this tree had been summoned through the Shadowed Arts. Though it appeared dead, it was very much alive, blazing in the evil magic which ran through its limbs.

The tree had twelve leafless branches protruding from its trunk. They were arranged in a circle around the tree, and the sight reminded the Elf of planets orbiting a sun. The tree was nearly seven feet tall with the branches circled around the top. The gnarled roots were growing straight down, right through the concrete of the warehouse floor. How far down they went, and what they drew nutrients from no mortal man could guess.

The Elf that had murdered Joseph Stanfield in shocking brutality earlier in the evening now stood before the tree in an almost religious fervor. This tree was the culmination of his years of study and work. This tree would bring forth his retribution… his salvation. This Tree of Sacrifice, as it was known, held the key to his ultimate revenge.

With the heart held aloft in his hand, the Elf began reciting the words to an incantation, his voice rising with each word in a fevered pitch. If anyone had been close enough to hear, it would have sounded like garbled nonsense, but to the obsessed Elf the words were beautiful poetry. This was his blessing, his prayer, his life.

With a final primal yell, the Elf raised the heart high over his head so it could touch the moonbeams creeping into the warehouse through a multitude of cracks and broken windows. The lifeless heart burst into flame as soon as it grazed the nearest beam of light the moon had offered.

The Elf assassin lowered his arm to stare at his prize burning in his palm. Though the heart burned brightly, it gave off no heat. Instead of the customary orange and yellow that is normally associated with fire, the heart burned with a blue flame. Also, the fire did not appear to consume it. The heart was aflame, but was not burning. The azure flames were bright, and for a moment the Elf was mesmerized by their brilliance.

With the blazing heart in his hand, the Elf approached the Tree of Sacrifice. When he was within a few feet of the trunk, a branch lowered itself down to the Elf's eye level. At the end of the gnarled limb were several little branches and twigs that looked very similar to a claw. The Elf placed the flaming heart into this claw with loving care. Once the burning organ had been placed, the branch rose back to its original position. The heart, now resting comfortably within the tree limb claw, began slowly beating once again. The spell was complete. The Elf was building a puzzle of revenge and he had just locked another piece into place.

The Elf surveyed the Tree of Sacrifice one last time. The beating heart of Joseph Stanfield was not alone. It now sat next to four other beating hearts that also burned with that same unearthly blue flame. Seven other branches remained empty and waiting. In due time they too would be filled with sacrifices. That thought brought a glint to the Elf's eye, and a wicked smile to his otherworldly face.

Now though was the time for a much-needed rest. The magic he had used that night had taken a heavy toll. The Elf knew his limitations, and he also knew he had stretched those limitations close to the breaking point. That was fine though, with Joseph Stanfield's heart, he had bought himself a night of rest. Another sacrifice could not be made for twenty-four hours. This did not really give the evil Elf enough time to fully replenish his strength along with his magical energies, but after the next sacrifice, the Elf knew he would have a month to rest. That would give him plenty of time to choose his next two victims.

Yes, this ritual that would give him his ultimate revenge required great patience. He had patience in abundance though, and revenge would be his. As the Humans were fond of saying, patience is a virtue, and all good things come to those that wait. Well, he would wait, one more month at least, and then he would unleash his magic once again. He so enjoyed the killing. The spilling of blood made him feel so alive.

With thoughts of Stanfield's blood spraying around the parking garage still in his head, the evil shadow assassin Stanfield himself had correctly named as Elf went to get his much-deserved rest.

Nobody knew he was among the Humans, and none of those fools would be able to trace any of the killings back to him. Oh yes, this rest would be long enough to get him through the next twenty-four hours, but it would also be undisturbed. The Elf laughed to himself as he went to prepare for his sleep.

# —Chapter 6

Kalen stared at the Human as he pushed himself from the nearby tree and began walking towards the Elf. Kalen had not moved an inch from the spot where he had emerged from the crossover portal. As the Human male came closer, Kalen was able to get a better idea of what he looked like.

The Human was not quite as tall as Kalen, but what he lacked in height, he more than made up for in girth. Kalen could tell the man was incredibly strong just by the way he moved. His body was almost square shaped. The Human's solidly built body reminded him of the great Ash Trees of his forest home. He felt a slight pang of worry as the image of the Ash Trees flashed across his mind. He was unsure if he would ever see the great and wondrous forest of his home again.

The man approached until he was within an arm's reach. He had not spoken a word since his first statement that had brought Kalen out of the shock of crossing realms. This would have been considered very rude in Elven customs, but Kalen reminded himself, he was no longer among his people.

A quick bright flash of lightning lit the evening sky up just enough that Kalen was able to make out the Human's facial features. The man had extremely short black hair. His eyes matched his hair in color, but the intensity of those eyes was a bit unnerving. The Human had a square jaw and no facial hair. His whole physical structure seemed to be square shaped. In Kalen's estimation, the man looked as solid as the stone walls of the Keep of the Full Moon.

The Human guide was wearing a long coat that almost touched the ground. It was the same color black as the man's soaked hair. He carried a bundle under one arm, and continued to smoke the odd rolled paper with his free hand. He stared back at Kalen, sizing him up much the same way Kalen had done to him. Kalen stood his ground. He did not want to show any sign of weakness, but at the same time he wanted to project an image of confidence and strength.

The man took one more quick puff off the rolled paper, and then casually threw it away. Kalen was appalled. He had never seen such blatant disregard for nature before in his life. He had always heard rumors about how the Humans were abusive to the land they lived on, and how that was one of the primary reasons for separating the two races all those centuries before. The shock must have registered plainly on his face because the Human took a quick step back as if he thought he was going to have to defend himself.

"Oh yeah," the man uttered as understanding sank in. "I forgot you Elves were nature lovers."

Before Kalen could speak, the man reached inside his coat and pulled out a little black square. *It must be some kind of book,* Kalen thought to himself as the man flipped it open.

"I'm Special Agent Reggie Blackburn, your guide. They did tell you about a guide didn't they?" he asked cautiously.

Kalen looked at the black book carefully. On one side was some sort of small parchment that had a picture of the man standing before him along with some information. He was surprised that he could read it, but then he remembered the amulet Chief Magister Caer'run had given him. On the other side of the little black book was a metal star. He took it to be some sort of military medal. This man must be a soldier of some sort. That made sense to Kalen as he too was a soldier.

"Yes, I was told I would be met by a guide." These were the first words he had spoken. He recognized his voice, but the words sounded funny. He knew the magical amulet was working, but he had not thought about how strange it would feel to speak such foreign words.

"Good," Special Agent Blackburn replied. "Then let's get to work. We have a lot to do this evening, and we are behind schedule already."

The rain had started to slow down by this time. It was more of a spitting drizzle than a steady downpour. The man took the bundle he had tucked under his arm and handed it to Kalen.

"Christ, you look like you just walked off the set of that *Lord of the Rings* movie," the man chuckled as he handed the bundle to Kalen. "Put those on and we will be on our way. I have a car waiting. I will fill you in more once we get on the road."

Kalen nodded in understanding as he took the bundle. As he unfolded it he recognized it to be a coat similar to the one Special Agent Blackburn was wearing. There was also a black hat that matched the color of the coat. It was made of a soft material and had a brim that went all the way round.

Kalen had no idea what a car was, but he figured he would find out soon enough. He slipped on the coat over his uniform and placed the hat on his head. Once it was on, he realized it was to help cover up his ears as he remembered Humans had strange, rounded ears. He could only shake his head in exasperation. This was going to be a lot harder than he could have ever imagined.

The coat fit pretty well. It was a bit baggy, but he did not mind. It would be easier for him to draw his sword if needed. It buttoned up the front, and also had a sash to tie at the waist. He tightened the sash as best he could. The coat and hat felt alien to him, but he understood they were necessary evils if he was going to be interacting with the Humans. His ability to remain incognito and keep his Elven heritage hidden was of the utmost importance.

"Am I wearing this correctly?" he asked Special Agent Blackburn once he had donned the garments.

"Yeah," the Special Agent answered back. "You look like a million bucks. Now let's get moving." With that being said, Blackburn turned and started walking away.

"What is a million bucks?" Kalen asked under his breath as he followed. Special Agent Blackburn glanced back over his right shoulder, shook his head, and smiled.

Kalen followed close behind the Special Agent as they made their way through the trees. He was still trying to figure out just what a car was when Agent Blackburn came to a stop. Kalen, who was still in a slight state of shock from everything that had been happening, almost walked right into the back of the burly Special Agent. Luckily, he was able to catch himself before he embarrassed his Elven heritage even further.

Agent Blackburn had come to a stop a few feet from a large metal object. It was quite long, and was a dirty, dark blue in color. The large metal object was sitting along a path, paved with a hardened tar-like substance. Kalen guessed this path was what passed for a road to the Humans, and the large metal object was the car that Agent Blackburn had been referring to. Making these assumptions however, did little to alleviate the confusion that was making his head spin in a seemingly endless state of altered reality.

Agent Blackburn walked around the front of the "car" and stood directly opposite Kalen. He took something from his pocket, and held the object or objects, as it appeared to be several small items, up to the sky in an attempt to use whatever light was available from the shadow-covered moon to help him see. Agent Blackburn then fumbled with these small items for a few seconds. They made a jingling sound, and Kalen thought the items to be small bells of some kind.

Agent Blackburn muttered something under his breath before he finally settled on one of the small pieces of metal. The agent then took the small item and placed it in some unseen opening on the side of the "car" that he was standing on. There was a slightly muffled popping and clicking sound that caught Kalen's attention. He realized the items Agent Blackburn had been toying with were keys. This was a small triumph for Kalen, but he was encouraged that he was able to figure this small puzzle out on his own. It gave him some small measure of hope that he would be able to find his way here in the Human realm. It was one small step, but as far as he was concerned, it was a step in the right direction.

Agent Blackburn pulled at something along the side of the "car", and a door opened. The agent then bent over slightly and stepped in. Kalen looked along the side of the car he was standing on. He did not know if he would need a key to get in as well, but since the Special Agent had not offered him one, he thought it would not be necessary. He did spot a lever of some kind. He could see through the window that Agent Blackburn was sitting in the car and waiting. He took a hesitant step forward and lifted up on the lever. To his surprise, the lever lifted rather easily. There was another slight popping sound, and the door swung open. The way the door opened with such ease caught Kalen off guard, and he again almost lost his balance. From inside the car Agent Blackburn snorted out a laugh.

"I thought you Elves were supposed to be graceful," he said condescendingly, and then laughed again at his own joke.

"I am glad you are finding humor at my apparent unease, Special Agent Blackburn," he said trying to stay emotionally on guard, but with all that had happened, his anger was starting to rise.

Agent Blackburn choked back another snort of laughter, and knowing he may have crossed the line, tried to apologize. "Look, I know this is all new for you, and can't be that easy. I didn't mean to offend you, and if I did, then I'm sorry."

Kalen took a deep breath to settle his anger, and then, trying his best to copy the Special Agent's movements from a few minutes before, he attempted to get into the car. He was used to climbing up into the saddle of his favorite horse however, and hadn't realized how much a hindrance the general's sword hanging at his waist would be. The only logical solution was to remove the blade, which he did quickly before stepping into the car. He rested the sword between his legs as he leaned back into the seat. He was immediately surprised by how soft and comfortable the seat was, and had to admit, this was better than being bounced around in the hard leather saddle he used back home.Agent Blackburn smiled to himself when he saw the surprised look on Kalen's face. Blackburn knew he would be seeing that look a lot in the days to come. This was going to be the biggest case of culture shock the agent had ever been witness to, and he had seen some pretty weird things in his time.

Seeing that Kalen was just sitting there patiently waiting while the passenger side door was still hanging wide open, Agent Blackburn realized it was up to him to fill in the blanks for the Elf.

"You have to reach over and shut the door yourself. Be careful though, you do not have to pull real hard," Agent Blackburn instructed hoping that he did not come across as condescending as he had before.

Kalen nodded in response. He did as he was told and reached out to grab the door. The door felt heavier than it had when he had opened it, but following the special agent's advice, he pulled the door towards him without using a great amount of force. He was again surprised with the ease in which the heavy metal door closed. It shut with a loud bang, and he was concerned that he may have broken something.

"Don't worry," Agent Blackburn said when he caught the look of concern on Kalen's face. "This baby is built Ford tough."

Having no idea what the special agent was talking about, Kalen did what came natural to him and just nodded his ascent. Special Agent Blackburn, once he felt Kalen understood, turned his attention back to the keys he had produced from his pocket when he opened the car door.

Kalen watched as the special agent repeated the scene that had played out just a few minutes earlier. The agent once again fumbled with the keys, and again muttered under his breath as he selected one. He then placed the key in a small portal on the side of the strange wheel that was in front of his wide frame. The agent then turned the key, and the car fired to life.

Kalen nearly jumped out of his seat. He was caught so off guard, he actually made a move to draw his sword in an attempt to defend himself and the special agent. He quickly turned to see if the special agent was all right, and was perplexed when he saw the agent was sitting calmly. The noise had dissipated, but Kalen could still feel a vibration coming from somewhere underneath him and the car.

"Oh, that's just the engine," Special Agent Blackburn remarked casually. "That's supposed to happen."

The small feeling of victory he had felt earlier upon being able to figure out what the keys were, was now gone. In its place, he felt embarrassment and, even more disconcerting, he felt resignation. He was never going to be able to fit in well enough to accomplish this mission. For the first time, he felt a real fear of failing. This was a new sensation for him. He never questioned himself, but this was an extraordinary experience and circumstance. He was a soldier though, and he was determined to see this mission through. He just hoped it would not be an unmitigated disaster.

Agent Blackburn, seeing that Kalen had visibly calmed, reached out to grab another lever that was coming off the strange wheel. He pulled the lever down and the car began to move. As it began to pull away, Agent Blackburn reached over his shoulder and grabbed some strap that was hanging by the door. He then clasped the strap to a previously unseen clip located at his opposite hip. Watching the special agent closely, Kalen mimicked the movement. He found the strap hanging by the door on his side, and pulled it over his lap just as the agent had. It took him a moment to find the clasp, but once he did, he was able to lock the strap together with ease. He figured this must be some sort of safety device due to the rate of speed that car was moving, which was incredible as far as he was concerned.

In all the recent confusion, Kalen had forgotten that he needed to know where it was he had crossed over. He felt a momentary hint of terror as he realized he had forgotten to mark the spot. If he could not find his way back to the tree, he would be stuck in the Human realm forever.

"Excuse me Special Agent Blackburn, but could you please tell me where I crossed over at. I need to know so I can return when my mission has been completed."

He hoped he sounded calm. He was giving away vital information that could be used against him if it fell into the wrong hands. He had to trust Special Agent Blackburn though. The burly Human was his guide after all, and the only person that knew he was an Elf.

"Yeah, they told me about that," Blackburn responded nonchalantly. "Don't worry, I already marked the tree, and this place is called Angeles National Forest."

He was not sure who the "they" that Agent Blackburn was speaking about were, but "they" seemed to have a working knowledge of the conditions that he was working under. This did little to assuage his feelings on giving away such important information though. He was definitely a stranger in a strange land.

He had never felt so out of place in his life. The monumental task and responsibility that had been so astonishingly and inexplicably placed on his shoulders was quickly becoming an almost unbearable burden.

"You know in the rush of things, I never did catch your name," Special Agent Blackburn said curiously.

Glad the silence in the car had been broken, Kalen answered back, "I am Kalen Or'wain."

"Nice to know ya, Kalen. As I mentioned before, I am Special Agent Blackburn, but you can call me Reggie," Blackburn replied in a friendly tone.

"That is kind of you, Reggie, and please just call me Kalen," he said hoping he sounded as friendly as Special Agent Blackburn had. "You mentioned earlier, before we got into this machine that you would 'fill me in' on the way. If I understood you right, we are under the way now. Any information you have could be most helpful."

"Oh yeah," Reggie replied remembering. "We have a bit of a drive before we get to the crime scene so I will tell you everything I know."

Kalen sat patiently staring at Special Agent Blackburn waiting for him to elaborate on the situation. Special Agent Blackburn, or Reggie as he wanted to be known, stared out of the big front window for a minute before he spoke again.

"I guess the first thing I should let you in on is that my government knows about yours, and your government knows about us. There are elements within each of our governments that have regular contact with the other. Who they are, and how they maintain this contact, I have no idea," Reggie said beginning his explanation.

Kalen was a bit taken a back. He stared at Special Agent Blackburn intently. The weight of the special agent's words began to settle heavily on his already overburdened shoulders. He had no idea the Elves and Humans even knew about each other let alone have some sort of regular communication. However, this did explain a few things. Like how Chief Magister Caer'run was able to follow Drè's progress, and how the council was able to arrange for a guide so quickly.

Special Agent Blackburn turned onto another road, and Kalen became somewhat unnerved as he felt the car begin to speed up. The images outside the windows became blurs as the speed of the machine increased. He was having a hard time discerning which was more troublesome, the speed with which he and Special Agent Blackburn were traveling, or the story he was being told.

Reggie could tell by the look on his passenger's face that Kalen was distressed. "Look, I am not trying to freak you out or anything, but you wanted to know."

"That is quite all right, Special Agent Blackburn – I mean Reggie – this is information I need to have." Though he was indeed "freaked out" as Reggie had put it, Kalen knew he needed to hear the rest.

Reggie nodded ascent, and continued. "I work for a special division of the U.S. Government. They are a security force that is run by a separate entity within the government. The section I work for is strictly black ops. It is so secretive no one but the top brass even know that it exists."

Kalen was having a hard time following what Reggie was saying, but he understood enough to know the agent worked for some specialized and secret security team, though he had no clue as to what "black ops" and "top brass" were. He sat and listened intently and did his best to continue to keep up with what Reggie was saying.

Reggie paused, and looked over at Kalen to make sure that the Elf understood. Kalen was staring back intensely. Reggie shrugged and continued.

"The division of the agency that I work for only handles problems of a, shall we say, paranormal persuasion. I investigate situations that are best kept quiet so as not to panic the rest of the country."

Kalen watched as Reggie turned the car onto a pretty busy road. He was caught off guard as other cars were passing by at a great speed. He heard Reggie mutter something under his breath about hating to drive on a freeway. Again, he was not sure what the Special Agent was talking about. He watched as Reggie took a deep breath and then continued on with his information.

"About three months ago, my division became aware of a large surge of magical energy, for lack of a better term. At the time we had no idea what caused this. Now we know that the surge was your friend crossing over."

Kalen did not want to interrupt, but hearing the word friend, he felt he had no choice. Through clenched teeth he whispered, "Drè Fao'lain is no friend of mine."

Reggie Blackburn was startled to hear such hatred escape the up-to-this-point relatively quiet Elf.

"Hey, I'm sorry. It's just an expression," he apologized.

Kalen was shocked at his own response. He knew his anger at Drè ran deep, but with all the events of the past few hours, he was reaching a boiling point, and his anger was starting to spill over. He was going to have to be more careful. He hoped he would be able to rely on his training to get him through this near impossible ordeal. It would have to if he ever hoped of returning home once again.

Reggie, sensing the tense moment had passed decided to tell Kalen everything else before he was interrupted again. "Shortly after the surge, the first body was found. It was a prostitute. She had been mutilated pretty badly, and her heart had been taken. That sounds bad, but things like that happen here more than you might think. One month later, another body showed up in LA. This time it was some hot shot lawyer; same MO as the hooker. He was cut up pretty badly and his heart had been taken. By this time the Agency was picking up on some strange readings. At the time we weren't sure what they were, but it did not take us long to figure out that we were picking up on the Dark Magic your fellow Elf was using."

Kalen could only stare at Reggie. He was still in shock over all the recent circumstances. Sitting here in this strange machine going faster than he ever thought was possible, he still could not believe Drè was involved in all this.

Special Agent Blackburn continued. "It was about this time that we were contacted by your people. Once we knew that we were dealing with an Elven killer, preparations were made. I volunteered to lead this investigation, and your people decided that we needed help from one of their own. I guess that's where you came in."

Reggie watched Kalen for any sign of understanding. To his credit however, Kalen sat perfectly still and did not give any indication he was surprised by any of this.

"You must be one heck of a poker player," Reggie said shaking his head as he chuckled under his breath. "Anyway, we still didn't really know what we were dealing with. I went to L.A. to poke around, but came up empty. The Agency and your government decided the only thing we could do, would be to wait for the next body to surface, and go from there. When this new stiff showed up tonight, the plan was set into motion, and you were brought over. I know that is kind of a vague overview, but it sums things up to this point. Any questions?"

Kalen sat in silence trying to digest everything he had just heard. He was having a hard time believing a few short hours ago, he had been sitting on his deck overlooking Lake Alorien, and enjoying a glass of wine. How he wished he had not answered his door, and let that young page into his home. He did not know what to say, so he just sat in silence staring out the large front window and watched as the other machines kept zooming on by.

Reggie did not quite know what to make of his passenger's silence. He too stared out the window for a minute before he added, "We will be there in a few minutes so I need to let you know what is going to happen. The LAPD are already there, and they will not be happy to see us since we are going to take over the investigation. Let me do the talking. If you need anything or have any questions, direct them towards me. I want you to have as little contact as possible with anyone else. It is bad enough that we have one Elf on the loose."

Kalen was a bit offended by this last remark, but quickly changed his expression when he saw that the Special Agent was smiling.

"Just kidding, Kalen," Reggie said. "You need to lighten up, it's only the possible end of the world as you know it that we are dealing with."

Kalen knew that was supposed to be a humorous remark, but there was nothing funny about it. He also knew the end of his world was exactly what they were going to have to deal with.

# CHAPTER 7

Miles away from Kalen Or'wain's and Special Agent Reggie Blackburn's initial meeting, Drè Fao'lain prepared for his replenishing sleep. The use of all the powerful Dark Magic and the completion of the ritual had taxed his strength mightily. The only way for the twisted Elf to regain that strength and restock his magical energy reserves was for him to take his rest. This evening had been a raging success, and it was time to give the devil his due.

Drè laughed out loud at that thought. Those words were truer than anyone could know. The Shadowed Arts he was invoking truly was born of evil. He intended to capitalize on that very same evil to see his revenge brought to fruition. If the payment for his revenge was his mortal soul, then so be it. It was a small price to pay as far as he was concerned. He would pay any price to see the Elves perish. He wanted them to suffer, and suffer they would.

Now, however, was a time for sleep. The Elves would suffer, but only if he had enough strength to complete the ritual. The only way to get that strength would be to use the replenishing sleep.

He went to his sleeping chamber located in the back room of this abandoned structure. It was the perfect site for him to use as his headquarters to launch his long awaited revenge on the Elven populace. This place had been abandoned for years so it was quite easy for him to take up residence here, and none were the wiser. The foolish Humans would never be able to trace him back to here, not with all the warding spells he had placed around this building.

The building had originally been called the New Getty Villa Warehouse. It was located between Topanga State Park and Topanga Beach. The surrounding neighborhood was not very affluent, and the people all kept to themselves. Not that it mattered that much to him. If he had to deal with a few wandering eyes, then so be it. That would be all the more fun. Torture could serve its purposes as a dire warning to those that may get too curious, but as of yet that had not really been a problem. He considered doing it anyway, just for fun. He could randomly pick one of his curious fellow city dwellers, and teach the rest a valuable lesson. He would give further thought to that matter upon awakening.

He felt himself becoming physically weaker by the moment. He hated that feeling, but again, it was a necessary evil he would have to deal with, a side effect he must endure.

He quickly began undressing and setting his equipment aside. He needed to rest badly. He was not only feeling extremely weak, but he was beginning to feel ill as well. The Dark Magic had fed off his life energies and taxed a heavy toll. That was how the magic worked, how it lived, and where its power was drawn from.

Just as he lay down on his pallet, he felt a slight tingling down deep in his abdomen. This was a new sensation; one he had never felt before, after using the Shadowed Arts. It was a curious feeling. It was not altogether unpleasant, but it was more of an annoyance. He thought it was just another side effect, and it would pass with the sleep.

Then without any warning, the tingling turned into a stabbing pain, and he cried out in excruciating agony. He fell from his pallet and writhed on the cold concrete floor of the abandoned warehouse. Wave after wave of agony came crashing over his body. He felt as if he was about to be torn completely asunder. His body was on fire, and it felt like he was burning from the inside out.

He again screamed in agony. He was laying face down completely prone, and he was unable move. Sweat was dripping from his forehead and dribbling into his eyes. Normally this would have caused a stinging, but he was already in such agony the minor stinging would have been a welcome relief. Now, it was just another factor in his equation of pain.

Just as quickly as it had occurred, the gut-wrenching pain stopped. It was as if someone had simply flipped a switch from the on position to the off. He remained on the floor, panting. He tried to catch his breath, but was unable to do anything more than gasp for air.

Once he was sure the worst was over, he scrambled back to his knees. He blinked away the tears that had come to his eyes, and wiped the sweat from his brow with his forearm. When he felt he had his composure once more, he pulled himself back to a sitting position on his pallet.

He stared straight ahead at the far wall of his sleeping chamber. There was only one thing that could have caused that kind of reaction within his system: magic. He knew immediately what had happened. He was not sure how those bumbling fools could have found him, but another Elf had crossed over.

This was definitely going to be a problem. He knew it would be a matter of time before this new Elf would be on his trail. He wondered who it was that had been foolish enough to cross over, and try to stop him. He knew the Elven Council would choose someone important. Well, that would be all the better. This new Elf would have a front row seat to the end of the Elven race.

He needed that rest now more than ever. He knew however, that his replenishing sleep would have to be cut short. His plans may be changing. He may have to adjust his timetable for the completion of the ritual.

He lay back on his pallet, and smiled. Those fools thought they could send one Elf to stop him. This may be a slight setback, but he was confident nothing could get in his way. He slipped into his sleep of replenishment, and dreamed of a wasteland that had once been the plush and green Elven forest.

# —CHAPTER 8

Amy was glad the rain had finally stopped. Due to the hour of night, and the fact that she had her siren on as she drove, she was able to make good time from her apartment in Encino to the scene of the murder at ChemCo in San Fernando. Traffic was still heavy, but traffic was always heavy in LA County.

She took the exit off the San Fernando Valley Freeway and drove southeast down Glenoaks Boulevard. It did not take her long to spot the crime scene. There were red and blue flashing lights along with that famous yellow tape with the black lettering that read "police crime scene" in big black block letters. They might as well have put up a huge neon sign with an arrow that said, "Murder."

Amy could see that all the commotion caused by the arriving police had already drawn a crowd. She could also see that the press had showed up in droves. There was no way the department was going to be able to keep this case under wraps any longer. A hooker and a lawyer showing up dead was not so unusual, but once you threw in this new murder of a major company's vice president and the added fact that all of the victims' hearts had been removed and taken, well that was front page news.

She pulled up next to a couple of patrol cruisers and parked. She had to show her badge and identification to the officer standing guard out front. He was a young kid, and she did not recognize him. He looked at her identification and waved her through.

"Where's Detective Hansen?" she asked as she ducked under the police tape.

"He's up there somewhere," the young officer answered, tilting his head back in the direction of the actual crime scene.

She nodded and made her way to the entrance of the parking garage. There were flashes of bright light as the news reporters began snapping off as many pictures as they could. Many shouted questions at Amy as she walked by. She did her professional best to ignore them and acted as if they were not there. There was no way she was going to give these vultures any information without getting the okay from the captain. She was already on a short leash and under constant scrutiny; she definitely did not need any more trouble.

Some of the officers on crowd control duty moved in and pushed the reporters back. There were, of course, the inevitable arguments about Freedom of the Press and all that other crap reporters often spewed in hopes of finding a sympathetic officer. This was the LAPD though; there was no sympathy. The reporters were pushed back to a respectable distance and that was the end of any arguments.

Since she was technically off duty, she really had no claim to be here any more than the reporters did. Detective Hansen had done her a favor by letting her in on the investigation. It was only fair though. She was the one that had investigated the prostitute, and she was the one who had made the connection between the lawyer and the hooker. She should be here this night, if for no other reason than her familiarity with the other cases. She knew however, if any other officer in Homicide Section I had been on call, she would never have been informed.

Just as she was about to enter into the parking garage, she noticed another vehicle pull up. It was navy blue, and it was so ordinary looking it immediately stood out and caught her attention. She knew what that meant, and she knew only one institution used cars that looked that plain. The Feds had caught wind of this case, and here they were. Man, Detective Hansen and especially the captain were going to be hot. Now that the press had picked up on this story, the case had moved to a high profile position. The captain would want his department to handle this. If the Feds got involved, they would steal the spotlight.

She did not care one way or another though. All she knew was that people were dying in a pretty gruesome manner, and so far not a thing had been done about it. There was absolutely no evidence to speak of. The killer and his or her motive was a complete mystery.

The bodies were starting to stack up, and in her estimation, the killer was just getting started.

She did not wait to see the Feds get out of their supposed undercover car. She entered the parking garage, and began her search for Detective Hansen. She needed to let him know that he was about to get some uninvited company. She knew the look on Detective Hansen's face when he found out about the Feds would be priceless, but she also felt a pang of guilt about taking pleasure in the detective's misery. He had thrown her a bone after all.

As she made her way to the actual crime scene, she could see quick flashes of light, and hear the loud clicking as the crime scene investigators were processing the scene with their cameras. The parking garage was of the underground variety, and was fairly small compared to most. It looked as if it would only hold fifty or so cars, twenty-five on each side with a drive cutting through the middle. The garage was pretty crowded with the crime scene investigators and the homicide officers that had been unlucky enough to be on duty.

At the very back of the parking garage, was an elevator, and this was where the flashes were coming from. She could see a lump of bloodied flesh propped up against the elevator doors. She could also smell the awful stench that always accompanied a murder scene. It was a combination of raw, spoiling meat, and a coppery metallic smell. It always made her sick to her stomach, and this instance was no different. She did not dare show weakness in front of these sharks though or she would never live it down. If word got out that she could not handle a crime scene, then she would find herself stuck in front of a desk answering phones. She was not about to let that happen. She had worked too hard.

As she slowly walked closer to the scene, she saw Detective Hansen off to the right. He was talking to one of the crime scene investigators. Hansen looked pretty haggard, but was definitely in control of the situation. She had always envied Detective Hansen's ability to be at ease no matter how strange the situation was. He was a natural leader, and so, as a byproduct, people just seemed to flock to him. They trusted him, and followed him without the detective really having to try and assert himself. It was a gift he possessed, and she hated him for it.

She continued to watch Detective Hansen as she made her way down the length of the garage. She tried to stay focused on Hansen so she would not have to look at the lump of flesh that was left of the victim. Detective Hansen, as if sensing her presence, looked up from his conversation and spotted her, and quickly waved her over. She tried to look confident as she sauntered over to where Detective Hansen was standing.

"Lovely night for a murder," she quipped, trying to sound at ease.

"Only you would think that, Sommers," Detective Hansen fired back without any hesitation. "About time you showed up. What did you do, stop off for a beer before you decided to grace us with your presence?"

The other officers that were within earshot laughed condescendingly.

"Well shoot, Hansen, if I had known you were in such a hurry to see me, I would have gussied up a bit for ya," she said mockingly. She was seething that Hansen had demeaned her in front of the other officers, but she felt better as she watched Hansen's face redden after her own condescending comment.

"Whatever, Sommers," Detective Hansen said tiredly. "I called you in on this because I knew you would want to be a part of the investigation, but if you would rather stand here and trade insults then maybe I made a mistake."

"Screw you, Hansen," she replied. "No way you are going to save face now, so cut the crap and give me the run down. Oh, and by the way, you are about to get some company."

"What are you talking about?"

Amy could tell Hansen had probably already guessed, but she said it anyway, "The Feds pulled in right after I did. They should be walking in any minute."

"Christ, what else can go wrong?" Hansen asked in a loud voice.

The look on his face was as priceless as Amy had predicted. She wanted to smirk at him, but decided to err on the side of caution and keep her thoughts to herself. There was no sense in committing career suicide just for the sake of a good chuckle.

Detective Hansen's outburst had pretty much summed up her own feelings as well. She stared at Hansen, and nodded her head in understanding. This case was hard enough, and with the Feds involved, it was going to become a real migraine headache fast. She could tell the mood in the garage had just gotten a bit more hostile, and the attitudes were growing chillier by the second.

"Well before those jerks get here and try to take over, let me give you the run down," Detective Hansen said as he regained his composure. "It's our guy, of that there is no doubt. It's the same MO. The victim was incapacitated by arrows, and sliced to pieces by an extremely sharp blade. The victim's heart was cut out and removed, probably postmortem. It's just like the other two. There is no evidence of the perp entering or leaving the scene. This victim, as far as we know, is completely unrelated to the other two. There are no fingerprints or any other forensic evidence other than what's left of the victim."

Amy could tell Detective Hansen was holding something back. He had a glimmer of excitement in his eyes that gave his secret away.

"You found something didn't you?" she asked.

She could feel herself getting excited as well. So far this case had turned up zero evidence that could help them identify and stop their killer. If Detective Hansen had found something, then it was possible they would be able to crack this case wide open.

"You know the arrows that this prick uses to disable his victims?" Detective Hansen asked teasingly.

"Yeah," she answered slowly.

"This time he screwed up. In his haste to get out of here, the stupid psycho left the bow behind." Detective's Hansen's eyes almost popped out of his head as he relayed this last nugget of information.

"Are you shitting me?" she asked in shock. This was exactly the big break this case needed. Now maybe they could make some headway in catching this piece of garbage.

"I wouldn't shit you, Sommers. You're my favorite turd," Hansen said jokingly before adding, "It's already been bagged and sent to the lab for processing. Let's see those Fed jerks get their hands on that."

Amy could tell Hansen was trying to sound triumphant, but she also knew that if the Feds wanted this piece of evidence, they would get it. She just hoped the investigation would be a joint effort between the two departments. Detective Hansen could sound as confident as he wanted, but once the Feds walked into the garage they would be running the show.

As if on cue, Amy saw the federal agents make their way into the parking garage. There were two of them. One was average height but looked as solid as a brick wall, and the other one was tall and skinny. The second agent appeared naturally graceful as he seemed to glide rather than walk. As the two agents closed the distance, she was taken aback by the tall skinny agent. There was something about him that was just not right. She could not quite put her finger on it, but he seemed out of place.

She continued to watch the two agents as they made their way down into the parking garage. They walked just at the edge of the actual murder scene. She could tell the tall skinny agent was unnerved, and that made her feel a little better about her own unease.

"I'm looking for a Detective Hansen," the solid looking agent said. His tone was not unfriendly, but it left no doubt as to who was in charge.

If the mood and the atmosphere in the parking garage had been growing cooler before, it was downright frosty now. Amy thought that if things got any chillier between the officers and their new visitors, the Feds, then she was going to be able to see her breath soon.

Upon hearing his name, Detective Hansen looked up, made eye contact with the federal agent that had asked about him, and walked over. He kept his stride quick and even. Amy, who was watching this scenario unfold, knew Hansen was nervous, but he would never let it show.

"I'm Detective Hansen. What can I do for you?" the detective's voice was calm, but not quite steady. Amy thought she could pick up a slight waver in his tone, which definitely belied his anger.

The larger of the two federal agents, who appeared to be the one in charge, turned to stare at Detective Hansen. The agent gave Hansen a good hard look over. It was obvious to all that were watching, which was pretty much everybody in the garage, the agent was clearly sizing Detective Hansen up.

After looking the detective over, and being satisfied with what he saw, the agent responded, "I am Special Agent Reggie Blackburn, FBI." Agent Blackburn then turned to look over his shoulder at the other taller yet skinnier agent. "This is Special Agent Kalen... Wain."

Amy immediately picked up on the fact that Agent Blackburn hesitated when he tried introducing his partner by name. Either these two did not work together very often or Agent Blackburn was lying. That did not seem logical, but if she had to lay a bet, she would put her money down on the lie.

Amy turned her attention to the quiet agent. He was fairly tall, maybe 6'4", and slender. She had mistaken his body type when she first saw him walk into the garage. He was slim, but he had an underlying strength. It was almost as if he had an aura that surrounded him that made him glow or shine. He wore an old-fashioned raincoat that he kept tied tightly at his waist. She thought she could make out a slight bulge at his hip. It did not look like a gun, but she was pretty sure it was a weapon of some kind. He also wore a fedora-style hat that was pulled down tight over his ears, and also pulled low over his face. He pulled it down even lower as she stared at him. This kept his eyes and most of his face in shadow. She was pretty sure this was intentional, but she had no idea why. Was he trying to hide something? She could not be sure. There was something about these two that did not feel right, but she usually got that vibe when the Feds were around. They just gave off that weird feeling of holding all the cards and knowing all the secrets. She was brought back to the moment by Detective Hansen's voice as it began to rise in anger.

"This is a load of crap!" Detective Hansen yelled. "You think I am just going to sit back while you stroll in here and take over our investigation? You must be outta your stinking mind if you think that's going to happen."

"You can think what you want, pal," Special Agent Blackburn fired back. "I don't care much for your tone either. Why don't give your captain a call and he will ease your burden over who is now running this investigation."

"You Feds really tick me off. We do all the work, and you guys come sweeping in to take all the glory." Detective Hansen was irate, and his tone matched his mood. "You bet your ass I'm calling my captain. This isn't over yet."

Detective Hansen turned towards Amy and aimed his finger at her chest. "Detective Sommers, watch these two while I call the captain. If they try and touch anything, arrest them for obstruction. He's not touching a damn thing until I get final confirmation."

Detective Hansen stormed out of the garage so he could get a signal on his cell phone and call the captain.

Kalen grew uneasy as he and Reggie neared the crime scene. The feeling had started creeping up on him once Reggie had turned onto the new road. According to the sign he had read as they made their turn; it was Glenoaks Boulevard.

Reggie continued to drive up this road, and the feeling of unease continued to increase. By the time Reggie stopped the car in front of the largest building Kalen had ever seen, the feeling of unease had turned into full-fledged nausea. He worried that he might even be sick.

Reggie had noticed that Kalen did not look well, and had made a brief inquiry as to how the Elf was feeling. Kalen just waved it off, and they proceeded to the scene. He was hoping the nausea was just a leftover side effect of the magic used in his crossing over, but he thought it was strange that it was affecting him now. Whatever it was, it was getting stronger.

Kalen and Reggie exited the car at the same time. Kalen looked around, and took several deep breaths to try and calm his stomach. It helped a little, but a new wave of nausea made his stomach roll anew. The air in that place seemed to smell of smoke and rot, which did not help much either. How the Humans could treat their world like this, he would never understand. To have this level of pollution where people actually lived was unforgivable in his opinion. He pushed those thoughts to the back of his mind. He was not here to judge the Humans, but to try and save his own people.

He was also surprised by how many people were here. It seemed as if this was some sort of attraction for all to see. Did these people have no respect for the dead? Whatever had transpired here was a tragedy, not a spectacle. He was amazed as he watched Humans in uniforms physically push the crowd back at times. He had never seen anything like it, and in his estimation, the whole scene was insane.

Kalen turned as Reggie called out to him and made a motion for the Elf to follow. He watched intently as Reggie showed his medal or badge to another officer that was standing guard to an entrance to some sort of manmade cave. It was dark, but he could tell this cave led underground. The man in uniform that was standing guard seemed angry, but he moved aside and Reggie again motioned for Kalen to follow him, this time into the underground cave.

They did not have to walk very far. The air in the cave-like structure was just as bad if not worse than the air outside. It tasted stale to him as he breathed it in. The nausea reached an all time high as he moved farther into the cave. Reggie walked ahead a few steps. He seemed confident in where he was going, so Kalen just followed behind.

Just ahead, he could see several people milling about. Some were using machines that caused bright flashes while others were diligently writing things down in some sort of notebooks, while still others seemed to just be standing around and observing. He was again surprised by how many people there were. He thought it was also odd that none of these people were wearing uniforms, even though it was clear by their actions that they were part of the security force. Not wearing a uniform to the scene of a crime would have been a terrible breach in protocol for the Elven Security Force. Strange seemed to be the word of the day for Kalen though, so he did his best to try and go with the flow.

As they reached the bottom of the manmade cave, Kalen could see the body, or more accurately, what was left of the body. An annoying buzzing in his head joined the nausea he had been experiencing to this point. It was like having a small insect slowly buzz around your ear, and no matter how many times you swatted at it, it kept dodging your blows and would slowly make its way back.

He brought his attention back to Reggie as the special agent made an inquiry. Another Human walked over to stand in front of Reggie. This Detective Hansen, as Reggie had named him, was not that imposing of a figure, but Kalen noted that he exuded confidence. He quickly surmised this was the person in charge.

It was just as Reggie had said it would be. Detective Hansen was angry that he and Reggie were there, so he stood silently out of the way as Special Agent Blackburn and Detective Hansen exchanged harsh comments.

Kalen did become aware of someone watching him at this point. Heeding Reggie's words, he tried to keep himself as inconspicuous as possible. He pulled his hat even lower, hoping this would not let anyone get a good look at his face. His own curiosity was piqued however, and he could not help himself. He took a quick look around. His eyes immediately were drawn to the person that was staring intently at him.

He was surprised to see this person was a woman. He was not surprised a woman would be involved in a proceeding such as this. Elven women were equals in every way, and many had served admirably for the Royal Guard. His surprise at seeing the woman was due more to the fact that she was the first Human female he had ever seen. On first glance, the curious Elf did not think she was as attractive as the Elven women he was more accustomed to, but she was not displeasing to the eye either. He made a mental note that this woman seemed to be a person of importance here as well.

He continued to watch from under the brim of his hat. Detective Hansen startled the woman when he barked out an order for her to watch him and Reggie before storming out of the underground cave. She was caught off guard at first, but recovered quickly.

She walked over to Reggie and in a friendly gesture shook hands with the special agent. Kalen listened intently as she spoke.

"Hi. I'm Detective Sommers. Don't mind Hansen, he always acts like that when he loses a peeing contest," she said amicably.

Special Agent Blackburn laughed out loud at her comment. Kalen stood transfixed and watched her closely as he continued to listen to their conversation.

"Detective Sommers, it's nice to know someone around here has a sense of humor," Agent Blackburn joked in an attempt to de-escalate the tension that had built up. "We are here to do a job just like you guys. I have my orders, and from this point on, Agent Wain and myself will be leading the investigation."

Amy looked over at Kalen curiously. "Does he ever talk?"

"Rarely," Reggie answered back quickly. "Special Agent Wain is a crime scene specialist and a profiler."

Kalen noted that Reggie's description of him seemed to impress Detective Sommers. If it was not for the incessant buzzing in his ears, and the strong desire to retch, he may have enjoyed that moment a lot more. Instead, he just nodded at Detective Sommers noncommittally. She smiled and nodded back.

The moment was broken, though, as Detective Hansen made his way back into the underground cave, "Well boys, shut her down. The big bad Feds are here to wipe our butts for us."

This brought a groan from the other officers. Detective Hansen turned his attention back to Special Agent Blackburn and said, "Well the captain confirmed your story. I still think it's a load of bull, and I want to be kept in the loop at all times. Is that clear?"

Special Agent Blackburn smiled back sarcastically. "That works both ways you know."

"Whatever," Detective Hansen rebutted before he walked away.

"Is he always such a prick?" Reggie asked Detective Sommers as he watched the disgruntled detective storm off.

Detective Sommers smiled and shrugged her shoulders.

"Pretty much," she answered back.

# —CHAPTER 9

Kalen was still queasy and the buzzing in his ears was still there. He took some small measure of comfort as these two sensations started to subside. He decided to turn his attention to the matter at hand. He needed to get a look at the body if he was going to be able to learn anything.

"Well Agent Wain, it's time to earn your keep," Reggie commented. "Let's go have a look at the deceased."

"The crime scene techs are just finishing up processing the scene so it might be few minutes before you can have access to the body," Amy replied.

"Okay, but we are going to need the reports of all your findings, and I don't just mean from this scene. We will need the others as well," Reggie was trying to sound authoritative.

"Sure, that's no problem. I have most of the files on my desk back at the station." Amy did her best to go along.

"Well since I doubt Mr. Congeniality down there is going to be much help tonight," Reggie said as he nodded his head in Detective Hansen's general direction. "You know what they say, Detective Sommers, you show me yours and I'll show you mine."

"You know Agent Blackburn, as sad as that was, it was still the best offer I have had in awhile," she said trying to sound funny.

Amy and Reggie both laughed. Kalen had no idea what was so funny so he continued standing quietly.

After she finished laughing, Amy began rattling off all the information she knew about the case. "Whoever this psycho is, he's a real whack job. He hunts his victims down with a bow and arrow, and then slices them to pieces. From there, he steals their hearts, and I don't mean in a good way." She aimed that last comment at Reggie and they again shared a laugh.

Kalen was surprised that he felt envious of how easily Special Agent Blackburn got along and carried on a conversation with Detective Sommers. He wanted to join in, but for one thing he had no idea what the joke was, and for another he knew it was better to heed Agent Blackburn's warning and keep a low profile. Still, he was unnerved by the pangs of envy that were joining the nausea at the pit of his stomach.

"The really odd thing is," Amy continued, "the killer has left next to no physical evidence at any of the crime scenes. And by no evidence, I mean no evidence; not one hair, fiber, fingerprint or anything else. The only thing we had, up until tonight, were the arrows that were left behind in the victims' bodies, and they are another mystery altogether. It's almost as if this guy is a ghost that wanders in, slaughters his victim, and then simply vanishes."

Reggie and Kalen shared a quick look upon hearing this. Kalen had picked up on one of Detective Sommers' comments, and decided to chance asking a question. "You said, 'up until tonight.' Did you find something new at this scene?"

"He speaks," Amy exclaimed in mock surprise.

Unbelievably, Kalen felt himself blushing. He desperately hoped his hat was pulled down far enough that no one would notice. At that moment, he would have rather had someone notice the fact his ears were pointed than see him turn a nice shade of red.

"Hey, you're good," Amy chimed back into the conversation. "Tonight, our killer may have screwed up big time. He left his bow behind. We found it not far from the victim's car."

Kalen immediately forgot about his embarrassment. He definitely needed to get a look at the bow. He hoped there was some way that he could use this to bring Drè down easily. Any edge he could get would be helpful at this point. He just hoped that this was good sign of things to come.

He turned to Reggie and in a hushed tone said, "I need to see that bow."

To his credit, Reggie nodded and calmly stated to Detective Sommers, "My partner is going to need to get a look at that bow, and we may have to keep it in our possession for awhile."

"Well, it has already been sent to the crime lab for processing," Detective Sommers replied. "If you guys want to swing by the department tomorrow, we can ride over to the lab and go over the results together."

Reggie was just starting to comment that he did not think that would be necessary when Kalen interrupted him. "That's a good idea, Detective Sommers. Now I need to look at the body."

"Sure, I think the techs are pretty much finished."

Reggie stared at Kalen in frustration. "I thought we agreed on a low profile."

"She knows these murders, and she will make it easier for us to get that bow," he explained.

"Maybe," Reggie said knowingly. "She's also not too hard on the eyes, but I am sure you are above such mundane things, being an Elf and all."

Kalen answered the accusation by shaking his head, while making his way to where the body of the third victim was propped up against the elevator doors. The nausea and buzzing had almost completely stopped. This unnerved him as he still had no explanation for the cause.

He approached the body carefully. Agent Blackburn and Detective Sommers stayed back at the periphery to give him room to work. He really had no idea what he was looking for. As he got closer to the body, he could see how severe and complete the mutilation was. Only one blade could make cuts that deep and precise. He knew because he carried such a blade at his hip at that very moment.

The curved scimitar of the Elven military was the most finely crafted sword the Elves could produce. He had one as Captain of the Royal Guard, and General Brandy'wine had one as leader of the Elven military. That was the very same sword he carried. He also knew Drè's father would have had one as well. That was more than likely the blade Drè was using to carve his victims into the mess that was laid out before him right now.

Kalen also took special note of the arrows that were protruding from this victim's body. The fletching was made from the tail feathers of a moon falcon. It was no wonder Detective Sommers had called the arrows a mystery. That particular type of falcon did not exist in the Human's realm. Neither did the Ash wood the arrow's shaft was made from. That wood was from one of the sacred Ash Trees that made up the forest the Elves called home. There was no way the security force Detective Sommers worked for could trace these arrows. They simply did not have anything to compare them to.

After he finished looking over the body, Kalen walked back to where Reggie and Detective Sommers were standing.

"Could you please show me where you found the bow?" He directed his question towards Detective Sommers.

"Hold on, I will have to get Hansen over here, he never showed me." Amy paused and looked around. She spotted Detective Hansen off to one side, brooding. "Hey Hansen, they need to know where you found the bow."

"Sure, maybe I could run and get them some sandwiches too since apparently that is all we're good for." He was still fuming over his altercation with Special Agent Blackburn and he made no attempt to hide his disdain.

Smiling, Agent Blackburn replied, "Sandwiches? That's a great idea. I like mine with extra mustard."

Detective Hansen glared back at Reggie. He muttered something under his breath, and from the tone, Kalen knew it was nothing nice.

"Just follow me so we can get this over with," Detective Hansen said after exhaling a deep breath.

He led them back up the drive, close to the entrance of the underground cave. He stopped next to the second-to-last car before the entrance.

"We found the bow right here," Detective Hansen uttered while pointing to the ground next to the driver side door of the car.

Kalen knelt to inspect the ground in hopes of finding any clue that might give him any information that could be used to help locate the whereabouts of Drè Fao'lain. What he got instead was another dose of gut-wrenching nausea. He actually swooned, and had to put his hands out to stop himself from toppling over.

Then it dawned on him what was causing these feelings. It was the residual side effect of magic, but not the magic that had been used to help him cross over, but from the Shadowed Arts Drè had employed to help carry out his evil plan. He knew that Elves had a certain sensitivity when it came to all things magic. He just had never been so aware of it before. He was unsure whether it was due to the power of the Shadowed Arts or if it had something to do with being in the Human realm.

"This is where he exited," he said to Reggie before he could catch himself.

"This is where who left?" Detective Hansen asked harshly. "The killer?"

He was not sure what to say. Instead he looked to Reggie for help in trying to put this fire out before it blew up in his face. Thankfully though, Detective Hansen was so angry over the whole situation he was willing to jump on anything he could use to make the Feds look bad.

"Sure this is where he left. He just snapped his fingers and vanished into thin air. Well this case is closed. Wow you federal agents sure are good," Detective Hansen rambled on sarcastically. "Give me a break. Sommers, I am appointing you department liaison with these guys. I've had my fill." With that said, Detective Hansen stomped out of the garage.

Detective Sommers on the other hand had not said a word. She looked at Kalen in a strange way. He knew she had heard his slip. He knew it was a relatively minor mistake, but anything that could give him or the reason why he was there away was problematic at best. He knew it was not enough to just disguise his appearance; he would have to choose his words carefully as well from now on.

Sensing that Detective Sommers was about to start asking questions, Reggie decided to head everything off at the pass. "Well, I think we're finished. Agent Wain and I will be in touch." Kalen watched as Reggie reached into his coat pocket and pulled out a rectangular piece of paper, and handed it to Detective Sommers before adding, "If you need to get hold of us with any information about the case, you can reach me here at this number."

Amy took the card and deftly slid it into her own coat pocket without so much as glancing at it.

"That's fine," she said, and then added, "I'm not going to get home until late so I won't be at my desk until late tomorrow morning. Call the department and they will patch you through, and we can set up a time when you want to go over to the lab."

"Will do," Reggie answered back.

Reggie then motioned for Kalen to follow him once again as he started making his way back outside. Kalen stood his ground for a few seconds longer, watching Detective Sommers as she walked back down to the murder scene to join her fellow security force officers. He was pleasantly surprised when Detective Sommers glanced back over her shoulder and gave him a smile. He smiled back, and then quickly turned and caught up with Reggie.

The two walked back to Reggie's car. It was still dark out, and the rain had started to fall once again. Neither one said a word as they both opened their doors and got back into the dirty blue car. Reggie dug in his pocket for the key, and fired the car up just like he had done back at the park where he had first met Kalen.

Before he started the car though, Reggie turned and smirked at the Elf. "So Romeo, you have only been in this world for a few hours and you have already been smitten by one of the natives."

Reggie started laughing out loud at his own joke. Kalen just glared back at the Human agent. He was not quite sure what Reggie was saying, but he knew enough to know he was being made fun of. The serious look on Kalen's face only caused Reggie to laugh louder as he put the car in gear and drove away.

# CHAPTER 10

Kalen awoke the next morning around 9 a.m. In those first few seconds of delirium one feels upon waking, the tired Elf thought the events that had transpired the previous evening were all part of some strange and elaborate dream. Unfortunately for him however, he opened his eyes and seeing his strange surroundings, it all came flooding back, and he realized that it had been all too real.

After leaving the crime scene the night before, Special Agent Blackburn explained he was going to get a room for the night at something called a hotel. Kalen figured that a hotel was the Human equivalent to an inn, and when Reggie pulled into a building with a large sign out front that named the building "Resident's Inn," he knew that he had figured correctly.

On the way to the inn, Reggie had also stopped and picked up some food. Kalen had thought it was magic when Reggie had talked into a little box and then drove around to the side and their food was there waiting for them. Reggie explained this was often referred to as fast food. Kalen had no idea what he was eating, but he was pleasantly surprised by how good the food was. He had not eaten anything since before he had gone to meet the Elven Council, and he was famished. He ate the fast food hurriedly; he even finished Reggie's fried vegetables. The agent had called them French-fries. Kalen did not care about the name; he just needed to replenish all the energy he had expended from the evening's continuously odd events.

When they had finally arrived at their hotel room, Kalen literally collapsed onto the bed and mercifully slipped into unconsciousness. He had slept straight through the night without even so much as a grunt or a snore. As with the food and his hunger, he did not realize how exhausted he was until he lay down on the bed. Sleep overtook him quickly, and he did not even bother trying to put up a fight. He welcomed sleep's embrace, and reveled in its serenity.

Once he was awake, and he assured himself the evening before had not been a bad dream, he climbed out of bed and stretched. He was surprised how sore he was and how cramped his muscles felt. He was reminded of how he felt after being involved in a major battle as it was the same kind of soreness and aching. He knew the soreness arose for the same reason, he had been running on adrenaline. From first hearing the news that Drè Fao'lain was back, to the crossing over and the initial meeting with Special Agent Blackburn, and then the drive to the murder scene and the meeting with Detective Sommers, he had been on a huge adrenaline rush. He had not had any down time until the moment he had collapsed in utter exhaustion.

He looked at himself in the mirror that was hanging on the wall above the chest of drawers. It was the only piece of furniture in the room other than the two beds. He looked as ragged as he could ever remember. He was still wearing his Royal Guard uniform that he had put on before going to the council. It was wrinkled and disheveled. He felt a slight pang of guilt when he saw the state his uniform was in. As a professional soldier, he had always taken great pride in his appearance, and tried to convey the importance of appearance to the Elves he commanded in the Royal Guard. If those Elves could only see him now.

He looked around the room. He saw General Brandy'wine's sword lying on the floor by the bed he had slept in. He had simply unbuckled the scabbard and let it fall to the floor before he had crawled into bed. He again felt the guilt that only a commanding officer could understand. He preached to his men all the time about taking care of their equipment; this especially pertained to their swords. He picked up the sword and gently laid it down on the bed. General Brandy'wine would be livid if he saw how he had simply tossed his sword away like it was nothing more than a piece of dirty laundry.

Just then, Kalen noticed he was alone in the room. Special Agent Blackburn had apparently left sometime before he had regained consciousness. He was not surprised. Reggie had told him the night before he was going to check in at the local agency office, and make some arrangements. He hoped Reggie would bring back some more of that fast food. He was starving again, and he knew he had a long day ahead of him. He had no idea of the time or even how time worked in the Human's realm. He did remember however that he and Reggie were supposed to meet Detective Sommers sometime in the morning so he could get a look at the bow the Human security force had found.

He was again struck by an odd feeling. He was not sure he knew the source of the excitement he felt. Possibly it was because he was going to be looking at a key piece of evidence that could help him find Drè Fao'lain and return home quickly. Alternatively, the tingling sensation in the pit of his stomach could be due to the fact he was going to see Detective Sommers again.

He had never before met a woman he felt such an instant connection with. Though they had barely spoken to each other, he was fascinated by Detective Sommers. She seemed to possess an inner strength and a strong sense of duty that definitely appealed to him. He had met plenty of women who had served in the military and had a sense of duty similar to his own, but Detective Sommers seemed to radiate a glow of assuredness in her actions. She had a job to do, and she was not going to let anyone stand in the way of completing that job. He respected that kind of attitude and could relate to it completely.

She also seemed to be a very observant person, and it was clear to him that she did not miss much. He remembered his slight slip of information from the previous evening, and knew he should be prepared to answer the questions that would be coming. Detective Sommers had picked up on it as well, and if he had guessed correctly about her personality, then she would not let that slip go without some kind of explanation. He would expect nothing less from Detective Sommers. This gave him something to ponder as he cleaned himself up and waited for Special Agent Blackburn to return.

Around the time Kalen was waking and stretching out his sore muscles, Drè Fao'lain had also awakened from his mildly replenishing sleep to start his day. The sleep had been nowhere near long enough, and Drè could still feel the effects of his prolonged use of the Shadowed Arts. He felt weak and unsteady. His thoughts were fuzzy, and it took several minutes for his head to clear enough for him to even start considering the implications of another Elf crossing over.

He remembered the sharp pain he had endured upon this new Elf's arrival into the Human's realm. This had the potential to cause serious problems for the murderous Elf's schedule. That is why he had to cut his sleep of replenishment short, and that is why he felt the way he did at the moment. He could not allow anything to interfere with his plans. He knew he was going to have to deal with this new problem quickly. He could only add sacrifices during the full moon phase, which only gave him two nights a month to work. With this new Elf in town, things could get difficult.

He had originally planned to sleep longer so he could use his Shadowed Arts to travel to another part of the Human realm for his next sacrifice. He had the victim picked out, and had worked to put his plan into motion. With this new predicament however, he dared not leave town. He would have to find another victim here in Los Angeles. He had never taken victims from the same area on back-to-back days. That could prove challenging. If successful though he would have six sacrifices. He was halfway to his revenge and his salvation. He was not going to let anything stand in his way, especially not another uninvited Elf.

The ritual called for the sacrifice of someone with a corrupted heart. It had been so easy finding Humans that met this requirement. He usually studied his prey closely. Tonight though, he was going to have to act quickly. There would not be time for detailed preparations. He also knew he would not have as great a command of the Shadowed Arts that he relied upon. That was fine though. The Humans were no match for the power he could wield, even if it was in small amounts.

He dressed quickly in his black suit. He began gathering the necessary tools for the evening's work. It was then that he realized he did not have his bow. He could not remember what had happened to it. His thoughts were still a little fuzzy. He searched every square inch of the warehouse, but came up empty. He decided to replay the events from the night before in an effort to retrace his steps. The realization of what had happened to the longbow slowly unfolded before him. He had dropped the bow in the garage, and in his fervor of the moment, had forgotten it.

He went into a frenzied rage. How could he have been so careless? He had planned his sacrifices out to minute detail. He left no evidence for the stupid Human police to find. Now they had the longbow, which gave them a direct link back to him.

He destroyed his sleeping quarters in his fit of rage. His well laid plans, for the moment anyway, seemed to be coming apart. This just would not do. He was torn between trying to retrieve his longbow from the police or concentrating what was left of his energy into finding his next sacrifice. In the end it was no contest. The ritual was what was important. The longbow would have to wait. He promised himself that whoever he chose as his sacrifice would suffer dearly for the trouble that this would cause.

He stepped outside to get some fresh air, attempting to clear his mind. There was no one outside or on the streets. This was another reason why he had chosen this location to call forth the Tree of Sacrifice. It was deserted. The neighborhood was made up of the poor and downtrodden. What people that were still around, kept to themselves. The Human world had already chewed them up and spit them out. He marveled at how the Humans treated each other. What a sick and deprived race they were. No wonder it was so easy for him to find victims that were corrupt. From what he had seen, they were all corrupt.

He walked to the corner of the street that his abandoned warehouse was located on. There he found what he was looking for. He had made it a habit of looking in the Human's newspapers for stories about his crimes. This always amused him.

On the corner was what was left of a stack of papers that had been dropped off for dispersal. When he looked at the front page, his mood changed from anger to ecstasy. Not only was the story of the grisly murder he had committed the night before on the front page of the paper, but the picture gave him the answer he was looking for. The picture had just given the vengeance-crazed Elf his next victim. It was time to prepare.

Special Agent Blackburn returned to the hotel a short time later while Kalen was in the bathroom washing up. He had indeed brought breakfast with him. It was something called an Egg McMuffin. Kalen devoured it much as he had done with the cheeseburger the night before. This was definitely one thing about the Human world he was enjoying. The food was fantastic. The coffee Reggie brought was another story. It was bitter, and he had a hard time getting it down. He forced himself to drink it though, knowing that he was going to need his strength to get him through the day. He sat on the bed and ate his food and drank the bitter coffee as Reggie laid out the plan for the morning.

"I checked in at the home office this morning, and there wasn't any news. This guy really covers his tracks well." Kalen nodded in agreement as he continued to chew the last bite of his Egg McMuffin. "I also brought you some different clothes. I had to guess the size, but they should fit. There is one more thing. You cannot be running around Los Angeles with that sword." Reggie emphasized this by pointing at the blade Kalen had placed on the bed.

This immediately caught the Elf's attention. "I have been charged with stopping Drè Fao'lain. Just what am I supposed to use to stop him or defend myself if the situation calls for it?"

"Calm down," Reggie interjected. "I don't plan on leaving you naked out in the cold. I got you a standard agency-issue firearm. This should also help your disguise."

Kalen guessed that a firearm must be some kind of weapon, but he was not crazy about having to try and defend himself with a weapon he had never used before and was therefore uncomfortable with. This was going to be a definite problem.

"I have never used a firearm before, and I do not think I would be very proficient in its use if we get into a situation that would call for us to go into battle," he tried to explain.

"I figured that, so let's just hope that we don't have to go into battle. All I know is that you cannot go around carrying that sword on your hip. If it makes you feel better, we can keep the sword in the car, but when we are out in public, you carry the gun," Reggie emphasized.

The way Reggie said this last statement left no room for argument. Kalen could see the logic in what Reggie was saying though. He did indeed need to do everything that he could do to try and fit in, and make himself as inconspicuous as possible.

"I agree, and I will comply with your wishes," he said conceding the point.

"Good. I'm glad that's settled," Reggie said as he handed Kalen the bag containing the clothes. "You should change. I called your new friend, and we are supposed to meet her at her office at 11:30."

Kalen felt that tingle of excitement again. He tried not to let it show, but one look at Special Agent Blackburn's face told him he had failed miserably. The Elf scowled at Reggie as he took the bag and walked into the bathroom to change. He could hear Reggie laughing through the closed door.

He dressed quickly. The clothes Reggie had gotten for him were a little big, but they fit well enough. It was similar attire to what Reggie wore. It consisted of dark blue slacks with a black belt, a white long-sleeved shirt that buttoned up the front, and a jacket that was the same color as the pants. There was also a long piece of cloth he was unfamiliar with. He had seen the same type of material around Reggie's neck. The material was tied in a loop so he slipped it over his head and under his collar as he had seen Reggie do. He then pulled the material until it was snug around his neck. Lastly, he slipped on the black shoes and socks that were in the bag. The shoes were a little small and they pinched his feet. He was used to wearing his uniform boots. These shoes did not seem very practical to him, but since he was trying to pretend to be Human, he knew he would have to deal with the discomfort.

When he finished, he walked out into the other room. There he saw Reggie handling a small black object. He watched as Reggie slid something into the handle and then pulled back on the front. This caused a clicking sound.

"This is a gun," Reggie explained. "It is loaded and ready to go. All you have to do is hold it like this, aim it using these sights, and then slowly squeeze the trigger."

Kalen took the gun in his hand. It felt heavy for such a small object. It was unwieldy in his opinion, and not very practical. He held it like Reggie had just shown him.

"Careful now, if you pull the trigger, the people in the next room will get a rude awakening," Reggie half-joked. "The way it works is, once you squeeze that trigger, you release a bullet. That's a projectile that travels at a very high speed. That bullet will create a pretty large hole in whatever it hits, and it does not stop traveling until it does hit something pretty solid."

Kalen lowered the gun, and understood why this weapon could be effective. He still preferred to carry his sword though. He planned on taking Reggie up on his offer of bringing the sword along. He knew he would feel better having his own weapon of choice around if things ever got out of hand and if a battle was imminent.

"Last but not least, you are going to want this." Reggie handed Kalen another hat. It was of the same style as the one he had worn the night before. This hat though was newer and was the same color as the clothes he was now wearing.

"Clothes make the man, you know," Reggie joked again.

Kalen shook his head in confusion, which just brought another round of chuckling from Reggie. He put the hat on his head, and pulled it down low so it would cover his ears. He then picked up the gun and started to slip it into his coat pocket.

"Oh, wait a minute, I forgot this. It's a shoulder holster. Take your coat off and I will put it on for you," Reggie said, holding a figure-eight looking black strap.

Kalen did as he was told, and when Reggie finished, he looked at himself in the mirror. He did not like what he saw. He felt as if he was staring at a complete stranger. He barely recognized himself. The shoulder holster was snug, and like the shoes, uncomfortable. He did not know how Humans walked around like this all day.

"If you're ready, then let's roll," Reggie said.

Kalen grabbed his sword and followed Reggie out the door. They walked out to the car and he placed the sword in the back seat where it would be within easy reach if he needed it. He then climbed into the passenger seat and buckled himself in. Reggie completed his ritual of patting himself down in an effort to find his keys, and then he too slid into the car.

"Are we going directly to Detective Sommers' office?" he asked in anticipation.

Reggie looked at the Elf and jokingly said, "Look at you, you're as nervous as a virgin on prom night."

Kalen stared open-mouthed at Reggie. He knew he had just been teased again, but the humor simply did not translate. He made a mental note to have Reggie explain some of his humor when a more appropriate time came. In the meantime, he shook his head in exasperation and exhaled loudly. Reggie snorted out a laugh as he put the car in gear, and they drove off to meet with Detective Sommers.

# —CHAPTER 11

After another harrowing drive in which Special Agent Blackburn used several colorful phrases, including what was apparently his favorite description – "morons on wheels" – to describe the other Humans that were driving, they arrived at a large stone building in relatively good time. According to words etched in a large, gray piece of granite, the building was the Los Angeles Police Department. These words had been so expertly etched into the large stone obelisk Kalen wondered if maybe the Humans also had contact with the Dwarfs as well as his own people. He recognized this as the name he had heard the Human security force use to describe themselves the night before at the crime scene, and he quickly surmised this building must be their headquarters. A smaller, metal sign next to the door said "Robbery-Homicide Division."

Reggie looked at a timepiece he kept strapped to his wrist. Kalen had thought this was an odd place to put an adornment such as that, in case he had to go into battle. It looked uncomfortable, and probably would not offer up much defense. He decided to put the matter off for another time. It was just one more item for an ever-growing list of things he would try and discuss with Reggie when they had a free moment. However, right then he needed to remain focused on what was important – seeing Detective Sommers again and catching Drè Fao'lain.

He smiled inwardly and shook his head slightly. Had he really mentally listed seeing Detective Sommers as more important than completing his mission? It had just been a mental slip. He knew what his priorities were. Still, he had to admit, the thought of spending some time with Detective Sommers while working on this case was not an altogether unpleasant prospect. He just hoped it did not detract from the greater problem at hand.

"Well, we are a bit early, but I don't think she'll mind," Reggie said after glancing at his watch. "Let's get going, and for Christ's sake please remember to let me do the talking. Let's not have any more little slips."

Kalen nodded his head in ascent, but he knew if Detective Sommers was half as perceptive as he thought she was, then some questions would shortly be coming their way. Reggie strode up the stone steps that led into the building. Kalen pulled his hat down a little tighter and followed.

They were able to enter the structure without any problems. The doors were not locked and Kalen paid close attention to the fact that no sentries were stationed in front of the entrance. This was just sloppy procedure in his estimation, especially for a security force.

Once inside, he had to gasp to catch his breath. The interior was huge. It was round much like the Keep of the Full Moon had been, but this place was impressively bigger. It was the largest structure he had ever been in, and that included the palace where King Shander and the Royal Family lived. Not only was this building huge, it was ornately decorated as well. The floor was a mosaic of colored marble that shined in the late morning sunlight that streamed through the glass front doors. The walls were shiny gray granite, the same color as the exterior of the building. He once again wondered if the Humans had access to Dwarven Masons. From what he had seen in his brief time in this realm, he just could not see Humans paying that much attention to detail.

There was a large central station in the center of the immense foyer. Inside, he could see several uniformed Humans milling about. The station was completely closed in by a thick stone base that was covered in some sort of black matting. He had no idea if this was for protection or if it was decorative in nature. There were large glass windows that went all the way round the station. The glass seemed to be unusually thick. He watched and followed as Reggie approached one of the windows in the station.

Reggie reached inside his coat, and in what was fast becoming a familiar routine to Kalen, pulled out the black book containing the gold badge. He was starting to get the impression this badge must be of some importance, for whenever Reggie showed it to another Human he generally got what he wanted. It was no different this time. He wondered if the badge might have some sort of magical charm on it. If there was magic, it didn't seem very potent, though. The man on the other side of the glass seemed unimpressed.

"We are here to see Detective Sommers. She is expecting us," Reggie said after the Human behind the glass took another look at the charmed badge.

"Sure thing, let me just phone ahead," the security officer said disinterestedly.

Kalen watched with curiosity as the Human behind the glass picked up an oblong object attached to a long cord of some type. The security officer then punched a few buttons. After a few seconds, the man began speaking into the oblong object. Watching the Human work the device, Kalen realized it must be some sort of communication machine.

"Hey Sommers, your new Fed buddies are here to see ya. You want me to send them on back?"

The soldier used a mocking tone much as the Detective from the previous night had done when he had referred to Reggie and Kalen. He could not hear Detective Sommers' reply, but the soldier seemed satisfied with the response. He hung up the communication device and returned his attention to Reggie and Kalen.

"She said for you guys to go ahead and go on back," he uttered, sounding bored.

"That's really great news there guy. Uh, if you aren't too busy shuffling papers you want to tell me just where I can *find* Detective Sommers?" Reggie asked sarcastically. He was agitated by the other man's lack of respect, and was starting to lose his patience.

The Human glared back through the window at Reggie, paused, and then said, "Look just because you are some hot shot federal agent doesn't mean I have to roll out the red carpet."

"Just point me in the right direction, Sergeant, and I will be out of your hair for the rest of the day," Reggie said, showing great restraint.

The sergeant reached his arm out through the window. Kalen tensed, thinking this might be some sort an attack. Instead the man pointed to the long hall that broke off to the left of the central station.

"You just head down that hall. Take the last right and follow it all the way to the end. That's Homicide, Section I and you can find Detective Sommers there."

"See that wasn't so hard," Reggie fired back as he began heading off to the left. Kalen thought he heard Reggie whisper "moron" under his breath as he turned his back to the not-too-cooperative desk sergeant.

Reggie motioned for Kalen to follow, and the two left the disgruntled Human behind as they made their way to the meeting with Detective Sommers. The corridor was not overly long, and there were only a couple of other doors that they passed. They ignored these as they continued on.

"Why is it, Reggie, that the Humans of the security force do not seem to like you because you are a 'Fed'?" Kalen asked curiously.

This was a point that had been bothering him since the previous night. He was used to all members of all the Elven security forces getting along and working together. He figured it would be the same for the Humans as well. Apparently he had figured wrong.

Reggie gave a slight shrug of his shoulders before he responded, "Well, basically they think I am going to steal all their glory. Usually when the Feds are called in, it is because the local police either cannot handle the job or they have screwed up the job. Me being here just reminds these officers of that."

"Can they not work with us in hopes of helping the greater good?" Kalen asked as they turned right per the directions they had been given.

Again Reggie shrugged his massive shoulders. "You would think, huh? What those little jerks don't realize is that the services I provide, they would want no part in anyways."

Kalen had been listening so intently to Reggie that he failed to notice the special agent had stopped in front of a door at the end of the hall. When he looked over, he saw the words "Homicide Division, Section I" written on the glass window that made up the top half of the door. Underneath the written words, someone had taped a piece of paper to the window that read "Enter at Your Own Risk" in bold black ink. He looked at Reggie unsure as to what their next move should be.

"Well aren't they all just a bunch of Joe Comedians," Reggie commented in response to the posted sign. He looked as if he was fighting a losing battle in trying to remain patient with the whole situation.

Kalen did his best imitation of Reggie by shrugging his shoulders in response to the special agent's comment. Then Reggie opened the door and they walked into Homicide, Section I.

The room they entered was alive with activity. There were Humans wandering around all over the place. The sounds were almost overwhelming. The cacophony of people all trying to talk at once and trying to talk over each other was deafening. The constant rustle of who knows how many papers and the incessant ringing of some unknown device just added to the commotion. There were desks scattered throughout the large room that were separated by partitions of some kind. There were Humans at each desk, and they all looked extremely busy. No one paid him or Reggie any attention, and the Elf was beginning to wonder if anyone had even noticed the two had walked in.

Finally one of the Humans at the closest desk looked up from a file and with little more than a passing curiosity, asked if they needed any help.

"We're looking for Detective Sommers," Reggie once again stated.

The Human stood up, looked out over the room, and then bellowed, "Hey Sommers, you have company."

Kalen looked anxiously to see if he could spot the detective. There was too much activity, though, for him to be able to sort anything out. As an Elf, he had pretty sensitive hearing, but with all the clamor he was unable to pick out the detective's voice. Instead he stood patiently and waited for Reggie to make the next move.

"She will be right up," the Human that had yelled for Detective Sommers said.

After a couple of minutes the detective appeared from around the closest cubicle to their right. Kalen could not help himself; he knew he was openly staring at Detective Sommers as she closed the distance. She was dressed in a black pantsuit with a white shirt. She looked slightly shorter than he remembered, but she was still just as captivating. He caught Reggie's smirk out of the corner of his eye, but chose to ignore it.

Detective Sommers walked right up to Reggie and shook his hand. She turned to look at a clock that was hanging on the wall just above the door that they had entered through. The clock read 11:30 a.m. exactly.

"Well aren't you two the punctual type," she said with a joking smile.

"Yeah, well, you know us Feds are all Boy Scouts – Be prepared and all that crap," Reggie joked back.

Kalen smiled at Detective Sommers. He wanted to join in the casual banter she and Reggie were sharing, but he knew he would probably not be able to keep up. Thanks to the amulet he wore around his neck he could speak the Human language, but he was still having an incredibly hard time understanding its nuances. So instead of saying something out of place, or even worse, something that would give away who and what he was, he just stood at attention and tried not to stare too hard at the female Human he found so intriguing.

Amy flashed him a quick smile as she teased, "At ease soldier."

She chuckled as Kalen actually took the military style stance for being at ease. Apparently, she thought his actions a jest, but in truth, Kalen was just doing what came natural to him, following orders.

With a sigh, she turned her attention back to Reggie. "Well Boy Scout, I hope you're prepared. I just got off the phone with the crime lab. They want us over there pronto. It seems we have some unexplained weirdness on our hands with that bow."

Reggie and Kalen shared a quick stare before the special agent replied. "This is Los Angeles, Detective, and everything here is weird and unexplained."

"My thoughts exactly," Detective Sommers answered back, "If you two are ready, let's go check out that bow."

"After you," Reggie said with a wave of his arm.

"Well, a Boy Scout and a gentleman, not bad for a meddling Fed," the detective fired right back with another smile. Then she turned and glanced at Kalen, "All right, Soldier. You're dismissed. It's time to move out."

It took Kalen a minute to realize she was not serious. She had just been joking with him. He was disappointed she felt the need to mock him. What really bothered the Elf however, was how jealous he felt of how easily Reggie communicated with the detective. Things seemed to be getting more complicated. The noise in the room was starting to really grate on his nerves, and he was most thankful when they left the room behind.

Once they were back out into the hallway, the silence was almost as deafening as the room had been. It took a couple of seconds for his hearing to clear. Once the ringing in his ears died down, he decided to ask some questions of his own.

"What was it that your lab found that they thought was so out of place?" he asked cautiously.

Startled by hearing the other agent speak, it took a moment for Amy to gather her thoughts before she could answer. "They didn't really say over the phone so I guess we will find out when we get there. Since it seems you have finally found your voice, I have a question for you. Last night at the crime scene you said something about knowing where the perp exited. What did you mean by that?"

He smiled knowingly. He had been correct in his intuition concerning Detective Sommers' observation skills. This only added to his growing attraction though. She was Human, but he felt that she would have made a good Royal Guard.

Sensing the moment was growing awkward, Reggie stopped in the middle of the hall, and did his best to cover up for Kalen's apparent momentary lapse. "He just meant that he knew the killer had had to leave the scene through the main entrance."

Amy stared at Reggie like he was a child telling a bad lie to get out of trouble, which really was not far from the truth.

"Huh?" was all she could get out as a reply.

Kalen also looked at Reggie confused. The special agent looked back at Kalen, equally confused. The moment that just seconds before had been slightly awkward was now fast becoming a full-blown incident. Kalen, not knowing what else to say, raised his hands palms-up to his waist in a gesture of resignation. The detective looked between the two, and threw up her own hands in exasperation.

"Yeah, it's a good thing you guys were called in. Its not as if this case was frustrating enough, now I get to work with Abbot and Costello," she said as she turned and once again began heading up the hall.

Reggie actually snorted out a chuckle before he too turned and followed the detective. Kalen, as confused as ever, just hung his head and brought up the rear as they made their way to the lab. He sincerely hoped things would get better once they were able to inspect the bow. He truly did not now how they could get any worse. Whatever thoughts he had had about working alongside Detective Sommers had flown out the window after that unintelligent show he and Reggie had just put on. He hoped that some answers about Drè Fao'lain would be forthcoming, but for the first time since crossing over to the Human realm, he was starting to feel homesick.

# CHAPTER 12

While his adversaries were meeting at the LAPD, Drè Fao'lain was beginning his preparations for the evening's gruesome festivities. After learning of another Elf crossing over, he had had to dismiss his original plan of taking the heart of a slum lord who lived in the Human city of San Diego.

Weakened by his over use of the Shadowed Arts, he knew he would have to find another victim that was close by. He would have to find someone that was corrupt enough in Los Angeles. He smiled to himself as that had proven far easier than he could have imagined. He knew it would not be a problem, and it had not been.

Upon seeing the front-page story of the *Los Angeles Times* newspaper, he had easily selected the next victim that would give their heart to the Tree of Sacrifice. His handiwork with that disgusting example of Human corruption from the night before had been splashed all over the front page. Accompanying the story were several pictures of the gory crime scene. Humans simply could not get enough of their depravity. They loved to see it in bright colors all over their forms of media. It made him sick, but it also made his selection process that much easier.

He had been able to select his next Human prey rather simply. Along with the pictures of the scene and all its gore, were several photographs of members of the Human security force. He had learned after his first killing, this force was called the LAPD, and he had also learned they were always the first ones on the scene after a killing. Most importantly though, through his vigilance of the Human's media outlets, he had heard that the LAPD was the most corrupt security force the Humans had to offer.

That was always the case, he thought to himself. The ones that were often in the highest seats of power were also the ones that were the most corruptible. Apparently the Human society had taken that ideal to heart. Not a day went by in this forsaken realm that he did not hear of some sort of corrupted official or politician that was being arrested or removed form their lofty position. He was starting to love these Humans for their vile and wicked ways. It was no wonder the spell that would call forth the Dying Moon required the hearts of Humans. It was pure genius. He smiled wickedly at the cleverness of it all.

He looked again at the photo he had torn out of the morning paper. Among the many pictures of his work from the previous evening, one photo had stood out, as if it had been calling to him, begging for his attention. It was a photograph of a solitary figure walking out of the underground garage that had become Joseph Stanfield's tomb. It was a photograph of his next victim.

Noticing the morning was starting to slip into early afternoon, he knew he needed to begin his preparations. The use of the Shadowed Arts had taxed him mightily, but it was necessary for him to draw on its power even more if he was to get through this evening's ceremonies. He placed the photograph into his pocket, and with a deep breath to settle his concentration, he began channeling the Shadowed Arts through his body once again.

The first tendrils of the magic felt like tiny pinpricks that ran up his spine. Then the pinpricks became nails, and lastly blades. He gasped from the sensation, not because he was in any pain, but because he was reveling in the magic-induced euphoria that only true agony can cause. The Shadowed Arts flooded through his body and took complete command over his senses. He surrendered to it openly and willingly.

When the magic found its center within his chest, and his heart felt as if it would explode from the pressure of the powerful and mystical force, he cast his arms toward the ceiling of his warehouse hideaway, and in a grand flourish brought his arms flinging down to the dirty concrete floor. Blue energy flew out from the palms of his hands and hit the concrete floor with incredible force. The massive and decrepit building gave a small tremble, but the entranced Elf hardly noticed. He was too caught up in the throes of his beloved Shadowed Arts to feel anything else.

At his feet, a small blue fire sprouted up from where the energy had struck the floor. The blaze grew larger and brighter, and seemed to hover just slightly off of the ground like some eerie, ghostly campfire. It had no fuel, but was burning brightly, nevertheless. He stared within the magical azure flames, mesmerized by their brilliance.

After a few seconds of marveling at his creation, he reached into his pocket and drew forth the photograph of his intended victim. He closed his eyes and waited for the briefest of seconds for the required incantation to come to him. With an evil smirk working at the edges of his mouth, he began speaking the words of the invocation.

The words were old even by Elven standards, the language all-but lost to a chosen few who made them their life's work as he had. To Drè the words were poetry. When he finished reciting the sweet flowing phrases, he cast the photograph into the magical fire. Once the photo touched the flames, blue sparks began shooting from the blaze. Then in brilliant white flash, the spell was complete.

He had to close his eyes against the burning glare. He could feel the spell begin to take effect. He dropped to his knees, and felt the magic expand his consciousness. He focused his mind on the image of the Human from the photograph and then, just like that, he could see into his soon-to-be prey's soul.

He could see everything; all the unnatural thoughts and acts were laid forth like an open book to be read. He devoured the images like some terrible carnivorous creature. The levels of deplorable corruption some Humans would let themselves sink to was not surprising anymore, and this Human was no different.

He was able to see how this supposed police officer rose through the ranks of the mundane to earn the title of detective. He saw this fraud of an officer of the law using the very same substances that others were being locked away for. He also was able to see his soon-to-be victim paying for pleasures of the flesh and then dishing out a violence that was unjustified. He was able to see into the darkest corners of his victim's soul, and he liked what he saw.

Corruption had eaten away and eroded his prey's morals until they almost did not exist. That was exactly what he was hoping for. This just further proved his point about power corrupting the powerful. This Detective Hanson's heart would fit nicely into the Tree of Sacrifice. Drè smiled openly. After this evening's work, he would be halfway to his most cherished goal.

When the magic of the spell dissipated, Drè slumped forward. He was able to catch himself with his hands before he fell on his face. The powerful magic had drained him, and he was exhausted. By the way the sun was shining through the windows near the roof of the warehouse, he could tell it was early afternoon. He had several hours before nightfall, and the full moon rose to its magnificence for the last time this cycle. He would need to rest.

He had been calling on the Shadowed Arts more frequently, and he was definitely feeling the strain. He knew that he was weakening, but when he completed his task of capturing this foolish and corrupt detective's heart, he would get his much-deserved rest.

He comforted himself with thoughts of this evening's upcoming hunt while he walked back to his destroyed bedchamber to sleep. He was going to need to call forth the Shadowed Arts, so he was going to have to be at full strength, or as close to full strength he could get.

When he entered his sleeping quarters he saw the destruction he had caused in his anger, but did not pay it any attention. The only thing he was interested in was the bed at the back of the room. He dragged his exhausted body over and collapsed into it. As he succumbed to the sleep that was overtaking him, he thought about his plans for the night, and once again let a wicked grin play across his face. All that blood – he so loved the blood – and with images of the lovely crimson liquid playing in his mind, he slept.

# Chapter 13

After a short drive, Kalen and his companions arrived at the Los Angeles Crime Lab. The drive over had been relatively quiet as none of the three had really spoken since the brief exchange in the hallway outside the Homicide Special Section I offices.

Detective Sommers had volunteered to drive since she knew where they were going. So Kalen and Reggie had followed the detective to the back of the police station and climbed in to a rather plain looking car.

Once they arrived at the crime lab, and Kalen began crawling out of the backseat, he clutched his stomach, as though struck by an overwhelming wave of nausea. He fell back down into the worn seat of the car, and let a quiet moan slip through his clenched teeth.

Reggie, hearing the sound, turned and asked, "You all right there, guy?"

The sound of Reggie's voice having broken the silence that had built up around the three since the bizarre exchange back at the police station caught Detective Sommers' attention. She turned and noticed that Reggie was focused on his partner. When she saw the supposed federal agent, she was taken aback by his suddenly pale appearance.

"Hey, are you okay?" she asked, concern creeping into her voice.

He had to hold his breath for a second before he could answer with another bad lie. "Yes, I will be fine. I am just not used to this weather."

Detective Sommers furrowed her brow in confusion at the strange response to her query.

"Uh… Okay," was all she could think to say.

Reggie once again had to butt in to try and save the situation. "Yeah, he's from up north, and the heat has made him sick lately."

The response sounded lame to Reggie, but when Detective Sommers made no further comment, he hoped she had bought the ridiculous lie.

In fact, Detective Sommers had not bought it, but she just chalked it up to the eccentricities of federal agents. She had dealt with a few Feds in her time on the force that were particularly strange, but she had to admit to herself that these two were the oddest by far. There was something unusual about this pair she could not quite put her finger on, especially the tall blonde one. He intrigued her in more ways than she cared to admit even to herself.

Kalen took a few more minutes to gather his legs under him. The nausea faded a bit but did not leave him completely. He was starting to think that this was more than just a side effect of his crossing over. This was more than just a random coincidence. These bouts of nausea had to be tied to something. He knew that it was somehow related to Drè Fao'lain.

Once he was able to move, he pulled himself from the back of the car. He had to use the open door for support, and once he regained his legs he felt better. It was early afternoon, and the warm California sun was beating down, which did not help his nausea. He almost pulled the hat from his head so he could wipe his brow. The sound of Reggie clearing his throat stopped him before he was able to make that fatal mistake however.

"Well boys, if everyone is up to it," Amy gazed in Kalen's direction as she said this, "we should go try and solve some murders."

Kalen nodded in approval while Reggie answered, "After you, Detective, this is your show."

"Don't you forget it, Fed," she said smiling and looking over her shoulder as she began walking to the crime lab building.

Reggie turned and winked at Kalen and quietly commented, "She sure has some sass, I will give her that."

"I heard that!" Amy yelled back from a little farther ahead.

The nausea finally starting to dissipate, Kalen asked, "What is sass?"

Reggie snorted a laugh, and just motioned for the Elf to follow.

Kalen was once again amazed by the immenseness of the structure they were nearing. It seemed to him each building they went to was bigger than the last. This monstrosity that Detective Sommers had called the LAPD Crime Lab was simply overwhelming in its massive size. It was also the oddest building that Kalen had seen yet. Even though this building was huge, it seemed to be made up mostly of glass windows. The roof, which hung over the side, was made up of some sort of cream-colored metal. He wondered why the Humans would make such an important building so indefensible. Unlike his visit to the Humans security force headquarters, he had no doubt that the Dwarves had absolutely nothing to do with this ridiculous structure. They would have found it offensive.

As they approached the entrance, Detective Sommers began commenting about the building, her voice full of pride. "This is the new crime lab. We share it with the University of California and the Sheriff's Department. Even some of your Fed buddies ship stuff here. It is probably the most advanced crime lab in the country."

Kalen was not sure what that meant, but the fact Detective Sommers was impressed was enough for him to be impressed as well. From the way she talked about the building, he noticed she took great pride in the accomplishments of her people when it came to her chosen profession. He could relate to that kind of pride. It was something that only true professional protectors could understand. As a member of the Royal Guard, his job was the protection of the Royal Family, and from what little information he had been able to gather, Detective Sommers' job was the protection of the citizens that lived in this city. It was definitely a bond and responsibility they could share.

"You speak with passion about this crime lab," he said to her. "I am sure they will provide the information we will need."

Amy glanced in his direction with rounded eyes, flashed him a big smile, and replied, "Yeah, if there are answers to our questions, these guys will find them."

Reggie gave Kalen a disapproving look and added, "I just hope they can give us a place to start looking."

They entered through large glass doors. Kalen watched as Detective Sommers imitated the ritual Reggie had so often used. She flashed her own badge to the man at the front desk.

"Detective Amy Sommers to see Doctor Bradley. He's expecting us."

The man inspected her badge for a second, and then ran his finger down a piece of paper that was attached to a small board. "Yes, here you are, Detective Sommers. He's back in the forensics lab. Do you know the way?"

"Yeah, this is not my first go round. People get murdered in LA almost everyday," she said sarcastically. She turned to Kalen and Reggie and instructed, "Follow me."

Kalen was surprised when she walked over to a wall off to the right. The wall was made up of a shiny metal, and had no apparent opening. He watched curiously as the detective reached out and pushed something on the wall, and he watched with even more curiosity as a button lit up. He felt foolish just standing there, staring at the shiny wall. He was beginning to hear the distant sound of something approaching. He looked around, but nothing seemed out of order. Reggie and Detective Sommers did not seem to notice the growing noise. Then with the ringing of a bell, a portion of the wall slid apart. Not being able to help himself, he jumped back and nearly lost his balance.

"It's just the elevator," Amy said when she noticed Kalen's startled expression. "You have seen an elevator before haven't you?"

Kalen looked at Reggie for support before he said, "Yes, of course I have. I am just not accustomed to them moving so fast."

Reggie shook his head as he stared up at the ceiling. His face contorted and it was difficult to tell whether he was about to laugh or cry.

Amy stared open-mouthed at Kalen. "Just how far north are you from?"

"If you only knew," Reggie answered as he stepped into the elevator. "If you only knew."

Once all three were inside, Detective Sommers pushed another button that had the letter "B" on it. The doors quickly slid shut, sealing them in. Then with a slight pause, the elevator lurched and began a quick descent to the basement. Once the elevator jerked into motion, Kalen reached out and grabbed the support rail with a death grip.

Reggie, seeing the detective staring at Kalen in wonderment, pointed toward the ceiling, and said, "Way, way up north."

"Apparently," was all she said in reply.

After what seemed an eternity to Kalen, the elevator slowed to a stop, and after another slight pause, the doors slid open. He nearly knocked Reggie to the ground trying to scramble out of the little cubicle. His legs felt weird, and it took him a few seconds to regain his equilibrium.

Amy cocked her head as she watched the duo. Finally, she shook her head. "What's with this Abbot and Costello routine? Can we just get to the forensic lab without any more drama?" she asked exasperated before she headed down a brightly lit hall.

"Look, you keep this ridiculous behavior up, and you're going to blow your cover, Elf," Reggie whispered sternly.

Embarrassed, Kalen quickly apologized. "I am sorry. I will try and control my actions, Special Agent."

"Well I hope so," Reggie admonished as he followed Detective Sommers down the hall.

It was not long before they were standing in front of a set of double doors. The words "Forensic Lab" were stenciled in large black letters over the windows of both doors. Underneath this, in slightly smaller lettering, was written, "Eugene Bradley, Ph.D., Department Head."

"I gotta warn you guys, Dr. Bradley is kind of a character, but he is the best in the business as far as I know," Amy informed her two companions.

"I don't care if the guy is Sponge Bob Squarepants, just as long as he can give us some information," Reggie replied.

Amy let out a loud laugh as she pushed through the double doors. Kalen and Reggie followed close behind. They entered into a large laboratory. Kalen was taken aback by all the odd looking machines and contraptions that filled the room. There were several Humans, all wearing long white coats, busily bent over some of the contraptions while others had their faces buried in stacks of paper. None of the Humans even seemed to notice they had walked in.

Amy cleared her throat loudly. "Can somebody point us to the mad scientist?"

"He's back in his dungeon," an anonymous voice answered her query.

Kalen looked over at Reggie, a little unsure of himself. From what he had seen of the Human culture – though admittedly it was limited – he was unaware that they utilized dungeons. These people were full of surprises.

He watched as Detective Sommers began making her way through the labyrinth of complicated looking machines to another set of double doors located in the back of the room. Without pausing, she pushed her way through. Kalen and Reggie followed right on her heels.

"Well Mr. Spock, we're here," she announced.

When Kalen had heard the detective call the man they were going to see a doctor, he presumed that he was a healer. In the Elven culture, healers were one step away from being Magisters, but instead of studying the mystical arts they devoted their lives to the power of healing. From his experience with the healers of his realm, he thought them to be a little quirky and slightly crazy. If the Human that was standing in front of him now was indeed a doctor, then he lived up to the expectation of being on the odd side.

Doctor Bradley looked up from the test that he was running when he heard Detective Sommers make her entrance. "Ah, Detective Sommers, nice of you to grace my presence."

Kalen could only stare at the man or rather stare up at the doctor, who was a good three inches taller than the Elf. The doctor was also incredibly thin. He looked emaciated, and Kalen guessed a strong wind could blow the guy over. The doctor's size was only the beginning, though. His hair was dyed neon green. He was not wearing a white coat like the other Humans that Kalen had seen in the room before. Instead the doctor was wearing black pants with copious amounts of buckles, zippers, and pockets. He wore dark black boots that any soldier would have been proud of. Lastly he was wearing a white shirt with no sleeves that read "Green Day" just under the collar, and "American Idiot" across the stomach. Kalen did not know what a "Green Day" was nor did he understand the word, "American", but idiot was something he recognized, and this Doctor Bradley looked like he fit that bill nicely.

"You're Dr. Bradley?" Reggie asked in astonishment. "Shoot, I got underwear older than you."

"Of that Special Agent, I have no doubt," Dr. Bradley quipped.

"He may be young, but he is in charge of the most sophisticated forensic lab in the country," Amy said in the doctor's defense.

"Yeah… whatever," Reggie replied. "Now that we are all done making nice, does the good doctor here have any information that can help us catch the crazy psycho?"

"Yeah Bradley, on the phone you said you had some strange findings," Amy said inquisitively.

"You could say that," the green-haired doctor replied condescendingly.

He led them over to a table where Kalen saw the bow laid out on a white cloth. He and Reggie shared a knowing look as they approached. In the light, Kalen could see a bow he knew all too well. He had seen it many times in his youth. The Elven bow had belonged to Drè's father.

"I know this looks like some kind of Hollywood prop, but what I found is some straight-up *X-Files* weirdness," Doctor Bradley said excitedly.

"Well don't hold back, Doc. Give us all the gory details," Amy said, unable to hide the excitement that she was clearly feeling.

"I ran this thing through every test we have to offer. I am talking about spectographs, chemical analysis, you name it. Heck, I even took a piece and was able to break it down to the cellular level," the doctor began.

"And …" Kalen, Reggie, and Amy all said at the same time.

"Hey, that was cool," Doctor Bradley commented. "Do you guys do parties?"

The look of contempt he received from Reggie was enough of an answer. "Just get on with it hotshot."

"Tough crowd," the doctor said under his breath before he continued. "Well, basically what I found out is that this thing should not exist."

"What are you talking about?" Amy asked.

"The wood that this bow is made from does not exist anywhere on this planet that I know of. The nearest type of wood that it comes close to comparing to is the ash tree," the doctor explained.

Kalen was listening intently. This could pose a problem if an explanation was not provided.

Reggie, seemingly thinking along those same lines, tried to reason, "Couldn't this thing come from a different variety of ash wood?"

"I thought of that, but that would be impossible," the doctor responded. "All known varieties of ash wood have been documented. It is a fairly common tree, and any different classifications would have been noted. It's more than that, though. When I ran this bow through a chemical analysis, the computer was unable to recognize many of the elements. So either this thing was engineered in some top secret lab, or it came from another planet. Even the string is a mystery."

"Its gossamer chord," Kalen said without thinking. He paled slightly as he noticed the others had all turned their attention towards him.

"And just what, pray tell, is gossamer chord?" Doctor Bradley asked skeptically.

"It is a rare form of sinew," was all that Kalen could think to say.

"You know this just by looking at it?" Doctor Bradley asked in frustration.

"I have seen it before," Kalen responded quietly.

"Is this guy for real?" The doctor asked, using his thumb to point in Kalen's direction.

"Special Agent Wain is an expert in this field," Reggie explained.

From the corner of his eye, Kalen could see Detective Sommers was staring at him. She had a confused look on her face as if she was trying to piece together a puzzle. He did his best not to return her stare, but he could feel her eyes boring into him.

"Look, besides your brilliant *X-Files* theory, is there anything helpful that you can give us?" Reggie asked. "You know like a fingerprint or some kind of fiber."

Still staring in Kalen's direction the doctor responded, "There were no fingerprints or fibers of any kind. I was, however able to extract a small soil sample. It seems that this thing has spent some time near the beach. From what I was able to analyze, the soil was actually sand."

"Well that's something I guess," Reggie said, though he sounded disappointed.

"Well, it is more than we had before," Amy commented, "and it might give us that starting point you were looking for."

"Is there anything else you can tell us?" Reggie asked the doctor.

"Not really, but I am sending this thing over to the university lab for further tests," Doctor Bradley answered.

"I'm sorry, Doc, but the bow is coming with us," Reggie said in a commanding voice.

"What!?" Doctor Bradley nearly yelled. "You can't just walk out of here with it. That bow is evidence and needs further testing."

"It's my evidence, and it's coming with me," Reggie argued.

"Bradley, he's right. This is his investigation, and we have been ordered to do as he says." Amy explained. "If he wants the bow now, he gets it."

Reggie nodded at Kalen, who in turn walked over and took the bow from the table.

Amy could not help but notice how familiar the quiet agent seemed to be with the bow. He had definitely seen this type of mysterious weapon before, but where, was the question. It was more than that though. The way he looked at the weapon was telling. She could not be sure of it, but she felt the agent had seen this particular weapon before. She knew more was going on here than she was being told. That was common practice for federal agents. There was more to this Special Agent Wain than what she had been told too. When she got back to the department, she was going to do a little investigating of her own. For now though, she decided to keep her mouth shut and her ears open.

Once Kalen had procured the bow, Reggie spoke quickly, "Well Doctor Bradley, the Federal Government thanks you for your help." To Amy, it seemed as though he was trying to make a hasty exit.

The doctor, too stunned by what was transpiring and disappointed that he would be denied his chance at a great conspiracy theory choked out a "Sure" as his response.

"Detective, will you lead us out of this rat maze?" Reggie half asked and half ordered.

Amy turned and led her strange entourage back through the crime lab with no further incident. She kept glancing back in Kalen's direction. He seemed unnerved by the close scrutiny the detective was showing him, especially on the elevator, where once again he held on for dear life.

When they got back out into the parking lot, and were heading for the car, Amy could not hold out any longer. "I know that you two are up to something. I recognize the fact that I am just a LAPD Detective, and you two are all-knowing federal agents, but this case is getting weird. I want to know just what the heck is going on, and I want to know now."

Reggie took a deep breath before he responded, sounding almost apologetic. "Detective, I will admit that both my partner's behavior and my own are a little out of place, but there are aspects of this case that I am just not at liberty to divulge. Your presence on this case is helpful, and I promise you that if at any time certain information becomes available I will pass it on to you. That's the best I can offer right now."

When Amy frowned doubtfully, Kalen continued. "Our actions may seem unorthodox, but I assure you, Detective Sommers, that stopping these slayings is of the utmost importance to us."

"I don't know why, but I believe you," Amy said, exasperated. "I just don't like being left in the dark."

"I know, Detective, but trust me when I say this. It is in your best interests," Reggie said.

With that, she unlocked the car and they all got in. Kalen gently laid the bow next to him on the back seat. Amy watched him for a moment in the rearview mirror. She thought she caught a hint of a smile as she turned her attention to starting the car.

"Well it's getting close to the end of my shift. You two want to grab something to eat?" she asked after releasing a breath that she was unaware she had been holding.

"I don't think ..." Reggie began, but was quickly interrupted.

"Yes, Detective, that sounds like a good idea," Kalen said from the back seat. "I like my food fast."

Reggie slapped his hand to his forehead and began rubbing his eyes slowly. Amy chuckled before she said, "Okay then, I like a man who knows what he wants."

She then dropped the car in gear and pulled away. The crime lab slowly disappeared from the rearview mirror.

# CHAPTER 14

Amy checked the digital clock set into the car's dashboard as she headed back downtown. It was not quite rush hour, but there was plenty of traffic out on the roads just the same. Though it was not a particularly long drive from the crime lab to the Robbery-Homicide Division office, it was a time-consuming one. The clock read 3:30 p.m. which meant she was almost off duty. Detective Hanson was once again taking the second shift duties that evening. After the long and weird day she had spent with her two passengers, she was glad her shift was about to end.

Since she was going to be taking the two space cadets out for some dinner, she figured she better follow procedure and call in her off-duty status. It would not do her any good to get Detective Hanson all riled up when he first came onto shift. Though, it might be fun to see the look on his face when he did not have her report to read.

She grabbed her cell phone and dialed the number for the Robbery-Homicide Division. It was answered after a couple of rings.

"This is Detective Sommers. I'm just calling in to say that I'm going off duty. I'm taking our friends out for some food, and then I'll return the car, and file my report. Tell Hanson not to get his shorts in a twist when he comes in," she said to the person on the other end.

Kalen watched from the back seat as Detective Sommers spoke into the small device that she normally wore clipped to her belt. He had to give the Humans credit in one aspect. Their forms of communication over long distances were far superior to anything the Elves had. He was amazed every time he saw Reggie or

Detective Sommers use some small and intricate gadget, and carry on a meaningful conversation with some anonymous person. A tool like that would be invaluable to the Royal Guard.

Once she finished her phone call, Amy turned her attention back to the two federal agents that were her traveling companions for the evening.

"So, what you boys hungry for?" she asked.

"Well Detective, this is your town so you lead the way," Reggie answered.

"This isn't my town, Special Agent. I just work here," Amy replied, somewhat strained.

Kalen, picking up on the tightness of her tone of voice, asked, "Is this place not your home then?"

Amy gasped a bit at the sound of Kalen's voice. The Elf suspected that was because she was used to speaking primarily with Reggie Blackburn. He felt his cheeks redden, as he realized that most of the things he had said must have sounded ridiculous to her. He saw her eyes in the rearview mirror.

"I live here if that is what you mean," she explained, "but I have never really considered LA my home. I'm originally from San Diego."

Kalen smiled and nodded in response. He had no idea where this San Diego place was, but he enjoyed listening to Detective Sommers talk. He wished he could have a more meaningful conversation with her, but he knew with his understanding of Human culture so lacking, any attempt would probably be an unmitigated disaster. So instead, as usual, he followed Reggie's advice and stayed quiet.

"I know you said you like fast food, Agent Wain, but I am in the mood for something a little more filling, plus I could use a drink," Amy said tiredly. It had been a long day, but she wanted the opportunity to sit down with these two and see if she could glean some new information especially if she could get a few drinks down them.

"Amen to that," Reggie said excitedly. "That is the best idea I've heard all day."

"I know a diner near the department that serves up a decent steak, and their beer is always cold," Amy said matching Reggie's excitement.

Kalen was little disappointed that he would not be having the fast food, but he liked the idea of sharing a meal with Detective Sommers.

"We will trust in your expert judgment, Detective," he said hoping he sounded as casual as Reggie had.

Amy giggled at Kalen's response before adding, "Depending on traffic, we should be there shortly."

They drove the rest of the way in relative silence. Other than Reggie's occasional complaint about the traffic or derogative name shouted out to the other drivers, the conversation was limited. Because of the traffic, it took Amy longer than she expected to get to the diner. It was nearing 4:30 p.m. when she finally pulled into the restaurant's parking lot.

Kalen looked up at the sign as they pulled in. It was a yellow circle surrounded by another yellow circle with the words Eat Well sprawled across the middle. To him, it seemed an appropriate name for a place with food. One thing he noticed that made him feel slightly more at ease, was that there was only one other car parked in the lot Detective Sommers had pulled in to. From his view through the large front window, he could also see the lighting seemed dim, which would also work in his favor.

Once Detective Sommers came to a stop, all three got out and made their way into the restaurant. Kalen had been right, the lights were darkened which created shadows that allowed him to hide his appearance. The restaurant was relatively empty except for one couple eating at a table. Kalen pulled his hat down even tighter over his ears when he noticed the couple looking in his direction. *Maybe this is not such a good idea, after all,* he thought to himself.

They stood patiently for a minute before a female Human met them. Kalen stood behind Reggie, trying to dodge any glances that may have been directed at him. He listened as Detective Sommers asked for a booth, and then kept his head down and eyes on the floor as they were led to the back of the restaurant. The female

Human advised them that someone would be there soon to take their order. Detective Sommers thanked the lady as they sat down.

The booth had been made for more than three people, but its size allowed for them to get comfortable. Reggie and Kalen sat on one side while Amy sat alone on the other. The booth was dark with plenty of shadows.

"Isn't this romantic," Reggie said jokingly.

"Why Special Agent, whatever do you mean?" Amy replied with a joke of her own.

They shared a laugh, while Kalen stared at them puzzled. This only caused further giggling. Luckily a waitress came to take their order, so he was spared the embarrassment of having to ask for an explanation.

Before the waitress could even ask, Amy ordered. "I'll have the steak special with a draft."

"That sounds good," Reggie followed. "I'll have the same."

Kalen, unsure of what to do, and not wanting to draw any more negative attention his way, simply said, "The same."

"How would you like those steaks cooked?" the waitress asked.

Amy and Reggie both said "medium" so when the waitress looked Kalen's way, he nodded his head in agreement.

"So that's three medium steak specials with drafts," the waitress repeated. "I will be back shortly with your drinks."

Once the waitress walked away, silence settled over the booth like a blanket. Each had thoughts on their minds, but all were unsure if they should be expressed. Kalen surprised the other two by taking the initiative and speaking first.

"If Doctor Bradley is an expert, why did he wear a shirt proclaiming himself to be an idiot?" Kalen asked with genuine curiosity.

Amy burst out laughing, and Reggie soon followed suit. Kalen had thought his query to be a logical question, and felt his face flush as embarrassment crept up on him once again. He found himself soon smiling however as his two companions' mirth became infectious.

The waitress returned and placed three frosty mugs in front of each of them. The laughter died down as each person took a drink. Kalen could not believe it. Human ale was incredible, and who knew that serving it cold only made it that much better. That was a tidbit he planned on utilizing once he returned home. It was then the weight of the seriousness of his mission settled into his foremost thoughts. The moment which had been so full of easy laughter a moment ago, was now once again deadly somber.

After taking a few more sips of her beer, Amy decided it was time to get down to business, "So I guess tomorrow we start combing the beaches."

"Yeah, I'll make sure I wear my Speedos," Reggie said sarcastically.

The look Amy leveled at Reggie clearly left no doubt that she did not appreciate his tone.

"Oh c'mon, the whole west coast of this state is made up of beaches. Talk about your needle in a haystack," Reggie tried to reason.

"Do you have any other ideas, Special Agent, or would you rather we just sit around and wait for this crazy nutcase to cut the heart out of another person?" Amy asked, starting to lose her temper.

Reggie stared back at his antagonist knowing she was right. He knew what was at stake here with this case, and the fact they had no answers and only one small lead was starting to get his ire up. He had hoped to get a clear starting point when they visited the crime lab earlier, but they had only run into more dead ends.

Kalen, sensing the growing tension, took a sip of his ale, and commented, "How great of a distance are we talking about, Detective Sommers?"

Amy, hoping she finally had someone on her side, took a deep breath before she handed out the frustrating news. "We are looking at hundreds of miles. Special Agent Blackburn is right; there is no way we could cover all the area. It would take all of the next few weeks that we have before the next full moon, and by then it will be too late."

"Why do you think he will wait until the next full moon?" Kalen asked.

"Some specialist you are," Amy snorted, "I thought you knew this case? This psycho only kills during the full moon."

"I know all that," Kalen responded patiently, "but was not last evening the first night of the full moon phase?"

"Yeah, so?" Amy said, her frustration growing.

"What are you getting at?" Reggie asked worriedly.

"Tonight is also a full moon. He might decide to kill again." Kalen finished his thought.

"We only have the two murders, well three after last night," Amy said. She was not following Kalen's train of thought. She continued to stare at him with a questioning look on her face.

"You have the three murders here, but is it not possible that he may have killed others elsewhere?" Kalen asked. He could feel the detective's staring eyes bore right into him. Instead of turning away however, he returned her stare in full.

"You think there are more?" Reggie asked, concern starting to creep into his voice. If Kalen was correct then the situation was worse than initially feared.

Their waitress returned carrying a tray with their plates. She seemed to sense that something important was transpiring, so she placed the dishes on the table, and quietly walked away.

Kalen looked at the piece of meat on his plate, and deciding that it looked fairly appetizing, picked up his utensils and cut a piece. The steak was juicy and he decided this was much better than the fast food he had eaten. He quickly cut another piece not realizing how famished he was.

He noticed that Detective Sommers and Reggie also seemed to be enjoying their respective meals. The conversation again waned as the food was being devoured. The point that he had made about the possibility of more killings still hung in the air, but it was put on hold as each enjoyed their succulent steak.

After she finished her meal, Amy downed the rest of her draft beer before asking, "So you think there are more murders that we do not know about?"

"I cannot say for certain, but I believe that our killer is under a time constraint, and he will use every opportunity available to him to satisfy his need," he answered gravely.

Amy pondered this for a minute before replying. "That does make sense. Maybe you *are* a specialist after all." She emphasized her statement by winking at Kalen.

Reggie, having been silent on the issue too long piped in. "Detective, is there a way you can check on this?"

"Yeah I think so. Let me make a call," she said before getting up from the table and walking outside.

The waitress arrived again. She cleared their plates, asked if anyone needed a refill, and when Reggie and Kalen declined, she left the check on the table.

"You've got to be kidding me," Reggie exclaimed. "I swear she planned that phone call just as the check was coming. I suppose you don't have any money. That would be too much to ask for, an Elf with cash."

"I have no form of compensation," Kalen said with disappointed concern.

"Yeah it figures," was the frustrated reply Reggie spit out as he dug in his wallet for some money to pay the bill with. "She is taking care of the tip, I can tell you that." He emphasized this by pointing out the window in the direction of Detective Sommers.

Amy checked the time on her cell phone. It was just after 6:00 p.m. The evening was really starting to slip by. She still had to return the Odd Couple, drop off her car, and write her report. Hanson was probably having fits that her report had not been there waiting for him when he came on duty. That thought made her smile. She loved making his life miserable even if he was the only other officer in Homicide Section I that treated her halfway decent.

She hoped he was not in the office as she began dialing. She was in no mood to get an earful. It had been a pretty long day, and with the questions that Agent Wain had just brought up, it looked like things were not going to get any better anytime soon. The phone rang three times before it was picked up.

"Homicide," the aged voice on the other end answered.

*Great,* Amy thought to herself. *It's the Detective that Time Forgot – Detective Killion.* He was the oldest detective in the whole department. He was way past his prime, and looked like he could drop dead at any minute. He came from the old school of policing when men were men and women were not allowed to be cops. So naturally he was not fond of Amy.

"Hey Killion," Amy tried to sound cordial. "I need you to check something for me if you get some time tonight."

"Ah, Detective Sommers," Killion rasped. "I thought you might be Detective Hanson calling."

"Why? Hasn't he showed up yet?" Amy asked, concerned. It was unlike Detective Hanson to ever be late.

"Wow, Sommers, did you detect that all by yourself?" was the sarcastic reply from Killion.

Amy decided to play it cool and ignore the pompous windbag's insults.

"Did you try calling him?" she asked instead.

"I never would have thought of that," Killion fired back. "Forty years on the force and I am too stupid to pick up a phone. Give me a break, Sommers."

"Well I wasn't sure, Killion. You know when you first joined the force I didn't think they had phones," Amy replied. She was tired of playing nice. If this jerk wanted to be an asshole, then he better be prepared to take what she could dish out.

"Kiss my wrinkled butt, Sommers," the disgruntled detective said in a defeated tone.

"Look Killion, I don't have time to waste while you try and get your palsy under control long enough to drop trow, and bare that wrinkled piece of sandpaper that you call a butt," Amy said as her anger was starting to get the best of her. "I need you to check and see if there has been any related killing like the one we had last night. Check all lines. I want to know if anybody else has had their heart cut out anywhere in this country in the last three months. This is for the case we are working with the Feds on."

Amy hoped this would deflect some of Killion's ire. If there was one thing the old fart hated worse than having women on the force, it was the Feds. If she could play the angle that the LAPD was getting information before the Feds were, then she knew the old coot would bust that wrinkled hind end of his to help out.

"If I can get this info for ya, Sommers, will it tick those Fed losers off?" Killion asked hopefully.

"You know it, Killion. There is nothing like scooping the Feds," Amy said, knowing that this would put the elder detective over the top.

"Damn straight," he said as expected. "I'll get on this right away."

"Thanks, Killion," Amy said, hoping that she had the right amount of appreciation in her voice. "Give me a call on my cell if you find anything."

"Will do, Sommers," Killion said, eager to get busy trying to out do the Feds he hated so much.

"I'll run by Hanson's place too, and check in on him," Amy said before she hung up. "What an old codger," she said under her breath as she made her way back into the restaurant.

Once she was back in the restaurant, Amy noticed Special Agent Blackburn was glaring at her over his mug. He drank down his last swallow and slammed the mug down onto the table. Amy noticed the waitress had come and cleared the table while she had been outside using the phone.

"Let me guess, Special Agent, you got stuck with the check," she teased.

"Oh, you're real funny, running out of here to use the phone," he put his hand up and emphasized his point by making the gestures for quotes with his fingers as he said the word phone.

"I thought you Feds made the big bucks. This should have been a pittance for you money bags," Amy said with a smile.

"Big Bucks my big fat rear," Reggie grumbled. "I left you the tip, smartass."

"You're such a gentleman," she replied as she dug in her pocket for some money. Once she located a couple of dollars she tossed them on the table. "I called in to the department, and they are going to check up on the Quiet Man's theory about there being more killings. They will call me if they find anything." Amy said trying to bring the conversation back to the importance of the murder investigation.

"Good. In the mean time, can you take my partner and I back to our own vehicle so we can get some rest before we hit the beaches tomorrow," Reggie complained.

"Sure, but first I need to stop by Detective Hanson's house. He hasn't shown up for work yet, and he is never late. It's on the way," she explained with more than a little concern.

Reggie was just starting to open his mouth to complain when Kalen cut him off. "That would be fine, Detective Sommers," he said with a little too much enthusiasm.

Amy half smiled, but she had to admit she enjoyed working with people who did not treat her like an outcast. These two were certainly odd, but they respected her opinion. It was a good feeling. The quiet one seemed to be enjoying himself as well. Amy was a little ashamed to admit to herself that she liked the attention.

"Well let's saddle up, and see if we can't get this evening over with," Amy said in mock frustration.

With that said, they all walked back outside into the evening air. They piled back in the car, and headed off. Amy pulled out of the parking lot, and quickly sped towards Detective Hanson's house out in the suburb. She could not shake a nagging feeling that something had happened. As a detective, one develops a sixth sense about certain things, and hers was tingling without abandon.

# Chapter 15

Drè awoke from a deep slumber with murder on his mind. He felt rested, but he also knew he had not totally regained his full strength. The use of such Shadowed Arts extracted a heavy toll on his body. However, the quick nap he had taken should be enough to see him through this evening's activities. He was confident he could secure his prize without needing to expend an extensive amount of energy.

He stretched out his muscles as best he could. They had tightened sharply while he had slept. He felt almost as if he had been in an extremely physical altercation. The aftereffects of the magic he commanded always left him feeling drained. It was fueled by his life energies, and every use forced him to pay a small price.

He caught his reflection in a broken shard of glass that he used as a mirror. He was disappointed with how disheveled his appearance had become. He had fallen asleep in the same clothes he had worn the previous evening. They were now wrinkled and he could spot stains that could only have been the blood of his last victim. That had been a glorious kill.

He had been in the Human's realm long enough to acquire several outfits that he could wear, and he quickly changed into one. It was similar to the one that had been removed in that it too, was completely black. He did not bother with the tie this time. He left the collar of his dark black shirt open to reveal his almost translucent skin underneath.

He looked at himself again in his broken mirror and smiled at his grim reflection. The black color of his clothing would help him adhere to the shadows, and hopefully hide his appearance until it was necessary to let his prey know that death had come calling. He did not even bother with the hat that he usually wore to cover up his features. This night's work would not be in a public place, but rather in the confines of his unsuspecting sacrifice's home.

He shook his head from side to side to untangle the unruly mess that had become of his hair. The almost blinding blonde locks cascaded across his slender shoulders. His smile widened when he saw the effect. He looked almost devilish. *So much the better,* he thought to himself.

"I will be the demon of the night that spells doom for all he meets," he said out loud for all the shadows to hear.

Finally, happy with how he looked, and feeling stronger by the minute, he walked out to the main floor of the warehouse. In the distance, in the far back, he could see the glimmering of the blazing hearts as they sat in their holds on the Tree of Sacrifice. Soon they would have the company of another. This night would mark the halfway point of his maniacal plans. The Dying Moon would be upon his loathsome kin in a few more cycles of the moon. He hoped they were enjoying their time like the unsuspecting fools they were.

From the way the shadows were slowly crawling along the floor and walls of his evil domicile, he knew the sun was moving across the sky, and that it was early evening. It was nearly time for his destiny to call him to work. He began gathering the tools that he would need.

He was still furious with himself for losing his precious bow. It made disabling his victims so much easier. It was no matter, though; he would be in close quarters tonight, and the bow may have proved cumbersome at any rate. He was relishing the thought of dispatching the worthless Human in a more grisly fashion anyway.

He gathered the precious ceremonial dagger he would use to carve out the heart he so desperately wanted to sacrifice, the special bag that would contain the heart once it had been removed, and lastly he buckled his sword around his waist. When it was tightly secured, he felt as powerful as a God ready to smite down the nonbelievers with his wrath. He was ready to dish out some pain.

From the use of the Shadowed Arts that he had called upon earlier in the day to determine the level of corruption in his intended victim, he was also able to learn the exact location of Detective

Hanson's dwelling. The Human's soul had been flayed open by Drè, and all the miserable detective's secrets had been laid bare. It was now just a matter of gathering what strength would be needed for him to call upon the magic to transport him to what was about to become Detective Hanson's final resting place.

He took several calming breaths to help him slip into the meditative state that was needed for him to draw on the Shadowed Arts. It did not take long before he felt the telltale tingling in the base of his spine that was the precursor to the magic coming home to roost in his body.

He formed a clear mental image of the small structure Detective Hanson called home. When the image was complete, he whispered the words of the spell that would carry him to exact his revenge. Once the incantation had been invoked, he closed his eyes. There was a bright flash of yellowish light, and he was gone. The only evidence that he had been present was the small blowing of dust that had gathered on the warehouse floor that might have marked a slight movement, and the scant charge that hung in the air for a few brief seconds that could only have meant the Shadowed Arts had been in use.

# CHAPTER 16

The California sun slowly moved across the skyline as late afternoon turned into early evening. The large decorative clock on the wall began chiming, marking the hour as 5:00 p.m.

"Damn," whispered Detective Hanson on the heels of the clock's last chime.

He quickly looked around to take in his surroundings. His thoughts were still fuzzy from the effects of the heroin he had injected into his body just an hour before. The heroin had been particularly pure and therefore a potent mix. The drug usually did not affect him so strongly, but he had slipped into unconsciousness mere seconds after shooting up. As evidence of that, the needle was still dangling from his right forearm.

Seeing this, Detective Hanson jumped to his feet, and pulled the needle out forcefully. He sucked air in through clenched teeth as he felt the stab of sharp pain as the needle was yanked out, then walked into his bathroom and tossed it in the trash. He caught his reflection in the mirror above the bathroom sink, and could see how ashy his skin had become, and how the circles around his eyes had multiplied.

He had considered himself to be a casual or recreational user the past year and a half, but he had to admit he had been using more and more, especially over the last six months. He would never come clean and say, but he had become a full blown heroin addict. So far, he had been successful in hiding his addiction, but with his physical appearance starting to deteriorate, it was only a matter of time before someone down at the department would put two and two together.

Thinking of the department brought him back into the reality of the moment, and the realization that he was late for his shift. He was never late. Things like this were only going to get the finger pointed at him quicker if he did not shape up. Since he was already late, he figured that he would go ahead and take a shower to clean up in hopes of being able to hide the effects of his dalliance.

After undressing, and throwing his clothes in a pile on the floor, he jumped in the shower and turned the hot water on full blast. He hoped the water would wash the guilt from his soul away as easily as it cleansed the dirt from his body. He watched the water circle down the drain, and prayed that his demons would disappear back into the depths with the water.

Back in the living room, a bright flash heralded the coming of certain death. The flash was quick, almost instantaneous, and would have blinded anyone unlucky enough to have seen it, but no one did.

Once the flash dissipated, Drè opened his eyes. He inhaled a deep breath taking in the odors of his corrupted sacrifice's dwelling. He felt slightly disorientated from the use of the Shadowed Arts; it took a full two minutes before the lingering effects of the transportation spell fully left his system.

Once he felt in control of his senses, he took note of the situation. The house was quiet except for the sound of running water that was coming from somewhere in the back of the detective's home. He was confident he had timed the transportation accordingly. He had caught his victim in the shower. This was going to be easier than he could have hoped for.

Drè knew he would have to be cautious with this attack. He knew that the Human police officers were always armed with their primitive firearms. These weapons were crude and in his opinion barbaric, but they could also pose a serious problem if he allowed himself to be caught off guard. He did not intend to let that happen however, and now with the knowledge of his victim being in the shower, he was confident that it would not.

He exited the living room, and slowly but deliberately crept down the short hallway. As he did, the sound of the running water grew louder. He listened carefully in case the water was suddenly turned off. This would cue him in on the detective's movements.

He stopped in front of an open doorway. From the hall he could see the queen-size bed that marked this room as the detective's sleeping quarters. How appropriate, he thought to himself. This bedroom would mark the place where Detective Hanson would take the deepest sleep of all – the never-ending sleep of death. This thought made him smile with a maniacal glee.

From directly across the hall, he heard the rushing water stop. He turned his head to stare at the closed door to the bathroom. The smile that was working its way across his face grew until the edges of the crazed Elf's mouth appeared to reach all the way around to his pointed ears.

He quickly stepped into the bedroom and hid behind the door. Once there, he drew forth the finely crafted Elven sword given to him by his father before he had died. This sword would spill the blood that would mark the halfway point to his ultimate release, the Ritual of the Dying Moon.

Feeling better after his hot shower, Detective Hanson shut the water off and stepped out of the tub. In his haste to get cleaned up, he had forgotten to grab a change of clothes or even his robe before he had entered the bathroom.

Dripping wet, he grabbed a towel off the rack next to the shower. He rubbed his face and body before wrapping the towel around his waist and securing it. The mirror above the sink had steamed over, so he used his hand to wipe away the aftereffects of the shower. Once he had cleared a path, he studied his face. The color had returned, and the circles around his eyes had faded somewhat, but he was disappointed that his eyes still looked sunken into his skull. If anyone at work noticed, he would have to come up with some excuse. It would not be the first time.

He grabbed the mirror and pulled the unseen cabinet open. There, lying on the shelf was a hypodermic. He felt his body respond, and knew he was in trouble when he wanted another fix so soon. He reached into the cabinet, but at the last second he grabbed his roll-on deodorant instead of the needle. This was a small victory, but one he hoped he could build on. It made him feel like he still had some control of the demon.

After applying the deodorant, he placed it back on the shelf, and with a final longing glance at the needle, he shut the door. He ran his fingers through his thinning hair to smooth it back. With a final wistful glance at his reflection he left the bathroom to cross the hall and enter his bedroom where destiny was waiting for him, and where death had come calling.

He headed straight for his closet to grab a suit for work. His attentions was so focused on deciding which shirt to choose that he never heard the soft footsteps until it was too late.

Drè heard the door from the bathroom open, and he heard the soft patter of bare feet on the plush hallway carpet as Detective Hanson walked into the bedroom. He stood statue-still as the detective walked over to his closet, never even sparing a glance at the door that he was using as a shield.

Drè crossed the room in three quick strides. He gripped the beautifully crafted and finely honed sword tightly in his right hand, and raised it up until that right hand was even with his left ear. With a final wicked grin and the evil gleam of insanity showing in his eyes, he brought the sword down in a diagonal slash.

The sharpened edge of the blade bit into the small of Detective Hanson's back. The blade of the sword had been sharpened to such a fine razor's edge, that the unsuspecting detective's brain did not even register any pain. He felt a tiny stinging sensation, before he lost complete control of his legs.

Drè was nothing if not studious. He had mastered the knowledge of Human anatomy. Other than a few small inconsistencies, Humans were not that much different from Elves. The one area he had paid specific attention to was the neurological system, and especially the spine. He knew if he could immobilize his intended victims quickly through paralysis, he could take his time removing their hearts while they were still alive to watch.

This is exactly what the possessed Elf had in mind for the detective. He wanted the torture of the moment to be drawn out. He intended to savor the experience as much and for as long as possible. That desire is what had driven the Elf to slash the detective's lower spine.

The exquisite sword was so sharp that the one slash from Drè had carried the blade through the tissue and muscle and into the spine where it severed the chord. Detective Hanson slumped to the floor in a pile like the dirty clothes he had tossed aside before his shower.

The cut had been so fine that blood barely started welling up around the wound. Drè was disappointed, but he would fix that soon enough. His thoughts drifted back to Joseph Stanfield's mutilated body and the pools of blood that had flowed from the many wounds he had inflicted. That had been glorious, and so too would this be.

Detective Hanson – still unsure as to what had just happened – tried to get back to his feet. When he realized there was no sensation in his legs, panic started to settle in, and when he turned his head to see the dark figure looming over him, he lost all sense of reason.

"Well, Detective, it is time to pay for your sins," Drè said in a calm voice that made the hairs on the back of Detective Hanson's neck stand up.

Staring open mouthed, Detective Hanson had a hard time finding his voice, "What the ..." was all he could think to utter.

"You Humans and your vulgarity," Drè admonished with disgust.

Hearing the way his attacker said the word "Human", Detective Hanson took a closer look at the appearance of the black-clad figure. There was something familiar about him. He was tall and slender, and that hair; it was so blonde that it was hard to look at. The eyes were the coldest blue that he had ever seen. Their intensity poured right into him, and if he could have moved, Detective Hanson would have shrunk back from their gaze.

"What do you want?" Detective Hanson asked, his voice trembling with terror.

"Nothing much, Detective," Drè replied in that eerie emotionless voice. "Just your heart."

Detective Hanson's eyes grew as large as saucers when he heard those words. The realization of who his attacker was hit him hard.

"You're him, aren't you?" Detective Hanson asked in a whisper.

"I am him, and so much more," Drè replied as he closed in.

Detective Hanson could only watch helplessly as the killer sheathed his long blade, and pulled out a shorter dagger that was at his hip. The murderous Elf squatted down so Detective Hanson had to look directly in his face. There was something not quite right about it. It was slender and less angular than most faces that he encountered. Then it dawned on him what was out of place – the ears. He could see that the tips of the killer's ears were pointed where they poked through the shiny blonde hair.

Seeing the realization dawn on the detective's face, Drè stood up and hovered over his prone victim for a moment savoring his helplessness. Then slipping his foot under the paralyzed body, he kicked the detective over onto his back. Detective Hanson still had limited use of his arms, and he began swinging them wildly in an attempt to keep his would-be killer at bay. Drè chuckled at the scene. He was reminded of a spoiled child throwing a tantrum to get his or her way.

There wasn't really any strength behind the blows, and Drè waited for the detective to exhaust what strength he had left. It actually took longer than he would have expected, a testament to the will to live that the detective still possessed, even if it was a futile hope at best.

Detective Hanson took one last desperate swing before his strength reserve played itself out. He knew he was dead, and that he was helpless to do anything about it. The killer was straddling his crippled body with the dagger held tightly at his side. The detective could find no pity in those cold dead eyes, and he did the only thing that could think of. He began to weep.

What little respect he had felt towards the detective's willingness to fight till the end disappeared when he saw the tears streaming from the defeated Human's eyes. His loathing for these pitiful creatures was now complete. With one last look of hatred, he bent down at the knees, gripped his ceremonial dagger tightly, and thrust it with all of his strength into the detective's heaving chest.

He watched with ecstasy as the light slowly dimmed in the detective's eyes. He shivered with pleasure as the blood began dribbling over his hand that was holding the dagger in the late detective's chest. He pulled the wicked dagger out, and plunged it into the lifeless body three more times. The blood began flowing out of the wounds like a mini red river. He threw his head back and closed his eyes as if he was experiencing a sexual release.

It took him some time to calm himself enough to finish his grisly task. His strong quick thrusts with the dagger had crushed the sternum and ribcage that surrounded their precious cargo. With the bones weakened, Drè was able to punch through the chest cavity with his fist, and pull back the shattered bones.

He was mesmerized by the beauty of the dark red liquid that was covering his hand and forearm. He felt vampire-like in a way, and he almost brought his hand covered in a glove of blood to his mouth for a taste. Realizing that his thoughts were beginning to stray, he returned to the more important task of removing the Tree of Sacrifice's precious gift.

With the dagger, he sliced away the skin and underlying tissue until he could see the invaluable component he so desperately needed for his ritual. It was still pink, and even though it was now dormant, he knew that with his help it would soon be beating again. Not in the body of some worthless Human though, but on the Tree of Sacrifice where it would have a place of honor. It would provide a service far more important than merely pumping beautiful blood through unworthy bodies; it would become a key component in bringing about the destruction of the Elves once and for all. This heart would beat again in the Ritual of the Dying Moon.

With a few last slices and cuts, he was able to pull the heart free from the lifeless corpse. The blood pooled around his feet, but he hardly noticed. He had in his possession what he had come for. The heart was all that was important now.

He removed the enchanted bag from his belt, loosened the drawstring, placed the heart inside, then pulled the string tight. He returned it to his belt, tying it securely. He trusted in the enchantments of the bag to keep the heart fresh and viable until he could get back to the warehouse, and complete the ritual when the moon would send its powerful beams down.

With the heart now secured, he spared a glance out the window. He was not sure how much time had passed since he had arrived at the detective's house. From the way the sun was positioned, he guessed it had only been an hour – an hour and a half, tops. He still had time before the moon would be out in all of its brilliance.

With the adrenaline rush from the thrill of the kill beginning to wear off, he once again felt weak. He had overworked his body the last two days with his use of the Shadowed Arts. If he could not get some extended rest soon, he would be in danger of causing himself great harm. The rush of killing did not help his strength either. It was a powerful narcotic in its own right. He thought he could now understand the detective's willingness to let himself become a shell of what he believed in so he could become a slave to the illegal substance. The compulsion to kill was overwhelming.

Trying to clear his thoughts, he left the dead detective behind, and returned to the room he had first arrived in. He was so tired and weak that he did not think he could draw on the magic to transport him back to the warehouse. He really had no other choice though. He tried to clear his thoughts enough to concentrate on calling forth the Shadowed Arts. Instead, all he could see were the gushes of blood as he had plunged his hand into the still-warm body of Detective Hanson.

Because he was so distracted, he did not hear the sound of an approaching car as it pulled into the driveway of Detective Hanson's house. The Human's communication device began to ring, making him focus on the here and now. After four rings, an automated machine answered the phone. He heard the voice of the now-dead detective answer.

"You know what this is and you know who you are, so leave me a message," the voice on the machine said.

There was a long pause before a loud beep registered from the machine. Then another voice, this one female, came over the answering machine.

"Hey Hanson, you're late. This is Sommers, Killion asked me to check up on ya. I'm just pulling in your driveway. You better be dead in there if you're planning on missing work because there is no way in hell I'm working for ya tonight."

There was an almost inaudible clicking sound, and then the house went silent once again. Hearing the female Human's message, he almost panicked. He was standing in the living room, and through the large front window, he could see that a car was indeed pulling into the driveway. Unable to concentrate enough to teleport out of the house, he smiled knowingly. He was going to get his chance to kill again. This time, though, it would not be for his higher cause. It would simply be for pleasure.

# CHAPTER 17

The drive from the diner to Detective Hanson's house was a relatively short one. It was a quick jaunt down the Harbor Freeway to get to Huntington Park where the detective lived. Neither Kalen nor Reggie were all that excited to have to deal with the "annoying little detective," as Reggie referred to him. Since it was not far though, they had both reluctantly – and in Special Agent Blackburn's case, begrudgingly – agreed to tag along.

"All I have to say is that he better not be as big of a prick as he was last night," Reggie commented in reference to Detective Hanson's less-than-friendly demeanor from the first time they had met.

"Oh, I'm sure he will be Mr. Manners," Amy replied sarcastically as Reggie snorted out a half laugh in response.

Kalen was about to ask Detective Sommers a question concerning her phone call about the other slayings when the nausea came back with a vengeance. Thankfully his two companions in the front seat did not notice his sudden sharp intake of breath. This was the most intense bout of sickness yet. He slammed back into his seat, and crossed his arms over his stomach to try and quell the pain. Something was happening. It had to be. There was just no other explanation for these seemingly random attacks. It had to be tied to Drè.

As he tried to regain his composure in the backseat, Amy turned off the freeway onto Florence Avenue. She reached into her coat pocket and pulled out her cell phone.

"If he is just hung over or overslept or something, I'm going to kick his punk butt," she said to no one in particular as she began dialing the number to Detective Hanson's house.

Kalen noticed that Detective Sommers was slowing down as she neared the end of the block. He watched as she began talking into the small cell phone, as she called it. Presumably she was speaking with Detective Hanson, but the tone in her voice was confusing to him. It was almost as if there was no one on the other end, and she was speaking to nothing but thin air. Amy hung up her phone and slipped it back into her pocket.

"I hate talking into those machines," she said as she pulled into Detective Hanson's driveway.

Kalen, still unsure as to what the detective was talking about, was momentarily disorientated as the nausea came on again with even more severity. Something was not right. The closer they got to the house, the more the nausea intensified. Whatever was causing the trauma to his system was emanating from the detective's home.

After several deep breaths, the gut-wrenching nausea lessened enough that Kalen was able to lift his head and see where they were. Detective Hanson lived in a small ranch-style house. It was an aesthetically pleasing earth tone he found soothing. He was also surprised to see a well kept flowerbed along the front of the dwelling. It seemed so out of character for a Human, especially one as distasteful as Detective Hanson had been.

From first impression, it appeared as if no one was home. The house was quiet, and there were no lights on. However, there was something wrong. Kalen could feel it. There was definitely an eerie quality to the whole scene. The nausea that just moments before had been almost debilitating, was completely gone. He wondered if he had been wrong about it being tied to Drè.

Detective Sommers put the car in park, and got out. She did a quick survey of the area before she approached the house. Whatever was out of place, Kalen could tell that she was picking up on it as well. She cautiously walked to the part of the house that was directly in front of the car.

"Something isn't right. It doesn't look like anyone is home, but his car is still in the garage," she said loudly enough so that Kalen and Reggie, who were still in the car, could hear.

"She is right, Reggie. There is something… out of place," Kalen tentatively commented.

That was sufficient warning for Reggie. He released his seatbelt, opened his door and got out. Kalen noticed that Reggie also slipped his hand into his jacket, where he kept his gun. Kalen also decided that staying behind in the car was not an option. Whatever was going on, he wanted to be in the forefront when it happened.

"I don't like this either," Reggie replied.

The air in the immediate vicinity of the dwelling seemed charged. It was thick and heavy, and Kalen thought he caught a slight smell of sulfur wafting on the early evening breeze. The leaves of the tree on the curb rustled quietly. The sun was still shining, but it was dimming from the brightness of the afternoon to the shadowy glare of early evening.

"I'm going to try the door," Amy said, her voice cutting through the tension like a knife.

Her tone, though quiet, seemed unusually loud in the unnaturally still evening, and it caused Reggie to jump slightly, causing him to laugh under his breath. He watched Detective Sommers approaching the front door, then turned to look at Kalen as the Elf got out of the car.

Kalen, watching the house the entire time, thought he caught some movement from inside, near the window. At first he thought it was Detective Hanson, but then the nausea hit him again, and Kalen turned to stare wide-eyed at Reggie.

"He's here," was all he could say before all hell broke loose.

Drè stood in the shadow of the living room, and watched out the window as the Human female exited her mechanical vehicle and began snooping around. He bided his time, and was rewarded when a second Human exited the automobile as well. This one was a male. He figured them both to be members of the same police force that Detective Hanson had belonged to.

Drè was about to spring his trap, when a third person stepped from the car. There was something different about this person. The way he moved, and the body type was so close to his own. Could it be? Could this be the one he had felt cross over? This was indeed going to be a special moment.

He moved quickly to the front door where the Human female was cautiously approaching. He knew his movement had been spotted by the other Elf, but for what he had planned, it would not matter. He paused for a second to call the black and orange flames to his hands, smiled, and attacked.

Amy was just about to knock on the door when she heard Agent Wain shout a warning from behind her. It probably saved her life as it gave her just enough time to gather her balance and leap to the side as the front door exploded in a black and orange fireball.

She landed in the flowerbed, showered in splinters of wood. The heat of the explosion washed over her, taking her breath away. With her eyes stinging from the heat and flying debris, she could barely make out the dark figure that looked like he was passing through the gates of Hell to enter into this world as he walked through the ruined doorframe.

When he had first gotten out of the car, Reggie had pulled the strap from his firearm so he would be able to remove it with ease. When he heard Kalen shout his warning to Detective Sommers, his training took over. He dropped to one knee and pulled the 9mm automatic free.

He was prepared to open fire on whatever had gotten the Elf so riled up when the front door exploded. The force from the explosion caused him to lose his balance. He was thrown back into the car, slamming the back of his head into the front quarter panel that he had been in front of. Stars exploded in his head, and he felt himself start to lose consciousness.

Seconds before the door exploded, Kalen felt a sharp pain in his stomach, and he knew what was coming. The explosion and ensuing fireball did not catch him off guard like it had with his Human partners. Nor was he surprised when the black-clad figure of Drè Fao'lain walked through the burning remains of the doorframe and stared directly at him.

Kalen walked around the car so he could face Drè without the barrier of the vehicle getting in between them. They stared at each other for a long time like two hated rivals preparing for a duel to the death. He could see the slumped form of Special Agent Blackburn lying against the car. He sincerely hoped the special agent was still alive, but at the moment, all he could focus on was the Elf standing a few feet away – the Elf that had murdered his father – the monster that meant to destroy their race.

Drè smiled when he recognized the other Elf. "Kalen, I should have known those old fools would send you."

"The only fool I see is you, Drè," Kalen said, surprised by how calm he was, but he could feel his anger starting to build.

"You cannot stop me Kalen, and if you try, I will kill you," Drè said determinedly. He emphasized his point by holding his open hands up at chest level and called forth the flames to burn small pyres in each palm.

Kalen, knowing that Drè would make good on his threat, reached to his waist to pull his sword free. He felt a sudden panic when he realized that his blade was back at the LAPD headquarters in the backseat of Reggie's car. Realizing his mistake, Kalen dove to the ground.

Drè, seeing his opening, flung the Shadowed Arts-fueled flames in Kalen's direction. However, his foe proved too quick, and the flames scorched the side of the car as Kalen rolled away.

He came to his knees and pulled the clumsy gun from his shoulder holster. He tried to remember the instructions that Reggie had given him. He hated using weapons that were not familiar, but he was out of options. Reggie had told him to just point and squeeze the trigger. He tried to aim by just pointing the barrel of the pistol in the general direction of Drè. He took a breath and pulled back on the small trigger. Nothing happened.

Kalen looked at the gun helplessly, almost pleading for something, anything to happen. He had no idea what he had done wrong, and he did not have the time to try and figure it out. Seeing that Drè was preparing to unleash another volley of burning magic, he stood up, and threw the gun at the other Elf.

It had the effect that he hoped for. The spiraling gun distracted Drè enough that his second burst of burning flame went wide, scorching the gravel of the driveway directly behind the car. Kalen, now completely weaponless, did the only thing he could think of, he charged the other Elf.

Amy finally cleared her eyes but she could not believe what she was seeing. Agent Wain and the strange-looking killer seemed to know each other. She overheard them exchange strained greetings, and watched in awe as the odd figure in black began throwing fire almost as if he was conjuring it himself.

She tried to stand up, but when she shifted her weight, she felt a sharp pain in her thigh. When she looked down, she saw a piece of the front door sticking out of her pants leg. She reached down without thinking and wrenched it free.

The pain turned from a wave of agony to a dull thumping roar, and she was able to follow what was going on. She saw Kalen attempt to fire his gun, and fail. Then she watched in horror as the crazy agent threw the gun, his only weapon, and charged headlong at the killer.

She tried to reach for her own gun, when the odd looking figure shot the blackish flames once again in the direction of Kalen. This time it was almost at point blank range.

She thought that the agent was dead for sure when, out of nowhere, he was dragged to the ground.

Kalen knew that he had almost zero chance of actually being able to close the distance and subdue his hated foe before another stream of burning flame was shot his way. Still, he was Captain of the Royal Guard and he had a duty to do, and if he lost his life in the process, then so be it.

What he did not see was that Reggie had regained consciousness and, seeing what was about to unfold, stood up and tackled Kalen. The flames springing from the hands of the other Elf were definitely meant for him, but they hit Reggie high on his shoulder, throwing him five feet across the yard where he lay without moving.

"NOOO!" Kalen screamed when he saw Reggie's lifeless body.

He was in the process of getting to his feet to resume his charge when a loud thunder-like noise caught him off guard. He looked in the direction of the sound, and saw Detective Sommers trying to steady herself as she leaned against the wall of the house for support. She had her gun drawn and had apparently fired at Drè.

Drè turned his attention towards Amy and laughed before announcing, "Your weapons are useless against my power."

Ignoring the maniac, Amy fired again. Her aim was off, though, and the bullet struck the windowsill that was behind their attacker. The barrel of the gun was shaking horribly as she could not maintain her balance with her injured leg. She was on the verge of attempting her third shot when the killer turned and stared directly at her.

Seeing the killer standing there with his hand on fire smiling at her was too much. She slipped, lost her balance, and slid down the side of the house to land in a sitting position. She dropped her gun instinctively when she put her hands down to break her fall.

It became crystal clear to her in that moment that the figure she was looking at was not Human. Though that seemed impossible, it was the only explanation that her already befuddled brain could come up with. Even scarier though, was how much the killer resembled Special Agent Wain, which could only mean one thing; he was not Human either.

Seeing what Drè was about to do, Kalen scrambled to his feet and began shouting for Detective Sommers to run. The words sounded strange, somehow. It took him a second to realize that he was speaking Elvish. He reached up to his neck to feel for the amulet, but it was gone. The implications of losing the amulet were too much for him to bear at the moment. Instead he focused his rage at Drè and prepared for another attack.

He was getting ready to charge when his foot brushed against something on the ground. When he looked down, he saw that it was Reggie's gun. It must have fallen from the agent's grip when he had saved Kalen and been hit by the magic flames. Kalen picked up the revolver, and hoping he had better success with this gun than he had had with his own, pulled the trigger.

This time, the gun fired. The recoil surprised him and it caused him to fire again. He had no idea where the projectiles were going, but he hoped that they found their way to Drè Fao'lain. He kept pulling the trigger, taking satisfaction in the thundering boom that marked the release of each bullet.

With bullets beginning to land all around him, Drè decided it was time for a hasty retreat. There was splintering wood flying in all directions from where the bullets were striking the house. The large front window that he had used to stare at the officers as they exited the vehicle, exploded into thousands of shards of glass. They rained down, cutting him in several places around his face. The burning magic in his hands disappeared as he lost his concentration.

He saw Kalen firing the weapon repeatedly, and even though he was sure that his former friend had no idea how to use the weapon properly, he could not take the chance of getting hit by a lucky shot. Instead, he ducked his head, and ran back through the destroyed doorway. He made for the rear of the house, and even though he was as tired as he had ever been, he began preparing for the spell that would take him out of that place.

Kalen fired the gun until he heard a repeated clicking sound instead of the loud bang. He watched as Drè ran back into the house to get away from the onslaught of projectiles that had been sent his way.

With the chaos of the moment suddenly gone, the world went eerily quiet. Kalen could hear the sounds of other members of the Human security force approaching. From the many sirens, it sounded as if a whole army was on the way. He tossed the empty gun aside, and ran to Detective Sommers side to see if she was all right before he chased after Drè into the house.

He ran to her asking, "Are you injured?"

She just looked up at him like he was a complete stranger. He understood though. Her world had just been shaken to the foundation by what she had seen, and now here he was asking her questions in Elvish, a language that she did not even know existed, let alone had ever heard before. He tried to smile reassuringly, and patted her on the shoulder. He grimaced as she pulled away from him out of fear. All he could do was stare at her, silently pleading for her to understand, but there was no way that she could. Frustrated with the futility of the situation, he got up and went after Drè.

He entered the house cautiously, not wanting to be taken off guard with a blast of the killing fire. Drè was nowhere to be seen however. He stood there and let his Elven hearing take over. He could just make out the quiet sound of someone whispering.

He followed the sound to the back of the house. There stood Drè at the end of a short hallway with his eyes closed, whispering something to himself.

"It is over, Drè," Kalen started to say, when a blinding white flash knocked him off his feet. When he opened his eyes, and the yellowish after glare went away he could see that Drè had gone. He let out a primal scream to vent off some of his frustration. As he turned to walk back through the house, he caught a glimpse of Detective Hanson's body.

He poked his head in the room, and saw the mutilated form of the Human who had greeted Reggie and him so rudely the night before. He had not liked the crude Human, but he did not deserve to die like this – nobody did. He shook his head in disgust and walked back through the dead detective's house to check on his friends outside.

In the time that he had been inside, several other officers had arrived on the scene. He was particularly happy to see that Detective Sommers had recovered from her shock, and had apparently taken charge. She was once again on her cell phone.

"Yes, this is an emergency," she was practically yelling into the tiny device. "I repeat we need an ambulance, we have at least two officers down and the situation is still volatile."

Kalen could not understand a word she was saying. Without the magical necklace, the spell that allowed him to speak and understand the Human language had no effect. When she noticed that he had exited the house, she ran over to him, and began asking questions that he had no way of knowing how to answer, and even if he did, she would not be able to understand him.

Without thinking, he ran his hands through his hair, and froze when he realized that he was not wearing his hat. It had probably fallen off when he had dived for cover. He looked around and saw the hat by the car. It had been trampled on, but he had to have it. He pulled his hair down to cover his ears as best as he could. Then with as much stealth as he could muster, he crossed the yard and recovered the hat. It was badly out of shape, but he placed it on his head, nevertheless and pulled it down tightly over his pointed ears.

The site of Detective Hanson's house had been chaotic just moments before while the battle ensued, but it was becoming more and more crazy as other officers continued to show up. There were at least a score of them milling about now.

Kalen was happy and surprised to see that Reggie was indeed still alive. He was being attended to by one of the other Human officers. However, he did not look good and Kalen was still worried. Once Reggie saw Kalen, he feebly waved him over.

Kalen sprinted to Reggie's side. The special agent was in a sitting position, leaning against the tree on the curb. Kalen knelt down, and was just as surprised when the wounded agent weakly lifted up his hand, and dangling from his fingers was the amulet. Kalen smiled mightily as he took the enchanted necklace and placed it around his neck.

"Sorry, I must have yanked it off when I tackled you," Reggie apologized. It took him several tries to get the statement out. He had to stop every few seconds and catch his breath.

"Save your strength, Special Agent," the attending officer said. "The ambulance will be here shortly."

After handing out orders and getting the news of Detective Hanson's death, Amy felt like she was in a bad dream. She was so confused by what she had seen. The killer and Agent Wain had definitely known each other – of that she was sure – and they both shared similar physical features including pointed ears. She had not remembered that odd bit of information until right now.

Then on top of that, the killer had flung some sort of fire around like he was a wizard straight out of a fairy tale. Then, Agent Wain had spoken to her in that strange melodic language. It was almost too much for her to handle, and she felt her anger rise.

The sound of more sirens caught her attention. She watched as the ambulance she had called finally arrived. The EMTs jumped out, and immediately ran over to attend to Special Agent Blackburn. She was relieved that he was still alive. She also saw Agent Wain standing near the ambulance.

Furious over Detective Hanson's death, and even more furious with her fear of what she had seen, she walked briskly across the yard to confront the strange and enigmatic FBI agent – if that was indeed what he really was.

When she was within an arm's length of Kalen, she could not hold back her anger any longer and she yelled vehemently, "Just what in the name of all that is holy happened here, and who, or should I say what, in the hell are you?"

Reggie, being worked on by the paramedics turned his head in her direction and said, "Trust me Detective, you don't want to know."

"Like hell I don't," she yelled right back, her anger beginning to boil over. "There is a dead cop – who just happens to be a friend of mine – in there with a hole in his chest big enough for me to put my leg through. There is some psychopath that could be your long lost brother," she emphasized this point by thrusting her finger in Kalen's face, "acting like this is some fairy tale family reunion, throwing fire around like he was Merlin the Magician. And then right when things get somewhat calm, you decide to start speaking gibberish. Now, I want some answers!"

Kalen hung his head before saying, "I will tell you everything, but not here. When Special Agent Blackburn is taken care of, we can go somewhere private and I will do my best to explain."

Surprised, Amy could only stare at Agent Wain questioningly. Now that he had agreed to tell her what she wanted to know, she was afraid that Agent Blackburn was right, and that she truly did not want to hear the strange agent's tale. Her anger began simmering back down, and she was able to regain her composure.

"Okay," was all she said.

Having dressed Reggie's wound as best they could, the paramedics loaded him into the ambulance. The special agent had lost consciousness from the pain, and from the medication that he had been administered.

"Take good care of him," Kalen said pleadingly.

"We will," the paramedic said, trying to sound optimistic.

Kalen and Amy watched as they put Reggie in the ambulance, closed the doors, and sped away with the sirens blaring. When the ambulance had disappeared back down the street, the duo turned their attention back to the crime scene. The former detective's house looked like a war zone. The yard had been taped off, and there were several officers with gloves on examining anything and everything. Kalen watched as an older Human approached.

"Hey Sommers, you all right?" the seemingly ancient Human asked.

Startled by the concern, Amy replied, "Yeah, Killion, I got a little poke in the leg, but I will live."

She regretted the words as soon as they came out of her mouth, and regretted them even more when she saw the look on the older detective's face.

"Yeah, well at least someone will," Killion responded maliciously.

"Look Killion, I need a car. I don't have time to explain," Amy said ignoring the malice that Killion had thrown her way.

"Why, do you have a lead?" he asked cautiously.

"Maybe. I just need a car," she said somewhat dejectedly.

The old detective stared at Amy for a second, then reached into his pants' pocket, pulled out his keys and tossed them to her.

"You know it is going to be your butt if you leave this scene," he warned.

"Don't worry, Killion, I can take care of my own hind end," Amy said. Then she turned her attention back to Kalen. "Come on, you promised me an explanation."

Kalen nodded his head in agreement and followed her as she made her way through the crowded commotion of the crime scene. There were several looks of confusion and disdain thrown her way by the other Human officers, but she ignored them all. When they got to Detective Killion's car, Amy unlocked the door.

"Get in," she ordered.

Kalen opened the door and sat down. Amy crawled in her side, put the key in the ignition and started the car. She stared at Kalen for awhile as if she was trying to figure something out. She looked as if she might ask him something, thought better of it, put the car in drive and sped away. They did not say a word to each other until they reached their destination.

# CHAPTER 18

If someone had been around to see the quick, almost supernova-bright flash appear and then just as quickly disappear leaving behind a black lump of flesh, they would have thought that a corpse had been regurgitated up from hell. In actuality that notion was not all that far from the truth.

His energy sapped, his strength reserves gone, Drè could only lie on the cold concrete floor of the warehouse. He was sick to his stomach, and had he the strength left, he would have wretched. Instead he lay in a heap much like the Humans he had left in his wake of destruction on his misguided path to vengeance.

Repeatedly conjuring the Shadowed Arts to fight off Kalen, and then using the magic once again to make a quick exit had taken a heavy toll. Drè knew that the Shadowed Arts fueled its unholy power by feeding off the user's life energy. If he was too careless and cavalier in its use, the Shadowed Arts would kill him. That was the double-edged sword an evoker of the magic had to handle.

What he needed right then was rest. God, how he needed the replenishment that only sleep could bring. He tried to raise himself up, but he simply did not have the strength, and he fell back onto his face where he passed out from exhaustion.

He awoke several hours later disoriented and feeling as if he had been trampled over by the entire Elven and Human races. His muscles ached, his head was pounding, and the nausea he had felt when he first returned had doubled in its forcefulness. He lay on the floor for an indeterminate amount of time and watched as the shadows moved across the walls marking the sun's descent.

He knew that he had come very close to dying and leaving his quest for vengeance unfulfilled. Even though he was fatigued, he managed a small smile of satisfaction. He got what he needed. He slowly moved his arm to his waist and felt for the bag that contained the heart of the corrupted police officer. He felt euphoria wash over him as his fingers brushed against the bag.

The smile faded rapidly, however, as he remembered the fight he had barely walked away from. Now that Kalen was here in the Human realm too, Drè knew he would have to make some changes. He would have to dispatch his former friend as soon as possible. He could not allow anything or anyone, for that matter, to interfere with his plans when they were so close to completion. That also meant he would have to get rid of the Human female as well. All that in due time, he plotted. Right now he had more important things to consider, like getting himself up off the filthy floor and adding his precious cargo to its most sacred of altars on the Tree of Sacrifice.

The moon was just starting to shine its brilliant light into the warehouse. He slowly gathered what energy he had left, and pulled his sore and battered body back into a standing position. He swooned somewhat before he could get his body back under control. The sense of disorientation passed, and he stumbled through the warehouse to where the Tree of Sacrifice was radiant in the glow of the moonbeams. He had to take several deep breaths to get his trembling under control before he could draw the heart out of the bag at his waist.

It took everything he had left, and then some for him to complete the ritual and add Detective Hanson's heart to Joseph Stanfield's and the others. Once the heart was burning in blue flames in its crook on the sacred Tree, Drè collapsed again. The reverent joy of the ceremony had carried him through, but now that it had been completed, he was completely spent.

Knowing that he needed to get to his sleeping chamber to restore his energy, the vengeance-crazed Elf crawled on his hands and knees across the filthy warehouse. He did not care though; all that mattered was his destination. After what felt like hours, he was able to cross the warehouse and make it to his sleeping chamber. It took him three times to get himself fully into his bed. He closed his eyes and slipped into the trance that would once again turn him into a vessel worthy of the gift of the Shadowed Arts.

# —Chapter 19

The silence in the car was uncomfortable at best as the two made their way through the traffic on the Harbor Freeway. Amy kept her eyes focused on the road outside her windshield. She was too unnerved by the death of Detective Hanson and from the queer events that had occurred in their confrontation with the strange looking killer to trust herself to speak. She would occasionally spare a quick glance from the corner of her eye to see if she could gauge what Agent Wain, now a complete stranger to her, was thinking. The agent sat unmoving as if he had been carved from stone, and this disturbed her even more. Something *Twilight Zone*-esque was going on, and she hated to admit it to herself, but she was afraid.

For his part, Kalen knew that once they reached their destination, he would have no choice but to tell her everything. His already-overwhelmed mind raced through scenarios that he might be able to use to explain the oddities the detective had seen, but deep down he knew they would never work. Detective Sommers was a professional investigator, and she would see through any lie he might come up with. That left him with just the one option – to tell her everything.

He was so lost in his thoughts that he did not feel the car stop or the hum of the engine suddenly go quiet. The jingling of the keys as Detective Sommers removed them from the ignition was what finally drew his attention back to the moment. He silently chastised himself for not paying closer attention. This was sloppy work for someone who was supposed to be the Captain of the Royal Guard, but the events of the past few hours had shaken him to the very core of his foundation.

Detective Sommers sat quiet and still for a minute, staring at Kalen. She had still not spoken to him, and from what he gathered, she was probably as lost in her emotions as he was in his. The driver's side door creaked loudly in the quiet evening as she opened it and stepped out. Kalen sat alone in the car trying to gather what was left of his wits before he too exited the automobile.

They had parked behind a large, square building. It was not quite as big as some of the other structures he had been to recently, but this one was still larger than anything he was used to seeing. As he looked up, he could see that many windows had lights glowing in them while others were as black as the evening sky. The building was made up of some sort of dark red rock that was cut into small rectangular shapes and then somehow mortared together. The red of the stone glowed eerily in the light of the full moon, and the darkness of the color made Kalen think of the blood he had seen at the home of the rude detective. This caused a cold shiver to make its way up his spine.

He stood transfixed as he stared at the building. His thoughts fleeing back to the events that had just occurred. It was almost too much for him to digest. He thought he was well prepared for having to face Drè Fao'lain again. Now, though, all the emotions of betrayal and anguish over his father's death came flooding back. He thought that he had been able to lay the memories to rest, but here in this foreign realm they came home to roost once again. They only fanned the flames of his growing hatred for Drè, and fueled his determination to put a stop to his former friend's madness once and for all. He had become so lost in his thoughts he had not seen Detective Sommers approach, and stand at his side.

Amy waited to see if he would acknowledge her presence. When he did not, she watched him closely for a few seconds. He seemed desperately lost in his thoughts. He was actually trembling, but if it was from the cool evening breeze or from something far more sinister, she could not tell.

After watching patiently for a full minute, she finally reached up, and touched the enigmatic agent on his arm. He jumped at the slightest hint of her touch. This in turn startled her as well. She was already on edge, and her nerves, which had already been frayed, were completely shot.

His eyes had glazed over and seemed to be staring straight through the apartment building. Slowly, he turned his gaze on her. She was taken aback by the intensity that shown in those endless blue orbs. She had never seen anything like it, and once again she wondered about this withdrawn and secretive man. Now, he seemed even more like a stranger than before. What was his true story?

Amy tried to match his intensity with a stare of her own, but she fell far short in her endeavor as his eyes bore right through her. Knowing she could not win this odd staring contest, she turned away and began walking towards the entrance of the apartment complex. After a few steps, she realized that Agent Wain had yet to follow. She looked over her shoulder only to see him standing impossibly still just where she had left him.

"Come on," she said somewhat forcibly without breaking her stride. Her voice sounded strange to her after the silence the two had shared on their drive over. What bothered her most, though, was the hint of trepidation she had heard.

She did not wait for a response. She was not going to give this cryptic agent the satisfaction of knowing how much she was intimidated. She did not want to admit it, but she was scared. What she had seen that night was something straight out of a horror novel, but yet Detective Hanson's death was not a work of fiction. She took solace in the fact that after taking a few more steps, she heard the sparse shuffling of the agent's feet as he began walking after her.

He followed Detective Sommers to the front door of the large Human superstructure. He knew that once they were inside, he would have to come clean about everything. He had no idea how the detective would respond. He understood that to her, his story would sound like the ramblings of a madman. What other choice did he have though? There was simply no other way he could explain what she had seen and been a part of.

Kalen felt that he could trust Detective Sommers. He would also have to trust in his instincts that the detective would be receptive to what he had to say. He knew that with Reggie clinging to life and out of action, he desperately needed Detective Sommers if he was going to be able to get around this city and stop Drè. He could only hope that she could look past the fantastic elements of his tale to the underlying danger – not just to his people but to the Humans as well. He silently prayed to Alorien that Detective Sommers would be able to fulfill her obligation as a protector of the Humans, and help him stop Drè before all was lost.

Amy waited for him at the front door. Once he caught up, she turned and unlocked the door and they entered together. Her apartment was to the left, all the way at the end of the hall. She had a brief flash of déjà vu as she recalled her sprint through the rain to get to the bathroom. That had only taken place around twenty-four hours before, but with all that had happened since then, it felt as if an eternity had passed.

They walked down the hall without speaking; neither wanted to break the cone of silence that had surrounded them. In the short walk from the entrance to Detective Sommers' apartment, the tension had steadily increased. Both Kalen and Amy knew that once they were inside the apartment the silence would most likely be shattered by whatever revelations were to be laid forth. They both secretly feared the consequences of what was going to happen next.

Amy methodically flipped through her keys until she found the correct one. Without hesitation, she fit the key into the slot on the handle, and unlocked the door. She paused to steel her nerves against the strain that was growing between herself and Agent Wain. She had not realized it, but she was holding her breath. She slowly exhaled as she pushed the door open.

"Welcome to my humble abode," she said. She knew it sounded lame, but it was the best she could come up with while under the immense stress.

Kalen stood patiently off to one side as Detective Sommers motioned for him to enter. He cocked his head to one side to get a better view into the interior of the detective's home. There were no lights on, and he was unable make out any specific characteristics. There was enough light from the full moon shining through a window that he was able to make out the dimensions. He was surprised by how small the detective's "humble abode" actually appeared to be.

After taking his quick survey, he decided to accept the detective's odd invitation, and entered the apartment. He stepped around Amy as she held the door open for him, and took several steps into the darkened interior. He had been correct in his earlier assumption. The detective's place of residence was indeed quite small.

Amy followed Kalen in without hesitating, and shut the door quietly behind her. She reached over to the light switch that was on the wall next to the door, but found herself pausing to stare at her strange companion. She knew there was something peculiar about this man, and the way he stood there – still as if he was a piece of petrified wood, giving off an inexplicable aura of power in the moonlit apartment helped to confirm her beliefs. The way he basked in the moonlight that crept through the drawn shades of her living room window – almost as if he was feeding on it and gaining strength from its illumination – gave him an inhuman quality. This only fed her own apprehension about the truth that he had promised to shed on the evening's events.

She finally decided enough was enough, and flipped the switch. The apartment was instantly flooded with light. She had to close her eyes for a few brief seconds so they could adjust to the sudden change. When she opened her eyes again, she was startled to see that Agent Wain had turned, and was once again staring directly at her. She shrank from his gaze. His eyes were aflame, and they were burning through her, right down to the very core of her being. She hated being made to feel so small and insignificant, especially here in her own home.

She turned away from his powerful glare and walked to the small closet that was just inside and to the right of the door. She slipped her coat off, and hung it up. Her motions felt stiff. She was nervous, and the tension was causing her muscles to ache. She could feel Agent Wain's eyes burning into her back as she maneuvered her jacket onto the hanger.

Hoping to break his impenetrable gaze's power over her, she turned to face him and asked, "Can I take your coat and hat?"

Kalen – who had been watching Detective Sommers intently and was trying to take measure of how strong she truly was – slipped off his suit jacket and handed it over. He still had his shoulder holster, but it was now empty. The gun Reggie had given him had been left and forgotten at the crime scene.

He reached up to remove the battered hat that had been a key part of his disguise, but stopped before he actually took it off. Then, realizing that in a matter of moments all would be revealed anyway, he grabbed the hat and handed it over as well. He shook his shoulder length blonde hair loose. It was matted with sweat and dirt from his fight with Drè, but it still held some of its original luster.

Amy placed the jacket and hat into the closet, and watched with great interest as Kalen's blonde mane settled into place around his slender shoulders. She had never really studied his face all that closely before, and was more than a little surprised by how exotic his facial features really were. His face was long and lean with sharp cheekbones that gave it an angular look. He was so closely shaved that it appeared no facial hair had ever grown on his chin. His eyes were the color of a perfectly cut aquamarine gemstone. She let her own gaze linger longer than anticipated, and she was reinvigorated with her own sense of power when he lowered his head to escape her own piercing stare.

When he lowered his head, she noticed two small flesh-colored points stick out of the almost feminine and pretty hair on either side of his head. She sucked in a startled breath when she realized that those points were actually the tips of his ears.

"What are you?" she asked in a whisper when she was finally able to find her voice.

Kalen jerked his head back up so he could look into Detective Sommers' eyes. Knowing that those investigative instincts of hers had taken in his physical characteristics, and namely his pointed ears, he offered up the only answer that was appropriate.

"I am an Elf," he answered truthfully, trying to sound as confident and reassuring as possible.

Upon hearing his response, Amy could only look at the Elf in confusion. She scowled back at him with a somewhat dumbfounded expression on her face. She was trying to desperately make sense of what she had just heard.

She scrunched up her face so that her brow was furrowed with wrinkles, and nodded slowly before she answered with the only reply that seemed appropriate. "I need a beer."

Kalen was unsure of what type of response he would receive from the detective upon making his revelation about his heritage, but he did know that her comment was completely unexpected. He had honestly thought she would have laughed at him in disbelief. He had actually been preparing himself to handle that contingency. As it stood now, he did not know how to proceed, so he just watched as Detective Sommers turned and moved into the kitchen area of her apartment.

Amy was stunned by Agent Wain's answer to her own question. The guy was obviously a complete whack job, but still it was pretty clear the demented agent honestly believed what he was saying. He had been as serious as a heart attack when he had made his crazy remark.

She stepped into her kitchen to get that much-needed beer. As she walked, she looked back to see him standing there in his own state of confusion at her own unusual behavior. She smiled at him in amusement over the comical frustration they were both experiencing.

"You want one too?" she asked. She figured they both could use a drink, after the way things had started. *Why not?*

Not knowing what else to say or do, Kalen nodded his head in compliance before answering. "Yes, Detective, I think I would."

She pulled two bottles of Bud Lite from the top shelf of her refrigerator, twisted off the caps, and tossed them into the garbage can that fit snuggly under the kitchen sink. She took a long pull from the bottle of beer she held tightly in her right hand. The alcoholic beverage went down cold and smooth. It did its job as it instantly made her feel a little less on edge. She took another quick drink as she prepared to listen to whatever "Mr. Elf" was going to throw out at her next. She shook her head in tired bemusement before she stepped out of the kitchen.

Kalen had not moved from the spot where he had first entered the apartment. His only movements had been when he had removed his jacket and hat. He was unsure how to proceed. The detective's unpredictable response had left him feeling stunned and befuddled. He desperately wanted to tell her everything so she would be able to get over the initial shock of his reality, and they could move on to the finding of Drè Fao'lain. He was just about to start his explanation when she walked out of the kitchen.

When he saw her exit the other room, he opened his mouth to begin, but stalled as she approached. She walked to within an arm's length, and handed him a cold wet bottle. He noticed that the bottle she was holding in her other hand was already at least half empty. When he took the offered drink, she brushed past him and continued on to the living area.

"Well Elf boy, come on in and have a seat," she said. "So far you've made a real impression. I can't wait to hear what's coming next."

With that said, Amy plopped down on the far end of her couch. The way the living room was set up, the couch ran parallel with the wall that was to Kalen's right. The far wall contained an entertainment center filled with pictures, a television, and a stereo system. The wall facing the couch had a small loveseat-style sofa. In between the sofa and the couch was a glass coffee table covered in a variety of magazines. Amy gestured towards the small sofa with the hand that had the beer in it.

Kalen understood this meant that she wanted him to sit down in the sofa so they could face each other. He took his first sip from his own beer, and crossed the room to sit down. He had had his first taste of Human ale back at the restaurant they had eaten dinner at. It had been incredibly good, but this beer was even better. He marveled at the smoothness of the drink as he sat down.

"I can say one thing for your people, they sure know how to brew a fine ale," he commented as he stared at the brown bottle in his hand.

Amy chuckled under her breath and asked, "This is going to be a whopper of a story isn't it?"

Kalen lifted his attention from the bottled ale and looked over at the detective before saying, "I know that what I am about to tell you will be hard for you to understand, but all I ask is that you hear me out."

"Oh, I am all ears," Amy said, "pointed ones even."

Kalen ignored the jab. He just chalked it up to the detective's apparent nervous frustration that she must be feeling. He leaned back into the small sofa, and tried to gather his thoughts to where it would be best to begin. He knew though, that to gain Detective Sommers' trust and confidence, he would have to be completely honest and hold nothing back.

Kalen could see Amy's shoulders tense up and then she slumped forward, as though feeling the weight of that increasing tension. After a moment, she spoke out. "Look, I just risked my career by walking away from a crime scene so I could let you try and explain just what the hell happened back there. I have a friend and co-worker dead. I better start getting some answers, and fast."

"The man who killed your friend, Detective Hanson, is named Drè Fao'lain," Kalen began.

"Wait a minute, you know him?" Amy interrupted angrily.

"Yes Detective Sommers, I do. All too well," Kalen said sadly.

Amy exhaled loudly. She drank what was left of her beer before setting the bottle down on the coffee table. She then rubbed her face with both hands and leaned back into the couch.

With a renewed interest in the supposed Elf's story she said, "Okay, tell me everything."

# Chapter 20

Kalen took a last look around the apartment before he began his explanation. He nodded his head in response to Amy's request before beginning once again. "As I said, the killer we confronted this evening is Drè Fao'lain. He is not Human. He is an Elf, like me. He has crossed over from our realm in hopes of completing a deadly ritual that will destroy my people. To complete this ritual, he needs the hearts of twelve corrupt individuals. That is what he was doing at Detective Hanson's house, and that is why your friend is now dead."

Amy's eyes were as large as saucers as she stared out at the man sitting directly across from her. This was just about the craziest story she had ever heard, and she had heard her fair share of doozies in her time as a homicide detective. There was no way this could be true. Still, she had to admit that this case was weird from top to bottom, so keeping an open mind was imperative.

She considered herself to be a fairly decent poker player; most detectives were. The same thing that made them good poker players is what made them good at their jobs. She had a knack for sniffing out a bluff. This came in handy when suspects would try to lie their way out of trouble. What gave her the creeps more than a little in this instance was that she did not get that sense from Agent Wain. He was either an exceptional poker player or he believed without a shadow of a doubt that what he was saying was one hundred percent true. She tended to lean towards the latter.

The apartment had grown as quiet as a morgue. Amy continued to stare at the supposed Elf, not knowing what to think or say. After a few minutes of her trying to understand, her frustration took over once again.

"Wait... wait... wait," she said as she waved her hands in front of her face for emphasis. "Are you trying to tell me you and this psycho are from another planet?"

"Not another planet, Detective, another *realm*," Kalen tried to explain. "Many generations ago our people shared realms with a variety of races. When it became apparent that the population of Humans was growing at an incredible rate, it was decided that the realms would be split. The great Elven Magisters of that time worked together and with their magic they created the Great Barrier that now separates your world from mine. The Humans have become a faint memory to the races of my realm. Some even believe that Humans are nothing but a myth."

Amy could not believe what she was hearing. His story was something out of a Hollywood movie plot, and it left her speechless. This was just utter nonsense. She had brought him here in hopes of learning the truth about the maniac that was running around Los Angeles carving out the hearts of the city's unsuspecting populace. Instead, what she got was a kook spinning some bizarre yarn.

"Look, you might have better luck selling this crap to Steven Spielberg. I'm not buying this," she snapped out of frustration.

"I know this sounds unbelievable, but Drè Fao'lain is real, and he will not stop until he has what he needs," Kalen tried to impress upon her how grave the situation really was.

"If you are indeed an Elf from another realm, then why were you running around with Special Agent Blackburn, and just how the heck did you get here?" Amy asked, exasperated.

"Agent Blackburn is my guide," Kalen tried to explain. "There are elements in both our people's governments that maintain contact with each other. Agent Blackburn works for one of those elements. He described it to me as black ops."

In an odd sort of way this made some sense to Amy. Special Agent Blackburn was a true federal agent, of that she had no doubt. Still, there was something different about the way he had handled this case. Also, when things had gotten pretty crazy at Detective Hanson's house, Agent Blackburn had not been surprised. He had acted as if he had seen that sort of thing before. Nobody is that well trained, are they?

Kalen appeared hopeful as Amy mulled over his words. He pursed his lips, apparently reaching a decision, and then continued.

"My name is Kalen Or'wain, and I am actually Captain of the Royal Guard. My job is the protection of the Elven Royal Family. I am not an agent like Reggie. Representatives of my people asked me to come here to track and stop Drè. Agent Blackburn's job was to help me assimilate into this city. We were also supposed to work together, and with our combined knowledge, it was hoped that we could stop Drè as quickly as possible," he said dejectedly.

"So you are saying that Reggie works for some secret government agency that handles Elf serial killers, and that he knew all along what you really were?" Amy asked trying her best to understand.

"That is correct," Kalen answered.

"That still does not answer the question of how you and this Drè got here," Amy stated. She had fallen deep into her investigative mode. She was hoping to trip Kalen up in his own story so she could prove him wrong.

"I can only guess as to how Drè crossed over," Kalen tried his best to offer up an acceptable explanation. "At one time, Drè Fao'lain was considered the most gifted Magister many had ever seen. His control over magic was unparalleled. I am sure that he has the power to create the spell that allowed him to cross over."

"Oh, so there is magic involved in all of this too," Amy scoffed.

"Yes, very powerful magic. We have seen a small sample of what Drè is capable of when he attacked us earlier," Kalen reminded the skeptical detective.

This statement caught Amy by surprise. Subconsciously, she had driven how the killer had manipulated the fire that had nearly killed Special Agent Blackburn from her mind. She also recalled that the killer had left no physical evidence other than the strange bow at any of the crime scenes. This had been one of the most troubling aspects of this madness. Still though, this story could not be true could it? She no longer knew what to think.

"If this Drè can use magic to – what did you call it – cross over? Then, can you use magic as well?" she tried to reason.

"No Detective, I have no magical abilities," Kalen answered.

"Then why would your government send you here to go after someone that is apparently pretty powerful?" Amy heard the question ringing in her ears. This whole thing smelled bad, yet here she was asking this guy questions like she was carrying out a real investigation. She could not wait to hear what was coming next.

"Though I cannot wield any magic, I was asked by the chief of the Elven Council to come after Drè. It was felt I was the best candidate," Kalen paused before he continued. The memories were hard enough, but somehow having to tell them to Detective Sommers was harder still.

"You said that you knew him. Is that why you were chosen?" Amy asked.

Kalen hung his head as if in shame before he breathed out an answer. "Yes, Drè and I grew up together. Our fathers were good friends so naturally Drè and I became friends as well. As we grew older, I followed in my father's footsteps and joined the Royal Guard. Drè began studying to become a Magister. It was thought that Drè would accomplish great things for the Elven people. When his father was killed in the service of the Royal Family, however, he began a descent into madness."

"What exactly is a Magister?" Amy interrupted.

"Magisters are Elves that have studied and learned to use and control magic," he answered.

"You mean sort of like a wizard?" Amy questioned.

"I guess that would be a fair comparison," Kalen replied. "Though an Elven Magister is capable of things that wizards can only dream of."

"More like a bad dream," Amy chastised. "Remember, your friend the Magister is running around LA collecting hearts."

"Drè Fao'lain is not my friend," Kalen said, his voice rising in anger. "The monster walking the streets of your city is no true Magister."

Amy was caught off guard by the flash of hatred that crossed over Kalen's face. If these two had been friends, that was far in the past. The pure hate Kalen had just shown left no doubt as to that. There had to be more to this fairy tale of a story, she thought to herself. Amy was surprised by how caught up she had become in what he was telling her.

"Is there more about this Drè that I should know?" Amy pried.

Kalen paused, apparently not sure how to respond. He seemed to be weighing options, trying to decide exactly what to tell her. She worried that her poker skills may have slipped and that she had given away that she was humoring him. She did her best to look earnest, imploring him to continue with her eyes.

"Drè Fao'lain is more dangerous than you could possibly know. He massacred an entire patrol of Elves, he tried to assassinate the Elven Royal Family, and," he had to choke back his emotions before he could continue, "he murdered my father."

*That explains the hatred,* Amy thought to herself. It still did not explain why he believed all of these delusions though. There was obviously some connection between this Kalen Or'wain and the killer, but the two being Elves from another realm was not the explanation she was hoping to get.

"You said something earlier about a ritual. What is he trying to do?" she asked.

"Drè is trying to complete the Ritual of the Dying Moon. If he succeeds, my people will be destroyed," Kalen answered.

"What is the Dying Moon?"

"Among the Elves, the Ritual of the Dying Moon is the most feared spell ever created. It is an anathema to my people. If completed, this ritual will darken the moon, turning its light into a poison, triggering a plague that will wipe out the Elves. Drè is obsessed with this. He is mad, and will stop at nothing to see it through," Kalen said, his voice containing a slight tremor as he spoke.

Amy could hear the pain and even a little fear in Kalen's voice as he finished. She had to give him credit. He had not slipped up once in his story. She had conducted countless interrogations with a variety of suspects and none of them had ever been able to stand up to scrutiny like Kalen had. That did not change the fact that she did not accept, or more importantly believe, this tall tale. Still, with the way he told the story with such conviction, she found herself wanting to.

"I need your help Detective Sommers if I am going to stop Drè. Whether you believe my story or not, Drè Fao'lain must be stopped." He was practically pleading with Amy for her to understand.

"I agree that this Drè needs to be brought to justice, but I cannot in good faith believe your story. You have offered up no proof other than those pointed ears of yours, but this is Los Angeles, the plastic surgery capital of the world," Amy stated.

"Think, Detective," Kalen implored. "Use the investigative techniques you have been trained in, and more importantly, use your instincts. You have a bow that is made from a wood that does not exist in this realm. You have a killer that can come and go at will, committing heinous murders without leaving a trace of himself behind. You yourself saw this killer use magic to shoot fire from his hands and nearly kill Special Agent Blackburn. You have spent the last couple of days laughing or wondering about my own strange behavior, and yes Detective Sommers, I have pointed ears. Ears that I was born with by the way, not surgically altered. It is all here before you. What do those instincts of yours tell you, Detective Sommers?"

Every instinct she had was screaming at her that he was telling the truth. It just could not be though. There was simply no way that what she was hearing could possibly be real because if it was, everything she believed in was going to change.

"This is crazy, Kalen. You know that don't ya?" she did her best to try and sound flippant.

"I can see how you would think that, Detective." Kalen tried to be understanding, but he was edging towards desperation. He needed her help, and if he could not make her believe soon, then he knew it may never happen.

"I'm a cop. I deal in facts and proof, and right now you are not giving me either."

Kalen dropped his head in frustration. He was running out of options. How could he give her the proof she required that would allow her to believe him? Just then, he remembered when Reggie tackled him.

"Do you remember when you heard me speak after the attack?" he asked Amy hopefully.

"Yeah," she answered hesitantly. "You were speaking gibberish."

"That was not gibberish; that was Elvish," he explained. He then slipped the enchanted medallion over his head and handed it to her.

Amy took the offered necklace not quite understanding. She looked at the pendant closely. On the front was the likeness of a woman bathing in moonlight. She flipped it over, and on the other side were some strange symbols. She looked at Kalen in hopes he would explain.

He smiled knowingly before he began to speak. "*Tier ano`ch a`breu.*"

Amy's mouth fell open when she heard the same strange guttural words that she had heard him use before.

"*Tier ano`ch a`breu,*" he repeated.

She had no idea what he was telling her. She just sat there looking from the necklace in her hand to Kalen speaking the strange language. This was almost too much for her to comprehend.

Kalen motioned with his hands for her to put the necklace over her head. He repeated the gesture several times to make sure she understood what he was instructing her to do.

Amy saw his gesture and, without thinking about it, placed the necklace over her head. She immediately felt a tingling sensation spread through her body. It was similar to feeling a low-level shock of electricity. She could not explain it, but she started feeling energized. She felt as if she was in the best shape she had ever been in. She was invigorated, and the only way she could describe the feeling was euphoric.

"I hope this is proof enough," Kalen said one more time after she had put the necklace on.

Amy half smiled when she heard him speak.

"All right, nice trick. How ..." she slowly trailed off when the shock of hearing what she was saying began to sink in. It was her voice, but the words she was saying were completely foreign. Yet, she understood them. The sudden realization of what was happening made her head spin. "Oh my God. This is for real isn't it?"

"Every word, Detective, every word," Kalen answered knowingly.

With trembling hands, she slowly removed the enchanted necklace and handed it back to the Elf. He took it, and in the same motion, slipped it back on.

"I can't believe this," she whispered.

"Will you help me, Detective Sommers?" Kalen asked.

Before she could answer, the telephone in the kitchen rang, breaking the tension. She got up from the couch and crossed the room to the phone, her mind still turning over the conversation. She was still in shock when she picked up the phone.

"Hello," she said.

The gravelly voice on the other end belonged to Detective Killion. "Hey, Sommers – boy, are you in deep trouble."

"Killion?" she asked a little surprised. He was about the last person she wanted to hear from at this moment. "What do you want?"

"The captain is mad as hell over you and that Fed leaving the scene," Killion said, ignoring her question. "If I were you, I would get your butt here first thing in the morning."

"Thanks for your concern. I am sure it comes from the heart," she replied. She was about to hang up when Killion spoke up again.

"I ran that cross check you asked for. I found two other cases that fit your profile."

That got her attention. She had forgotten all about her request. "What did you find Killion?"

"Like I said, there are two other cases. A drug dealer in Las Vegas and a convicted rapist in Phoenix were both found dead with their hearts cut out, and they both happened during full moon phases. You think it could be our guy?" the old detective asked.

"I'll let you know," Amy said stunned, before she hung up. She turned to see that Kalen had also stood up and followed her into the kitchen. He was now staring at her intently, with a look of concern etched on his face.

"What is it?" he asked quietly.

"You were right, he has killed others. Two other bodies were found with the hearts removed. Both individuals were criminals. With Hanson's murder tonight, that makes six," she noted.

"He is halfway there," Kalen said, grimly.

"Okay, Kalen Or'wain, I'm in. Whatever you need, we have to stop this," she said, finally giving in to the madness this Elf had brought into her life.

# —CHAPTER 21

Kalen awoke the next morning stiff and sore from having slept curled up on Detective Sommers' couch. He stood up to stretch out his aching muscles. A sharp yet comforting aroma wafted through the air, and he prayed to Alorien that it was coffee, or at least the Human equivalent. Their ale was pretty good so hopefully this coffee would follow suit, unlike the cup he had been given back at the hotel.

After the phone call from Detective Killion the previous evening Amy finally said she believed in his story. She had an endless stream of questions for him, and he stayed up well into the early morning hours trying to satisfy her curiosity. She sat through most of his explanation with a look of stunned yet skeptical awe on her face.

True to her word though, once she had decided he was telling the truth, she had accepted everything else he had told her. Her questions had been poignant and sincere. It felt good to talk about his people and culture with someone who was genuinely interested. He had spent all of his time in this realm trying to hide his heritage. Now, though, with Detective Sommers at least, he did not have to pretend anymore.

He liked Detective Sommers – or Amy as she had asked him to call her – from the first time he met her. He found her to be fascinating. Talking with her through the night only reaffirmed those initial feelings. He was more than a little embarrassed to admit, even to himself, he had become quite attracted to her.

"Well, the dead have arisen," Amy said as she walked into the living room. "You look like you were rolled hard and put away wet."

"I am not sure what that means, but I am guessing that it has to do with the state of my appearance," Kalen said. He knew he must look awful. The shirt and pants that Reggie had given him were spotted with dirt, and wrinkled from having been slept in.

Amy chuckled at his comment, and handed him a mug of steaming coffee. "I don't know if they have coffee where you come from, but here it is a necessity for those of us in the law enforcement business."

Kalen took the offered mug. He took in the strong, rich aroma before gingerly taking a sip of the hot liquid. The taste was so exquisite that he closed his eyes to better savor the moment. This coffee was infinitely better than the cup Reggie had given him.

He took two more quick sips. "Ale and coffee, you Humans are definitely more advanced than Elves in these two areas."

"It's Starbucks," she replied taking a drink from her own cup. "The best there is."

He smiled in response before taking another drink. He could not help but stare at Amy in wonder. Even standing there in a bathrobe with wet hair she was still quite striking.

An awkward silence built up between them causing Amy to shift her weight from foot to foot nervously. After a brief pause she could not take the quiet any longer.

"I need to get to work by eight. I am probably in pretty big trouble already. Why don't you go get cleaned up, and I will see what I can do about your clothes. You can throw them out of the bathroom before you shower. There should be plenty of towels."

"Thank you, Amy. You have been more than generous with your hospitality," he said before heading to the bathroom.

"Yeah, well, I'm not Suzy Homemaker, but I try," she said with a lilt.

She watched him walk away, and knew that things were about to get extremely complicated. *How do you track a crazed Elf that has the ability to use the Shadowed Arts,* she thought to herself. She was an LAPD detective, but she knew that she was in way over her head this time. To top it all off, she found herself becoming more and more attracted to the exotic Elf that was showering in her bathroom.

Kalen felt infinitely better after the hot coffee, and the even hotter shower. His clothes, though still somewhat dirty, had been ironed and were at least presentable. They had been hung on the inside of the bathroom door, and were waiting for him when he exited the shower.

Amy was also ready. She had dressed, and was waiting for him. She handed him his jacket and hat. He noticed his hat had also been reshaped so it would once again cover his pointed ears. He had not bothered with the shoulder holster this time so he slipped the jacket on with ease. After placing the hat back on his head, he gave Amy a smile of thanks.

"Don't mention it," she said upon seeing the smile. "Now let's go catch us a serial killer."

He could not help but feel energized. He felt much better about their chances of success now that Amy understood the truth of the situation.

Amy had explained she needed to check in at the police station, and then they would go see Reggie. The special agent had been admitted to Cedars Sinai Hospital, and by all accounts was doing better than expected.

The drive to the Robbery-Homicide Division office was completely unlike the previous evening, when the tension had been thick. The mood during the morning's drive was light and jovial.

When Amy pulled into the station, the lighthearted mood made him feel even more confident his mission would be a success. Unfortunately, that feeling did not last.

Amy escorted Kalen to her desk in the Homicide Section I office. She was unnerved by the looks her fellow officers were leveling in her direction. When an officer was killed, it always put everyone on edge. The whole division became hypersensitive to every minute detail. She was sure that her leaving the scene of Detective Hanson's death had been noticed and scrutinized heavily over the last several hours. She tried not to let on that the looks bothered her more than a little, but it did make her wonder if she was in more trouble than she had originally anticipated.

"You better wait here," she said to Kalen. "I'm going to go see my captain, and then we'll go see Agent Blackburn."

Kalen nodded his head in agreement and she could see the worry in his eyes. He was a soldier and must have some idea of what she was facing. He moved from one foot to the other, as though trying to decide whether to follow her or not. Finally, he leaned up against her desk and did his best to look casual.

She left Kalen, and smirked at his attempt to try and look inconspicuous. She did not have the heart to tell him that despite his best efforts, he still stuck out like a sore thumb. She laughed under her breath despite her nervousness about having to confront Captain Mulligan.

The captain was not generally an understanding man. He was short in stature, being only about 5'5" tall, but what he lacked in height, he made up for in attitude. He had never really liked Amy's promotion to detective. He had considered her rise through the ranks as a political maneuver made by the commissioner, and had resented Amy from day one. This did not, however, keep him from pandering to the cameras whenever she made the news for making an important arrest. They had a love-hate relationship in that they both loved to hate the other.

Amy walked the short distance from her desk to the captain's office in the rear of the department. She could see through the window in the door that he was sitting at his desk. He was a smarmy little man with his slicked back hair and pseudo-expensive suits. She tapped lightly on the glass of the window, and watched as the captain snapped his head up from the report laid open on his desk, and upon seeing her through the window smiled like a predator before waving her in.

She opened the door, and tried her best to look confident. The office smelled like a mixture of cheap cigar smoke and bad aftershave. Just being in this office made her skin crawl. She silently hoped whatever reprimand the captain was assuredly going to give her would be quick and painless. The stink of the office was making her queasy.

The captain eyed her sharply like he was a cat about to pounce on a poor, unsuspecting mouse. "Well, Detective Sommers, I will try to be brief."

She did not like the tone in his voice. There was something hidden in it just under the surface. He was deriving too much pleasure in this. He was always such an angry little man, yet now he seemed on top of the world. This worried her more than a little. She figured she better try and explain before he could climb up on his soapbox and browbeat her.

"Captain, I know my leaving last night was unprofessional, but I was trying to track down a lead."

"Quiet, Detective," the captain ordered. "I have a dead officer that was carved up like a Thanksgiving turkey, and the only officer on the scene is the almighty Detective Sommers, and what do you do? You leave!"

He punctuated his statement by banging his fist on his desk as he finished.

"Captain, I really thought …"

"I don't care what you thought, Sommers," he interrupted angrily.

The fact he had referred to her as Sommers and not Detective Sommers was not lost on her. It was going to be worse than she feared.

"You have been dragging this division down ever since you were promoted, which was against my wishes by the way. You think you can prance around here doing whatever you please, thumbing your nose at procedure every chance you get just because you are the commissioner's sweetheart." The captain was on a roll. His voice continued to rise as he went on, "Well I am here to tell you, Sommers, not anymore. I have the death of a murdered detective on my side, and not even the commissioner can save you this time. As of right now you are on administrative leave pending an internal investigation. I need your gun and badge."

She was stunned. She had figured that she was going to get raked over the coals, but she had never thought in her wildest dreams the captain would take it this far.

"You can't do this," she said aghast.

"Oh yes I can. I'm the captain, remember," he replied with a weird sense of glee. "Then again, you always did have a problem with knowing exactly who was in charge."

She stood there, frozen in place. The timing of this could not have been worse. Never mind that all she had ever wanted to do was be a cop. There was a killer on the loose more dangerous than anyone in the entire police department knew about, and this smug little jerk had just cost the LAPD the one person who knew the truth.

"You have no idea what you're up against," she said dismayed.

The captain, misunderstanding, quickly replied, "Don't threaten me, Sommers. Before all is said and done, I will see to it that you never get the chance to carry that badge again."

She did not want to give the captain the satisfaction of seeing how defeated she really was. She reached into her holster and removed the 9mm revolver, and then unclipped the badge attached to her belt. She looked at both objects for a couple of seconds before tossing them on the desk, in front of the captain. Then, without another word, she turned and exited the office.

She prided herself on being tough, but she was almost in tears by the time she made it back to her desk. Kalen was still leaning on the desk waiting patiently. The last thing she wanted to do was break down in front of the usually stoic Elf.

"Is everything all right, Detective?" he asked, his voice filled with concern.

"Not really. It seems my services are no longer required," she answered. She tried to sound nonchalant, but failed miserably.

"I do not understand," he said. His brow wrinkled with worry.

"I've been suspended," Amy tried to explain. Her anger was starting to get the best of her, and she had to fight to maintain control of her boiling emotions.

"They cannot do that," he exclaimed, stunned.

"Oh they can and did. This has been coming for awhile. That insufferable prick has been looking for a reason to get rid of me, and last night apparently, I gave him one." She sounded so dejected that she felt embarrassed. The last thing she wanted was Kalen's pity.

"I do not mean to sound callous, Amy, but what do we do now?" he asked.

"We stick to our original plan," she answered with determination. "I check in at the office, which I just did, and now we go see Special Agent Blackburn."

She knew that was not what Kalen was asking, but it was the only answer she had for him. She needed time to think, and a visit to the hospital would give her what she needed. Besides, maybe Reggie had some insight they could go on concerning the killer.

She took one last look at her desk, and then walked out with Kalen close on her heels. They exited the same way they had entered. The sun was shining brightly, but her mood did not reflect the cheery sunlight.

When they reached the parking lot, Kalen spotted Reggie's car. Remembering that his sword was still in the backseat, he made the decision to retrieve it.

"Excuse me Amy, but there is something I need to get from Reggie's automobile, but I am afraid I do not have the key."

Amy thought for a second before answering, "No problem. Follow me."

She walked over to the car, looked inside, and then stepped back and kicked the driver's side window. It shattered instantly upon impact. She reached in through the gaping hole that resulted from her well placed kick and unlocked the door.

"No keys necessary," she said triumphantly.

Kalen's mouth hung agape. It was a good thirty seconds before he could speak.

"Uh, thank you... I think," he said both shocked and confused.

"No problem. Grab what you want and let's go," she said looking around to see if anyone had noticed her handiwork.

Still shocked by Amy's unpredictability, Kalen opened the rear door, and pulled out his sword. He unsheathed the deadly weapon, and marveled at the shine as the blade caught the bright morning sun and threw it back at him.

"Now, I am ready to go," he said replacing the sword in its scabbard.

They shared a quick glance at each other, each smiling at the other's strange behavior before climbing back into the car Amy had borrowed from Detective Killion the night before and driving off to the hospital to see Reggie.

# Chapter 22

After suffering the near fatal wound in the battle with Drè, Reggie was transported by ambulance and then admitted to Cedars Sinai Hospital. The blast of magical fire had been a glancing blow to the left shoulder blade area, but it caused severe second-degree burns across most of his upper back. The pain had been horrendous, causing him to lose consciousness several times on his trip to the emergency room. The paramedics had given him morphine, but nothing seemed to take the edge off.

The last thing he remembered was being wheeled into a brightly lit emergency room with powder-blue-clad individuals running around, yelling out frantic instructions to each other. He had blissfully passed out shortly after.

When he awoke, he found himself heavily bandaged, all across his back, neck, and chest. He was as sore as he had ever been; he felt like he had been hit by a Mack truck while recovering from the worst hangover one could imagine.

He was not quite sure where he was, but seeing the white, sterile walls and soft white lights of a hospital room, he was able to guess that the events he had thought were a dream were all too real. The images of the attack with the renegade Elf came flooding back. The initial explosion, tackling Kalen, and getting hit by the fire were once again fresh in his memory.

The quick flashback caused a fresh round of nausea making the room spin. He remembered banging his head pretty hard, and wondered if he might have a nice little concussion to go along with his collection of burns. He reached over to find the nurse call button when the door to his room swung open, and two blurry individuals entered.

"Look, it's Sleeping Beauty waiting for a kiss from his Prince Charming. Go ahead Kalen, give the special agent a little lip action," Amy teased.

"Great," Reggie croaked. "With your pleasant personality, I'm sure I'll recover in no time."

"Yeah, well my bedside manner could do wonders for you," Amy said, playing along.

Reggie rolled his eyes before responding. "Where's an anesthesiologist when you need one?"

Kalen stood quietly beside Amy, and enjoyed the moment of friendly banter. Things had been extremely serious over the last twenty-four hours, and were more than likely going to get worse in the coming days. He was immensely relieved to see Reggie alive, and this brief moment of mirth was a nice distraction.

"Let me guess, that person skulking behind you, Detective Sommers, is Agent Wain," Reggie commented hesitantly. He had no idea how, in his absence, the Elf had fared, but apparently he had stuck with the detective.

"Don't you mean Kalen Or'wain?" Amy asked, her head inclined.

Reggie eyed her cautiously before replying, "I'm not sure I know what you mean."

"It is okay, Reggie," Kalen spoke up. "I have told Amy everything and she believes."

Amy smiled impishly before adding, "Yeah, I am up on the whole Elf controversy thing."

Reggie laughed out loud when he heard her comment. This in turn made his chest and back hurt. He winced in pain as his laughter turned from humorous chuckles to a rasping cough.

When the fit passed, he joked, "You two are going to be the death of me yet. So you think you are ready for what we are up against, Sommers?"

She stared at Reggie, apparently not knowing how to answer.

Reggie watched her closely and then said, "Good, because I was getting tired of all that pussyfooting around. Fill me in on what's been going on while I was out."

Kalen and Amy took turns telling Reggie everything that had happened since the attack. They told him how Kalen came clean about his heritage and the killer's, Detective Killion's revelation that two other murders had been discovered, and lastly they informed Reggie of Amy being suspended. Kalen finished up by telling Reggie about his car window.

"I can't believe they suspended you," Reggie said to Amy in disbelief. "And I really can't believe you kicked my window in!"

"I'm sorry, Agent Blackburn, but it really felt good," she said, trying to sound apologetic.

"Don't worry about it," Reggie said. "You should have kicked the captain's teeth in while you were at it. What a prick! One call from me, and I can have you back on the force."

"Thanks Reggie, but that's not necessary, at least not right now," she replied. "Right now we need to focus on stopping this Drè Fao'lain. I'll worry about my job later. Besides we can work faster without having the entire LAPD looking over our shoulders and breathing down our necks."

"I hear ya, Sommers. I don't think I'm getting out of here anytime soon though, so it looks like its going to be up to you two to do the leg work," Reggie explained.

"That is one reason why we are here," Kalen said. "We are trying to figure out our next move."

Reggie leaned back on the stack of pillows that were piled behind his neck and back. Their situation had grown complicated and extremely dire with his being injured and Detective Sommers getting suspended. This would limit their access to valuable resources. They would just have to make do, and go on the information they already had.

"Let's look at the facts that we already know," he reasoned.

"We know he has four confirmed murders, and probably at least two others that he can be tied to. He kills over a two-day period during the full moon," Amy said.

"We know that he is aided in his efforts by the use of the Shadowed Arts. I also believe that it is his conjuring of the Shadowed Arts that is triggering my spells of nausea," Kalen added.

"We may be able to use that to help track him," Amy added. "If anything, we will know when he becomes active."

"Yes, but we still don't have any idea where to find him," Reggie muttered in frustration.

"What about Amy's strange doctor friend?" Kalen reminded them. "He mentioned something about finding sand."

"That's right," Amy exclaimed excitedly. "Dr. Bradley said that bow had sand from a beach on it."

She paused, and Kalen and Reggie waited quietly, giving her time to try and sort the facts out. A couple of times she shook her head in frustration. If they only had a little more information to go on. It seemed to dawn on her how hard this was going to be without the resources of the LAPD.

"The majority of his killings have been here in L.A. right?" she asked no one in particular. "The sand from the bow was from a beach, so I think he has to be right here somewhere. What if he is hiding out somewhere near Los Angeles, on the ocean?"

"That sounds reasonable, and it gives us someplace to start," Reggie said trying to be optimistic.

"Drè will have used his magic to hide and protect himself," Kalen said, bursting the bubble of hope they had been trying to build on. "It will not be as easy as going door to door."

"We could always inform Homicide of what we know. With enough manpower, they may be able to locate him," Amy said trying to come up with an alternative.

"I do not think that is a wise decision," Kalen warned. "If Drè is cornered, he will attack with everything he has in his arsenal. The results would be devastating to your fellow officers."

"Then how can we stop him, Kalen?" Reggie asked.

"I believe if we can locate him soon, he may be too weak to call on the Shadowed Arts. Back at Detective Hanson's home, Drè lost control of his magic fire. That was why he fled back into the house. When I saw him right before he disappeared, he looked haggard, the magic is taking a heavy toll. He will need to replenish his strength before he can kill again. If we can find him fast, I will confront him, and without his magic, I will defeat him," he finished with a determined scowl.

"That's not much of a plan," Reggie complained.

"That's where I come in," Amy offered. "You distract the maniac, and together we'll stop him."

"Well aren't you two a cute couple of heroes," Reggie laughed. "Let's just worry about finding this piece of trash, and then we'll figure out how to stop him."

While Agent Blackburn was talking, Amy frowned as she thought of someone they could turn to for help. It was a long shot, but the whole situation seemed crazy, so why not give it a try? She just hoped her luck would not run out, and that one too many favors would not be called in.

"I think I might know someone that could help us," she said with renewed energy. "The problem is that he is not exactly a trustworthy person, and I am not sure if I can still get a hold of him."

"At this point we have to try anything," Reggie said. "If there is any chance, I say go for it."

"I agree," Kalen added.

"You two better get busy," Reggie urged. "Besides, I think its time for my sponge bath."

Kalen looked at Reggie like the special agent had just sprouted a second head. Reggie and Amy burst out laughing at the Elf's confusion. Kalen smiled, knowing he had once again been the butt of some Human joke. However, the laughter sounded good. and Kalen feared it would be a long time before they would have the opportunity to share another laugh. Amy and Kalen turned to leave when Reggie, called out, stopping them.

"Wait you two," he said pointing to a small closet inside the room. "My clothes should be in there. Take the hotel key, and use the room as a base of operations. Sommers, look in the top drawer of the dresser. There should be a little present for you, and Kalen, for God's sake, change your clothes."

They all shared a final giggle as Kalen and Amy left.

After they left, Reggie lay in bed, lost in his thoughts. He hoped the Elf and the detective could handle what was ahead of them. He had a bad feeling that things were going to go sour before all was said and done. He always got that feeling with cases like this one though.

A nurse came in, and gave Reggie some pills for his discomfort. He swallowed the pills down, and continued to ponder the possible scenarios Kalen and Amy could face, none of which were promising. He continued to plan until the pills took hold, and he drifted off to sleep.

As Kalen and Amy made their way out of the hospital and back to the car, she took out her cell phone, punched in some numbers, waited a couple of seconds before punching in several more numbers, and then hung up.

Amy caught the Elf eyeing her curiously and explained. "I am paging that person I thought might be able to help us."

Kalen smiled before responding. "In my realm, pages are usually young assistants." He told her of the young page that had brought him the summons from the Elven Council.

Amy returned the smile knowing it was probably a waste of time to try and explain any further. Instead, she unlocked the car door, got in, and started it up, waiting patiently as Kalen climbed in the passenger side.

They sped off toward the hotel he and Reggie had shared. The late morning sun beating down on the car was so bright, it hurt his sensitive eyes. They spoke sparingly, as both were lost in their own introspections on how best to solve the case.

The drive to the hotel took longer than expected, thanks to the midday L.A. traffic. Kalen noticed that unlike Reggie, Amy did not yell and call the other drivers colorful and derogatory names. She was able to remain calm and focused. He admired that about her, which only fed his growing attraction.

When they finally reached the Resident's Inn hotel and pulled into the near-empty parking lot, Amy's phone began to ring. The sound caught her so off guard that she fumbled with the phone before she could answer it.

"Sommers here," she said.

Kalen watched with interest. He hoped this was the person they had been waiting for. He was anxious to get out there and find Drè before the crazed Elf could do any more damage. So far though, his mission had been a series of failures, and his patience was growing thin. All of his instincts as a soldier told him that now was the time to strike, while Drè was trying to recuperate. He was pulled out of his thoughts by the sound of Amy's voice as she spoke into her small phone.

"I need a meeting," she said to whoever was on the other end of the line. "Just tell him Detective Sommers is requesting a face to face. Trust me, he will agree to it. Call me back at this number with the specifics."

She did not wait for an answer. Instead, she clicked her phone off and replaced it back into her pocket before getting out of the car.

"Is everything all right?" Kalen asked anxiously, as he too exited the automobile.

"Not yet, but it will be," she answered. "Don't worry, he will see us. He owes me."

Kalen did not know who the "he" was she had referred to, but he did not question her further. He knew that she would explain everything in due time. Right now, he followed her as she made her way to the correct room. He did not remember the exact number, but thankfully it was imprinted on the folder containing the small card that passed for a key.

Kalen had been so exhausted the first night that he barely remembered the hotel. Then, he and Reggie had been in such a hurry the following morning that he had not had time to commit many details to memory.

Thankfully, the room was on the first floor, and did not take long to find. Amy slipped the key card in the slot, and let herself and Kalen in.

"It's nice to see that Special Agent Blackburn spared no expense," she commented sarcastically as she looked around the small room.

The sarcasm was lost on Kalen, though, as he brushed past Amy, and headed straight for the bathroom.

"Hey, if you had to go that bad, we could have stopped somewhere along the way," she teased.

"Huh?" He blinked a couple of times at the sound of her voice. Then realizing what she was referring to, he noticeably blushed with embarrassment.

"Well, I just learned that Elves turn red when they blush just like we simple Humans do," she continued teasing.

Kalen, seeing he was being teased, regained his composure and tried to give Amy a look of admonishment before trying to explain his behavior. "I was checking on my belongings, and I wanted to change my clothes."

"Don't let me stop you," Amy answered back.

Kalen, still embarrassed, hurriedly shut the door to the bathroom. It was not so much that he was in a hurry for privacy, but he did not want Amy to see him turning another shade of red. He stood quietly looking at himself in the mirror, wondering how he, Kalen the Bold, Captain of the Royal Guard, could be outdone and get so flustered time and time again by this Human female. He smiled at his reflection and shook his head when he was unable to come up with an acceptable answer.

His Royal Guard uniform was folded neatly on the counter where he had left it along with the leather boots he had stored under the bathroom counter. He knew his uniform would make him stick out like a sore thumb, but he no longer cared. It was not about trying to stay incognito any longer. If he was going to have to face down and beat Drè, he would rather do it with the equipment he was most comfortable with, and in this case that meant his own boots and uniform.

He began undressing. He was most grateful to get rid of the black shoes that had hurt his feet. They were so impractical and uncomfortable; he could not believe Humans like Reggie could get anything done. As he finished taking the suit off, he could hear the faint ringing of Amy's cell phone. He also heard the detective's voice as she carried on a short conversation with her unknown contact. Hoping she was able to set up a meeting, he finished dressing as quickly as he could. Amy was just hanging up her phone when he walked out of the bathroom.

"Now that is a bold fashion statement," she said, taking in his outfit.

The black leggings tucked into his knee-length brown leather boots, the matching black vest over a white, ruffled, button-down shirt topped off with a red overcoat that came down to the Elf's knees, were almost too cliché for her too stand.

"All I need is my sword, and I will be ready for battle," he said, ignoring her comment.

"It's still in the backseat of the car," Amy informed him.

"Good," he said. Then motioning towards the small phone that was still in her hand, he asked, "Was that the call you were waiting for?"

"Yeah, everything is set. Someone will be here to pick us up in an hour," she answered.

Another hour, Kalen thought to himself. This waiting game was growing old. As a soldier, he had learned the virtue of patience, but he preferred action.

Amy could see the prospect of having to wait a little longer did not sit well with the Elf. He wanted to go charging off like some misguided cavalry to find and kill this Drè. She did not know if this was a trait that all Elves shared, or if this was just a side effect of the hatred Kalen felt towards the Elf that had murdered his father.

"It's only an hour," she sympathized.

"I know," he responded. "I have this feeling, though, that if we do not get to Drè soon, we may not get another chance to stop him."

"If anyone can help us find him, this guy can," she said trying to reassure the Elf before he began feeling too desperate.

He appreciated the effort Amy was making to try and alleviate some of his frustration, and put him at ease. It was a futile gesture however, as he would be unable to relax until Drè Fao'lain was stopped. He did not like the idea of Amy feeling sorry for him either.

"Did you check the drawer like Reggie said?" he asked, trying to deflect her from the well meant intentions of appeasing his frustrations.

"I completely forgot," she said in astonishment as she made her way over to the dresser.

She opened the top drawer just as Reggie had instructed, and there lying in the bottom was a Glock 20 10mm automatic and two full clips of ammunition.

"Oh Reggie, you really shouldn't have," she whispered under her breath as she removed the gun.

She popped one clip into handle of the gun and the other into her front pants pocket. Then, after checking to make sure the safety was on, she tucked the Glock into the back of her pants under her jacket.

"You have your weapon of choice, Detective. I am going to go get mine," he said with a fierce determination as he headed out to retrieve his sword.

"Whatever floats your boat, soldier boy," she said trying to sound flippant. "It won't be long now. They should be here soon."

# Chapter 23

Drè Fao'lain sat bolt upright in his bed. He was disorientated as to where he was. After a brief pause, the fog began to lift, and he was able to recognize his dingy sleeping quarters. The chamber was not pitch-black, which told him it was daylight outside.

He felt terrible. His body still ached as if he had been involved in some kind of strenuous physical activity for an insane amount of time. He was sick to his stomach, and after moving too quickly, his head began to spin. Things got blurry, and he felt like he was trapped under water. Eventually, the effects lessened, and he once more felt in control of his faculties. All of these little things added up to tell him that he had not been asleep long.

He had no idea what had drawn him out of his replenishing trance. He panicked briefly, wondering if Kalen Or'wain had found him. This was not good. He was nowhere near ready to face his former friend. He was entirely too weak to draw upon the Shadowed Arts.

He slid out of his bed, much like a serpent slides out of its hole in the ground. He had been so depleted of strength that he had not even bothered undressing. He was still wearing the suit he had worn at the now-deceased detective's house. It was splattered with dried blood, and crackled when he moved.

He quickly located his sword and dagger, and secured them around his waist. He had come too far and was too close to his objective to go down without a fight. If he could not use the Shadowed Arts, he would cut Kalen down like the mongrel that he was. He pulled his father's sword from the scabbard, and began to stalk out of his sleeping chamber.

As he neared the doorway, he was hit with a wave of magical energy. This is what had awoken him. He had set powerful warding spells all over the warehouse to warn him of any unwanted visitors. The magical wave was the warning that someone had breached the perimeter and set off one such spell.

He could tell by deciphering the effects of the wave that it was not Kalen Or'wain. He was relieved, but there was still the problem of someone entering his sanctuary without an invitation. This was unacceptable, and an example needed to be made. Whoever this person was, they were going to suffer mightily. This made him smile. If there had ever been any questions as to whether or not he had slipped from a rational being to an evil, insane one, that grin would have answered them.

Two more waves washed over him. That meant there were at least three unwanted visitors. *Well, so much the better,* he thought to himself, sadistically. This was better than he hoped. He would not even need the magic. He was more than a match for three puny Humans. This was almost an insult to his warped sense of pride.

He had noticed with his comings and goings over the past couple of days that certain street rabble had taken an interest in him. He paid them no heed. They were no more a threat to him than the incompetent Magisters the Elven Council had sent after him so many years ago. They were insects to him, and he would swat them accordingly.

The one mistake he made, though, was in gauging the level of his Human neighbors' stupidity. Like moths, these urchins had been drawn to the eerie blue light that leaked out of the warehouse. He had figured them too weak-willed to attempt a break in, but Human depravity never ceased to amaze him.

This could actually work in his favor. A few grizzly and brutal slayings of some local thugs would put the rest on notice. He only needed three more months, and these three fools would buy him those months with their blood.

The rest of this wretched neighborhood would see the killings for what they were – a warning for all to steer clear of their mysterious neighbor lest they suffer the same fate.

He was actually surprised how much he was looking forward to this. This was a rare opportunity for him. Since he had crossed over, his killings had been done for the sole purpose of completing the ritual. He had enjoyed them immensely, but he was unable to savor them like he truly wanted. However, this was different. This would be killing simply for the sake of killing. It would be killing for pleasure.

He grabbed the handle of the curved saber-styled sword even tighter. His knuckles turned white as the blood drained out of them due to his vise-like grip. He still did not feel as strong as he would have liked, but he would make due. They were only Humans after all.

He leaned his head out of his sleeping chamber's door and peered out into the sunlit warehouse to see if there was any movement. The warehouse was too large for him to be able to see into every corner. The leftover refuse from the building's previous occupants provided plenty of places to hide oneself. This was going to be one evil little game of cat and mouse.

Whoever these fools were, hiding out here, he refused to play their silly little game. He would not scurry about in the shadows like some vermin. He was Drè Fao'lain, the greatest Magister his miserable race had ever produced. He stepped out of his chambers, sword held firmly in his hand, pointing towards the ground. The crackle of his suit filled his ears. It reminded him of the blood he had already spilled, and made him smile anew at the blood he was on the verge of spilling. He so loved the blood.

"All right, foolish Humans," he announced as he exited his sleeping quarters. "It is no use hiding. Come out and face your doom."

He waited for the three intruders to show themselves. He was disappointed when they did not appear. He walked farther out into the warehouse. He could see the Tree of Sacrifice in its magnificence at the far end. At least they had not attempted to tamper with it. On the other hand, that would have been an interesting show to watch.

"Yo, man, there he is," the young gang member whispered to his two fellow gang bangers.

"Keep it down, fool," the oldest of the trio responded. "T said that we were just supposed to check him out."

"This place freaks me out," the third banger said timidly. "We've seen him, now let's get outta here."

"Yeah. I'm with W-Dog," the first banger that had spoken said.

They were hiding behind a stack of old steel drums. From their vantage point, they could see Drè as he walked out into the middle of the concrete floor. They had climbed in through one of the myriad of broken windows. Little did they know that they had set off the maniac Elf's protection spell.

"Is he carrying a *sword*?" the one called W-Dog asked.

"Yeah, I think he is. What'cha make of that, Bone?" the other banger asked the oldest and the leader of the trio.

"I thought I told you to keep it down, Taz," Bone scolded. "Between you and W-Dog, it's no wonder that fool knows we're here."

They watched with increased fascination as the pale stranger made his way out of the back room. He was indeed carrying a sword, which only added to the fascination. They had been sent to scout out this mysterious stranger that had taken up residence on their turf. They were not supposed to approach or get into an altercation of any kind with the stranger if it could be helped.

When the pale man spoke out, challenging the three gang members, they froze. They were here to gather information, not carry out an execution. The only one that was armed was Bone. If they went against T's orders, they would be in serious trouble, but at this point a fight looked inevitable.

"What now, Bone?" W-Dog asked, afraid.

With his sensitive ears, Drè heard their whispered conversation. He knew exactly where they were hiding. Now all he needed to do was draw them out. Then he could have his fun, dispatching them at will.

He closed his eyes and reached out with some minor streamers of the Shadowed Arts. The effort was more than he had anticipated, and he staggered back a step. Nevertheless, he was satisfied with the results. With that small feeler of magic, he had been able to ascertain that there were indeed only three individuals and only one had a weapon.

"Who are you that dare enter my dwelling?" he challenged.

He looked directly at the barrels the three Human youths were hiding behind. He raised his sword, and pointed it at the same spot before saying, "Leave now, and I might spare your lives."

Bone decided to cut his losses and get out of the warehouse. He pulled his 9mm out, and motioned for his fellow bangers to follow him. He may have been told not to interact with this crazy guy, but he was creeped out beyond belief and wanted to leave.

"Look dude, I don't want any trouble. This is just a big mistake. We're gonna walk outta here, and we can forget that we ever saw each other." Bone held the 9mm at his side, but made sure it was within the weird looking guy's sight.

Drè smiled maliciously as he saw the intruders finally come out from their hiding place. The one that had spoken was carrying a primitive weapon. If he were able to call forth the magic, he would have used the fire to light the fool up like a torch. Instead he slipped his dagger – the same one he used to cut out the hearts of his sacrificial victims – free from its sheath at his belt. He balanced the dagger lightly in his palm to better judge the weight. Then with a sharp flick of his wrist, he sent the knife hurtling towards the Human holding the weapon.

Bone saw the motion, but had no chance to react. The dagger hit him square in the stomach, knocking him off his feet. The 9mm dropped from his hand and slid across the floor to the base of the Tree of Sacrifice.

Seeing Bone, their leader, lying on the ground writhing in agony, W-Dog and Taz froze. This gave Drè the opening he needed. He charged the two remaining young gang members, sword held at the ready.

Taz, seeing the crazed Elf coming at him swinging the sword, tried to run, but lost his footing and fell. He hit the ground hard, knocking the wind out of him. He saw Bone's gun and began to slowly crawl towards it. He was so scared, he failed to notice the Tree of Sacrifice.

W-Dog, not wanting to end up like Bone, decided to take his chances. He charged Drè, and when he was within reach, he brought his fist back and threw a wild right hook. Instead of connecting on the Elf's chin like he had wanted, his misguided punch was intercepted by cold-tempered Elven steel. Drè's sword cut through W-Dog's arm smoothly as if it was made of paper. W-Dog lost his balance when his weight shifted and his punch was suddenly cut short. He fell forward, and was able to roll over in time to see the majority of his right arm land in a pile of rags off to his left.

Seeing the ruin that was his right arm, W-Dog began screaming in panic. This was music to Drè's pointed ears. He walked over to the young Human, stood over him, and laughed. This only made W-Dog scream with even more intensity.

Taz saw what had happened to W-Dog, got his wind back, and ran for the gun. He reached it quickly and grabbed it like a drowning person would grab the lifeline of a preserver.

"All right you sick freak," Taz screamed. He was near hysterics at this point. "Let's see how you like it."

He finished his threat by squeezing off two rounds from the 9mm. He was shaking so badly though, the shots did not come anywhere close to their intended target.

Hearing the loud discharge of the gun, and the ricocheting of the projectiles as they jumped around the warehouse, Drè turned his attention from the screaming W-Dog. He needed to finish off the Human with the gun before he was able to get off a lucky shot. Drè thought he might have to try and call the magical fire. Even if he could manage to use it for a few seconds, it would be enough to incapacitate the last of the three individuals long enough for him to finish the Human off at his leisure. Just as he was about to try an attempt to call upon the fire, something glorious happened, and he got the show he had wanted.

Taz was trying to steady his nerves long enough to get off a clean shot when the ground at his feet began to shake. There was a deep rumbling sound from directly underneath his feet. For the first time, Taz realized he was standing in front of a large tree. When he saw the burning blue flames, he began screaming like a child trying to wake up from a nightmare.

Drè watched, mesmerized. This was more than he could have hoped for. Two thick black roots broke free from the concrete floor of the warehouse. The roots began wrapping themselves around the young gang banger's legs. They moved as if they were alive. They were like two large boa constrictors on the verge of squeezing the life out of their captured prey. This moment was pure rapture for the crazed Elf.

The Shadowed Arts-sustained roots continued to wind their way up the Human youth's body. They encircled Taz's midsection, and wrapped around his arms. By the time they were done, Taz looked as if he had been swaddled in some kind of black rope like some perverse mummy.

Taz had stopped screaming by this time. He was so frightened, he had literally been frozen with fear. He would not have been able to move even if the fear had not petrified him. He had become so entwined in the roots that he no longer had any control over his muscles.

The roots wound their way up Taz's body until the small tapered points of the roots were even with the youth's two eyes. Then without hesitation, they plunged into the two orbs that mere seconds before had been opened wide with fear. There was an ungodly sucking sound and Taz began screaming anew.

Drè stood by and watched as the Tree of Sacrifice literally sucked the life out of Taz. The horrible suction sound continued far longer than the shrieks of pain. Taz's body seemed to cave in on itself yet the sucking continued. It would have been an obscene sight for anyone else to see, but Drè stood transfixed in passionate ecstacy, watching with the rapt attention a Christian would give Jesus, or a Buddhist would give Gautama Siddhartha.

When the roots were sated, they slowly began to unwind, and like the serpents they resembled, they slithered down the now-emaciated form of Taz's body. There was nothing left of the Human gang banger except a skin-like husk. When the roots were completely untangled from what was left of Taz, the husk fell to the floor and dispersed into countless pieces. The roots then drove themselves back into the floor and down into the depths with another trembling rumble.

Drè was so caught up in the religious-like fervor of the moment that he gasped in exhilaration when it was over. A groan from Bone grabbed his attention however, and he walked over to where the elder gang banger was on the ground, slowly bleeding to death from the stab wound. The Human had pulled the dagger from his body, and was trying to keep his life's blood from pouring out by holding his hands over the puncture hole. It was about as effective as trying to plug a hole in a dam with a finger. With a gleam of insanity shining brightly in his eyes, Drè lifted his sword and began hacking.

W-Dog, who was still in shock from the sudden and violent loss of his right arm, could only watch in horror as the madman sliced his friend to pieces. He could not scream or even call out for help, his fear causing him to wet himself. It was like his worst nightmare had taken form and come to life. The most terrifying aspect of it all was the laugh of joyous glee W-Dog could hear coming from the maniac as he continued to butcher his friend.

When Drè had spent his energy, he dropped his sword. It splattered in the growing pool of blood that was surrounding what was left of the intruder. He had hacked Bone into pieces of bloodied meat that were unrecognizable as Human. The blood was glorious. The metallic scent of it filled his nostrils and he felt intoxicated from the aroma.

W-Dog knew if he did not get up and try to run that a similar fate awaited him. He was weak from shock and loss of blood; if this madman did not kill him, he knew the loss of blood would. He had to leave, and get medical attention. If he could just get back to T, he would help.

Trying to summon any strength that he still might have, W-Dog pushed himself up with his left hand, and was able to get back to his feet. He stumbled around like one of those drunken, homeless bums he and Taz used to make fun of. He was not exactly sure what had happened to Taz, but he had heard the screams, and he knew whatever it was, it had not been good.

He slowly made his way to the window that had brought him and his two fellow gang members into this den of horrors. He staggered around, losing his balance. He fell into some old crates and caused them to fall with a loud clattering that caught Drè's attention. W-Dog knew he was done for, and he did the most embarrassing thing he could. He began to cry.

Drè heard the noise from the falling crates, and the sobs of utter despair. This brought a malicious smile back to his face. He had fed his blood hunger with the first intruder, and the Tree of Sacrifice had gorged on the life essence of the other. This one, he would send out as a warning.

He retrieved his sword, walked over to the weeping Human, and placed the point of the blade on the youth's chest. He pushed down hard enough that the tip drew a tiny line of blood. This made W-Dog whimper even more. Drè looked on the Human with disgust and contempt. These pitiful wretches were prime examples of how corruption could ruin a race.

"Go and tell your fellow Humans what happens when they meddle in my affairs," he commanded with as much menace in his voice he could muster.

With that, he withdrew the sword, and walked back to his sleeping quarters. He could feel the exhaustion taking hold and settling on him once again as the adrenaline rush subsided. He did not bother checking to see if the last intruder was able to make it out or not. If he did die from his wound before warning the others so be it. That could mean that others might try where these three had failed, and that meant more fun for him.

If he thought his suit had been bloodied before, it was completely saturated now. This time he did remove his clothing before settling back into his replenishing trance. However, he kept the soiled outfit piled by his bed. He slipped back into the trance with the sickly sweet smell of drying blood filling his nostrils.

W-Dog could not believe it when the crazy murderer spoke his warning and then walked away. He kept waiting for the stranger to come back and finish him off. When it became apparent that he was actually going to be allowed to walk away, W-Dog half stumbled and half crawled out of the warehouse.

He was found two blocks away by a couple of kids that had been out tossing a football around. An ambulance arrived a short time later, and W-Dog was whisked away. The paramedics could only shake their heads as they listened to W-Doghis ramblings about a madman with pointed ears.

"It's a crying shame what these gang bangers do to each other," one paramedic said sadly.

"It's the drugs," the other replied. "Just listen to this poor kid. He must be high as a kite."

# CHAPTER 24

Kalen had retrieved the general's sword from the backseat of Detective Sommers' car, and he was now sitting at the foot of the bed he had slept in a couple of nights ago, wiping the sharpened blade down with a white washcloth he had found in the bathroom. He was attempting to occupy his time until their ride arrived to take him and Amy to their much-anticipated meeting.

Amy was lying down on the other bed. She had her hands resting comfortably behind her head. At first glance, she appeared relaxed, but Kalen recognized the tension in her neck and shoulders. He got the impression that their contact was a dangerous ally.

"So who is this mysterious person of yours that we are going to see?" Kalen asked, his curiosity finally getting the better of him.

Amy opened her eyes and looked over at the Elf. He kept his eyes focused on his sword, examining it carefully and avoiding Amy's questioning stare.

Finally, Kalen stopped cleaning the razor-sharp blade, and returned her gaze with one of his own as he waited for an answer to his question. He respected Amy, and wanted to show her some professional courtesy, but he disliked the idea of walking into a potentially hazardous situation without being fully informed.

When Kalen's eyes met and held Amy's, she took a deep breath and then answered. "The person that we'll be meeting with is James Royalton Thompson or Royal T as he is known on the streets."

"And this 'Royal T' can help us find Drè?" Kalen pressed.

Amy sat up, and swung her feet off the bed and onto the floor so that she faced the Elf more directly. Kalen slid the sword back in its scabbard and then laid it on the bed reverently so he could give the detective his full attention.

"James Thompson, or Royal T if you prefer, is the leader of the Down Hood Mob street gang. They are the largest street gang affiliated with the Bloods. There are even rumors that Royal T is in line to take over leadership of the entire Bloods gang. He currently resides in the Venice area, and nothing goes down on the streets of Los Angeles that Royal T doesn't know about. He is probably better informed than all of the LAPD. With a name like Royal T, and with all the flows of information that he has coming in, Mr. Thompson likes to refer to himself as the King of the Streets," she finished.

"You are sure this 'King of the Streets' will be willing to help us? It sounds like from your description that this Royal T is in a position of power. He may not be as forthcoming as we would like him to be."

He had some experience in dealing with individuals who thought they were more important than they actually were. Those who tended to exaggerate their self worth usually liked to play at being coy with people they thought were beneath them. This is what he feared was going to happen with this gang leader. He did not know him per se, but he did know the type.

"Oh, he will help us. He owes me, and according to their warped sense of street justice, he will repay his debt," she explained confidently.

Kalen was unsure what to think of this. He knew that the organization Amy worked for was responsible for the enforcement of Human laws. From her secrecy about this meeting, he gathered that Royal T was probably not a law-abiding citizen. This meant that if Amy had helped the gang leader in some way to earn this debt, she may have been going against her own ethical code.

"What did you do for this individual?" he asked with more than a passing curiosity and concern.

"About a little more than a year ago, I arrested Royal T's little brother Billy – he goes by the street name Baby T – for the murder of two rival gang members." Kalen noted that her answer was casual and businesslike.

"You imprisoned his younger brother, and now he owes you?" he asked in disbelief.

"No," she answered while chuckling. "He owes me because I testified at Baby T's sentencing hearing on his behalf. He was just a seventeen-year-old kid trying to live up to his big brother's example. Thanks to my testimony, Baby T was spared the gas chamber, and was given a life sentence instead. So, in a way, I saved Baby T's life, and *that* is why Royal T owes me, and that is why he will help us."

Kalen nodded his head in understanding. He felt ashamed of himself for doubting Amy's character. He should have known better and he silently scolded himself. She had not broken any of her people's laws. She had, in fact, enforced those laws, and shown mercy at the same time. She was an incredible woman, and even though he was unaware of it, a goofy looking smile began to break out on his face.

"What're you smiling at, Elf boy?" Amy asked as her own smile began to spread.

Kalen surprised himself by answering, "You are a very special woman, Detective Sommers."

Amy's cheeks flushed bright red. She opened her mouth to say something but no words came out. Kalen was afraid he had been too forward. The bond between them had been growing stronger ever since the attack at Detective Hanson's house. He was sure she must feel it too, but was not sure what to make of her reaction. She swallowed hard and he could see her eyes soften as she seemed to search for a response. Before any words came out, there was a loud banging on the hotel room's door.

Kalen instinctively grabbed his sword, and jumped up from the bed, ready to face whatever challenge was going to be coming through the door.

"Easy there, big fella," Amy said, attempting to alleviate the tension. "That's probably just our ride."

Kalen relaxed as Amy moved to open the door. Whoever was on the outside must have been impatient as they began pounding on the door again before Amy could get there to answer it.

The knocking was so loud, it seemed to make the entire room shake. Kalen feared the door would crack and splinter apart from the onslaught. Though he had relaxed some after Amy's admonishment, he still kept a tight grip on his sword, just in case.

The second round of loud knocking ended just as Amy reached the door. She peered out of the tiny peephole to see who was on the other side. Seemingly satisfied, she nodded her head. She looked over her shoulder at Kalen, as though telling him not to do anything stupid.

"It's them," she confirmed before opening the door.

"You Sommers?" one of the youths asked as soon as he saw Amy standing in the doorway.

Kalen had to look around Amy to see the two young, dark-skinned Humans. He wanted to measure them up, in case there was going to be trouble. They were very young; not much more than teenagers. They were both dressed in dark, baggy shorts, and both were also wearing bright white shoes. The one that had spoken was wearing a white t-shirt with a design Kalen was unfamiliar with. It looked like a large, curved emblem of some kind, like a scimitar or the blade of a skate. The other Human was wearing a heavier black and silver shirt with large numbers on the front and back. The two were also both wearing red bandanas in a do-rag fashion on their heads.

Though they were young, they definitely had an air of confidence about them. Kalen took a mental note that they did not display any outward signs of fear. They were here to fulfill orders they had been given, and see their mission through. In an odd sort of way, he could relate to these two Humans, and he respected their sense of duty.

"Yeah, I'm Detective Sommers," Amy answered, putting an extra emphasis on the word, "detective."

"Cool. We're here to take you to Royal T," the gang member that had spoken earlier explained.

"All right. My partner and I will be right out," Amy offered.

"We'll be waiting for ya in the parking lot. Hurry though, T doesn't like to be kept waiting," with that said, the two bangers walked out to the parking lot and stood by a shiny black Suburban.

Amy left the door open so as not to raise any suspicion that she and Kalen may be up to something. Kalen could see the two gang bangers were watching the room closely.

"From here on out, let me do the talking," Amy ordered Kalen. "These guys are real big on respect so if you do have to speak, remember that. They have probably killed people over what were perceived slights. A lot of these kids have itchy trigger fingers and sometimes they feel the need to scratch that itch."

"I understand," Kalen said.

Amy looked at the Elf for a couple of seconds longer before nodding her head, seemingly satisfied. "No time like the present. Let's go," she said, walking out the door. Kalen paused long enough to shut the door behind him before he followed her to the large automobile.

As they approached the black Suburban, Kalen could hear a loud thumping. It was so loud he could feel the vibrations all the way into his chest. He thought he could pick out faint traces of what he guessed was music, but with the overwhelming thumping, he could not be sure.

When the two gang members saw the strained look on Kalen's face, they burst out laughing. The one that had not spoken walked around to the other side and got in while his partner waited for Amy and Kalen. When they got close, he motioned for them to get in as well.

They did as they had been instructed, and climbed into the backseat. Amy got in first and slid all the way over until she was behind the passenger seat. Kalen followed her in through the same door. Once inside, the loud bass-filled music made his head swim.

The driver also got in, and looked back over the seat to check on his passengers. Seeing that Kalen was in discomfort he teased, "Hope ya'll like Snoop Dogg."

"Oh yeah, sure, he's my all time favorite," Amy replied sarcastically. She had to practically yell to be heard over the pounding rap music. "My friend here is not a real music lover though."

The driver laughed again, but he reached over and turned the music down before dropping the gearshift into drive and speeding off.

Kalen watched the hotel get smaller through the tinted window as they drove away. He hoped this meeting of Amy's would bear fruit. He had a nagging feeling that if they did not find and stop Drè soon, they would not get another opportunity, and that would doom his people to an unspeakable fate.

*Shawn Oetzel*

# CHAPTER 25

Kalen and Amy held on tight as their driver weaved in and out of traffic at breakneck speed. The music thumped and the Suburban's tires squealed as they made their way to Venice. Amy had no idea how she was going to pull this off with Royal T. They were out of options though. She had meant what she had said about the gang leader knowing everything that happened out on the streets. The tricky part was going to be getting him to tell what he knew. Hopefully, her street credit was still good or else this could be a very short meeting.

James "Royal T" Thompson ran the Down Hood Mob from the Crenshaw Projects apartment complex. The gang ran everything from military style guns to crack cocaine, and they had recently branched out into the production and distribution of crystal meth. Royal T may have lived in the projects, but with the money his gang had rolling in, he lived like the king he referred to himself as.

The Down Hood Mob had grown into the largest and most influential street gang that was affiliated with the better known street gang called the Bloods. They were incredibly well organized, and just as incredibly dangerous. This had been Royal T's influence. He had spent six years in the US Army, and upon his return home, he took what he had learned and applied it to the local gang culture. Within a year, he had transformed the Down Hood Mob from a group of thugs into a well oiled machine that ran with military efficiency.

Everything had been running smoothly until his younger brother had been stupid enough to get himself busted. He hated to admit it, but if it had not been for the female cop, Baby T would have been gassed for sure. He hated owing a pig anything, but it was his brother's life.

Royal T had been shocked she would actually reach out to him for help. With his informants inside the LAPD, he had already learned about the detective's suspension, which had made him laugh. Sommers had always been a spitfire. Under different circumstances he may have pursued her, but as things were, that was simply out of the question. Besides, with his power and money he could have practically any woman in his hood. It was good being the king, and rank definitely had its privileges.

He was guessing that Sommers was coming to him about the unsolved murders, though why she still cared after getting suspended, he did not understand. He had some information she would probably find extremely valuable, but he was not sure if he wanted to share and give it to her. He preferred to handle situations himself, and the last thing he wanted to do was make things easier for the cops, even suspended ones.

He could see the black Suburban as it turned the corner onto his block. His two soldiers had followed their orders admirably, and had returned earlier than he had anticipated. He would have to remember to reward them. A couple of the high school girls that were always hanging around hoping he would notice them were always willing to do him favors. They would do the trick nicely.

He was a little surprised as to how much he was looking forward to meeting with Detective Sommers. This could prove interesting, and was definitely going to be fun.

Kalen had been trying to pay close attention to his surroundings when they had pulled into the Human neighborhood. From what little information he had been given, he gathered that the place they were in was called Venice. He watched with a renewed interest as the Suburban slowly came to a stop in front of several closely spaced, three-story brick buildings.

The buildings looked dilapidated, and were in major need of some updating. There were young children running around playing without a care in the world. Clothes had been hung out on lines to dry. Elderly Humans were sitting on stoops or hanging out of windows, casually watching as the world went by. It looked serene, but to the professionally trained eye of a soldier, Kalen could see the underlying signs of a military compound. The carefree picture the tenants had painted was merely a facade to cover the corruption that was truly running this place.

He could see sentries posted periodically throughout the Crenshaw Projects. They were all young, dark skinned, and wearing the now-familiar red bandanas. The occupants of these projects were more prisoners than they were tenants. This situation was going to be a little more serious than he had originally anticipated. He ran his hand down to the sword secured at his waist. He grasped the pommel firmly. The touch and feel of cold steel made him feel better.

When they had come to a complete stop in front of the Crenshaw Projects, their driver and escort got out. Kalen and Amy followed suit. The sun was still bright, and the humidity had grown to a sticky, uncomfortable level as the afternoon waned.

"Wait here. I'll go see if T is ready for ya'll," the driver of the Suburban told them before walking through the yard, and into the nearest apartment building.

The other youth walked around the large SUV, and leaned against it casually. He had not spoken to them at all during the whole trip, so neither Kalen nor Amy felt the need to try and be social. He was clearly there to keep an eye on them until Royal T was ready. They left the young gang banger to his duty. After about ten minutes their driver returned.

"Follow me," he said. "Royal T is waiting for you two around back."

"Lead the way," Amy responded, trying to sound confident.

As they began following their assigned guide, Kalen became worried when the other Human climbed into the large vehicle that had brought them and drove off, leaving him and Amy trapped, for all intents and purposes. *It will probably not matter,* he thought to himself. If things got bad enough where they would have to consider an escape, the vehicle's existence outside would not help them.

He watched Amy as she followed the young Human. Her stride was full of purpose, and she did her best to appear confident and in control. She was so sure of herself, it made him ease up a little bit in his own posture. It would do them no good if he appeared intimidated. Amy had said these men held respect in a high regard. He hoped their concepts of respect worked both ways.

They walked towards the first building. They had to go up a small flight of stairs, passing another red-bandana-clad youth, who was sitting on the top step. He barely recognized they were even there. He was too intent on doing his job watching the street to pay any attention to their presence.

They continued past the lone sentry without any kind of acknowledgement and walked inside the building. The first thing Kalen noted was the heat. The building was not ventilated very well, and it had become stifling. It was like a large brick oven. It was also deathly quiet. There were three stories of apartments filled with families, but not a sound was heard. These people were definitely being forced to live in a constant state of fear. He thought this Royal T may fancy himself to be a king, but from all the outward signs, the gang leader was more like a tyrant.

The trio entered a long narrow hallway with a staircase off to their right that led to the second floor and beyond. To their left were a series of doors Kalen guessed were the entrances to these apartments Amy had told him about. The inside of the building was in no better shape than the outside. The once-white paint was dirty and had begun peeling in a number of places. The walls showed signs of some kind of water damage that had gone unfixed for quite some time. He could only shake his head in disgust over the filth these poor people were forced to live in. It was an affront to his sensibilities, and for the first time since coming to this realm, he began to feel sorry for these Humans.

They walked straight through the hallway, past the entrances of the apartments, and out a backdoor that led outside once again. There was another set of steps with another sentry posted. He – much like his counterpart out front – did not even bother glancing in their direction as they walked on by. He could say what he wanted about Royal T's men and their methods, but he could not say that they were not well trained. Despite the depravity he had witnessed, Kalen once again found himself admiring the militaristic style and approach that this street gang took.

Their guide led them to a round patio table with a large umbrella that was providing the shade. The table was the only thing Kalen had seen that looked new, and it stuck out accordingly. At this table was perhaps the most intimidating person he had ever seen in any realm. He had thought Reggie was a huge wall of a man when they had first met, but this Human made the special agent look like a Dwarf from his own world.

Even while seated, Royal T looked as tall as Amy. From what Kalen could see, Royal T was wearing a white tank top shirt with several large silver chains hanging around his neck. He also had what appeared to be an overly large diamond pierced into his left earlobe. On his shaved head was the requisite red bandana.

During his short time in the Human realm, Kalen had already noted much diversity among the people. Elves were generally fair-skinned, as were many Humans. However, Human skin tones varied greatly and Royal T had the darkest skin the Elf had ever seen. It made the simple white shirt he was wearing stand out, almost as if it was glowing in the late afternoon sun.

His arms were rippled with muscle. He looked like he could pick one of his fellow gang members up, and rip them in half. He was simply a massive example of a Human being. It was no wonder he was recognized as the leader. If the rules of these Human streets were similar to what they were in his own realm, and it was survival of the fittest, then Royal T was going to win every time.

As they approached the table, Royal T stood up to greet his guests in a nice imitation of a polite and gracious host. When he stood, they were able to see all of his enormous 6'10" frame. He was extremely tall, broad, and his entire body radiated a massive amount of power. He smiled in an attempt to appear friendly, but it was the smile of a predator. His teeth, like his shirt, seemed to glow.

"Detective Sommers, so nice to see you again," Royal T said when they were standing in front of the table. He had a deep voice that matched his girth. There was also a slight metallic ring to his tone.

"Thank you, T," Amy tried to reciprocate their host's friendly demeanor. "We appreciate you granting us this meeting."

"Easy, girl," Royal T scolded. "Only my soldiers get to call me T."

Amy smiled jovially, trying to show she had not meant any disrespect before replying. "No problem. This is your backyard, so it's your rules."

"Now ya see, that's why I always liked you, Sommers," he explained condescendingly. "You always were smart, especially for a cop."

Amy let the backhanded insult slip. She had expected as much from someone who was so pompous. She could let a few digs against her go if it meant that she and Kalen would get the information they needed. Though she would have liked nothing more than to put this big oaf in his place by walking over to the great redwood of a man and felling him with a well placed knee to his groin. Instead, she just smiled prettily.

"Aren't you going to introduce me to your friend?" the large gang leader asked, motioning toward Kalen.

"This is Agent Wain of the FBI," she said, also motioning towards the Elf. "Though something tells me that you probably already knew that."

Royal T flashed that knowing smile again before he waved his guests over to two chairs that had been provided. He then made a dismissive gesture to the youth that had been their driver and impromptu guide. The youth, in turn, quickly walked away.

"Your men follow orders well," Kalen complimented.

Royal T beamed in response to the unexpected comment before he responded. "Only a fellow soldier could have respect for the importance of following orders."

Kalen nodded his head in agreement, but did not comment further. Amy was glad that he did not give away any more information. Royal T was the type of person to use every advantage he could gain against you. There was no need to give him any more ammunition. Instead, Kalen sat statue-still with an emotionless countenance. Amy understood that he was trying to give the impression that he, too, was someone that was used to giving orders, and having them followed without question.

"How's Baby T doing?" Amy asked, trying to break the tension that was building. She also hoped this question would serve as a reminder of her help, and that Royal T owed her.

"He is doing as well as can be expected for someone who is rotting away in prison," Royal T answered, his voice full of scorn.

He knew what Amy was up to, and his reply let her know that yes she had saved Baby T from being executed, but his situation was still not ideal.

"It's still better than winding up on a slab in the morgue," Amy continued, reminding the gang leader of the road his younger brother had been headed down.

Royal T clearly did not appreciate that this female cop was flaunting the fact that she had saved his baby brother's life. He straightened up in his plastic lawn chair and switched his attitude from one of casual indifference to one of perturbed annoyance. Amy narrowed her eyes and evaluated Royal T. When they came in, he had been playing with them – having fun. Now, he was growing angry.

"Let's cut through the garbage, and you tell me why exactly you're here," he said trying to keep his voice even toned. He was trying hard not to let Detective Sommers know she was getting under his skin.

Kalen picked up on the large Human's change in demeanor right away. He hoped Amy knew what she was doing by baiting the volatile Royal T. If the gang leader grew tired of Amy's persistence, he could call down a small army on top of them before either he or Amy could react. He decided to play it calm, but he watched the Human even closer for any signs of impending danger.

"All right, Royal T," she began. "Since you're tired of mincing words, I will get right down to the point. We are here because the LAPD needs your help; we need some information."

Royal T smiled his best predatory grin before asking, "What makes you think that I have this information, *Detective?*"

Amy did not like the way he had emphasized the word, "detective." The gang leader's voice had a teasing quality to it. She was worried about what kind of game Royal T could be playing, but she pressed on.

"You're the King of the Streets aren't you?" she asked, hoping that by invoking his heralded nickname she might win back a few brownie points. "If anyone would have the information we need, it would be you."

A genuine smile appeared on Royal T's face and he straightened a little. Amy could tell that he loved the flattery. However, there was a glint in his eye and his smile took on the predatory edge again. He knew something. The question was what did he know and how would he use the information.

"Tell me, Sommers, why would the LAPD send an officer that is on an administrative leave here to get information?" he asked wrapping himself up in his superiority as if it was some kind of security blanket.

"Damn," Amy whispered in frustration. "I should have known."

"Don't feel bad, Sommers," Royal T said in a mock-consoling tone. "The LAPD is the most corrupt police force in this entire despicable country. Some of those cops would sell their own children out for a few dollars."

The sad part was Amy knew he was right. More information leaked out of the department than anyone could imagine. There were more holes in the LAPD's security net than a piece of Swiss cheese, and they were all large enough to drive a Suburban through. It was the one aspect of her job she had never learned to stomach.

"Okay, so you know my dirty little secret, but that does not change the fact that I need some information," she said trying to reason with the gang leader.

"First thing's first, Sommers," Royal T said trying not to laugh, but failing. "You've got to tell me what you did."

"Let's just say that I have a problem with authority, especially when that authority is a moron," she answered, her voice full of scorn.

Royal T did not even bother trying to stop his laughter. He chuckled loudly at her indignation before inquiring, "The little guy finally got fed up with your smart mouth or did you screw up and give the little midget the reason to get rid of you that he's been looking for?"

"I screwed up," was all the answer she was willing to give.

"Poor Sommers, she doesn't have her gun and badge to play with anymore," he mocked. "Actually that works in your favor, Sommers. There is no way I would ever waste my valuable time helping those LAPD pigs do anything. Now that you are no longer one of the porcine, I can see you in a new light. I think I like the idea of helping you, Sommers, now that you're a renegade."

Amy knew that Royal T would help her because of his sense of honor and duty. However, the fact that she had been suspended gave him an even better excuse, and made him look even better in the eyes of his followers. Helping a cop would not have settled well with the members of his Down Hood Mob crew, but helping a renegade cop would be considered cool and dangerous. It would only add to his already over-inflated reputation.

"So, does this mean that you are going to help us?" she asked hopefully.

Royal T's eyes narrowed as he evaluated the detective. "Sure, Sommers, why not," he said cavalierly. "What is it that I can do for you and your Broadway Dancer-looking friend here and please do not further insult my intelligence by continuing the charade of him being an FBI agent."

Kalen frowned deeply. He knew that he had just been insulted in some fashion, but Amy was glad that he didn't comment. Royal T was on the verge of helping them and she didn't want any distractions. However, she did find herself wondering if the Elf liked to dance.

"Like I said, we need some information," Amy reiterated.

She also deliberately ignored the slight verbal jab that had been thrown Kalen's way. She also decided not to belabor the point about Kalen being FBI. Royal T obviously had a problem with law enforcement in general so there was no point trying to use that angle.

"Let's hear it, and I'll see what I can do," Royal T instructed.

Amy glanced quickly at Kalen, and when the Elf nodded his head in approval, she continued. "I know that you are aware of the serial killer running around LA."

"Which one?" Royal T jokingly interrupted, but when his two guests did not join in his amusement, he shrugged his massive shoulders, and gestured for Amy to continue.

"The one that has been collecting hearts like they were baseball cards," she answered in exasperation before continuing, "And the one that killed a detective last night."

"Ah yes, Detective Addict himself. Sorry to hear about that," he replied with a sarcastic grin spread wide across his face. "He was a good customer."

Amy glared in the gang leader's general direction. She and Hanson had not been the best of friends, but he had not deserved to die like he had. She bit back a heated reply, and instead responded, "This killer has also murdered five other people, three of them right here in Los Angeles. He likes to prey on the morally corrupt, so I'm sure some of the victims were also customers of yours. That can't be good for business."

She could give as good as she got, and Amy finished her statement by smiling maliciously back at Royal T. They both knew he had become rich by trafficking and selling illegal narcotics. His gang had more than likely killed more people with their drugs than they ever could have with their gang wars, especially now with the introduction of crystal meth. The LAPD had been cleaning the bodies of meth heads off the streets more frequently the past few months.

"You sure have a funny way of asking for help," Royal T commented while looking down at Amy. This was his way of showing the detective he was the one in control.

"Look, you and I can sit here and trade barbs all night long, but that isn't going to help me," Amy tried to reason with the moody gang leader.

"The information that we require is of a great importance. It could save countless lives," Kalen interjected, with just a note of desperation and frustration.

Royal T stared at Kalen after hearing him speak. He really had not paid much attention to the Elf. Kalen had been sitting quietly, letting the detective do all the talking. Now though, the quiet partner had struck a chord with his words.

"What exactly do you want to know about this killer?" Royal T asked, getting back to the point of their conversation.

Amy smiled at Kalen. She immediately felt bad about her childish behavior. She knew how important this was to the Elf, and what was at stake if they failed. With his simple statements, he had put her in her place, and put it all back into perspective. Thanks to him, she was once again able to focus on their mission.

"We have reason to believe that this psycho is staying someplace near the beach, pretty close to your territory. We were hoping that you could help us locate this lunatic before he can kill again," she said, almost imploring Royal T to help them.

Kalen and Amy watched intently as Royal T leaned back in his chair, and appeared to be deep in thought. He rubbed his chin repeatedly, trying to decide his course of action before saying, "I may be able to help you."

Kalen practically leapt out of his chair, hardly able to contain his excitement. He wanted to confront and stop his father's murderer as soon as possible. He gripped the armrests of his chair tightly, as though doing everything in his power not to leap up and shake the information out of Royal T.

Amy was excited, too. She had not known what to expect from Royal T, though she had banked on the prospect that he would be willing to help her as a payment for his brother's life. For a minute, she thought she had over-stepped the boundaries and gone too far, but thankfully, Kalen had been able to jump in and change the tide, and now it appeared help was finally on the way.

Just as Royal T was about to divulge what information he had concerning the serial killer, a gang member appeared, interrupting them. Neither Amy nor Kalen could tell where he had appeared from.

The youth walked around the circular table to stand at Royal T's side. He bent over, and whispered something into his leader's ear.

Amy could tell by Royal T's facial expression that the news was completely unexpected, and it was not particularly good. This did not bode well for her and Kalen. Her bad feeling began to grow worse.

"What happened?" Royal T said out loud in disbelief.

The messenger bent down again, and resumed whatever tale he had been relaying. Amy could not hear a word that was being said. She looked up at Kalen to see if he had picked up anything with his sensitive ears. He shrugged and shook his head.

"Where is he now?" Royal T questioned his messenger forcefully, and when he got an answer he ordered, "Take me to him."

With that said, the gang leader stood up from the table and towered over his guests. He was clearly upset and irate over whatever his fellow gang member had told him. He had a look of fierce determination marked on his face. Amy was glad she had not been the one to get this giant of a man's ire up.

Royal T waved another one of his soldiers over. This one had been the sentry that was sitting on the back step when Kalen and Amy had been brought out.

"Take Detective Sommers and her partner to my apartment. They can wait there until I return." he commanded.

"Wait a minute," Amy butted in. "We're not staying anywhere, and you said you would help us."

"Please, Detective, something important has come up," he said gravely. "Please wait. I will be back shortly and more than likely with the very information that you requested."

This caught Amy off guard. Whatever had happened had affected Royal T immensely. He was clearly upset, and his politeness in asking them to stay was genuine. She peeked over at Kalen who was disappointed by this turn of events. What choice did they have though? If Royal T was willing to give them what they wanted, then they would have to do as he bade them.

"Okay, we'll wait for you," Amy said somewhat confused over the whole situation.

"Follow me," the sentry that Royal T had brought over instructed.

"I will be back as soon as I can," Royal T said almost apologetically before he walked off to a separate building.

Amy and Kalen did the only thing they could. They followed the sentry-turned-guide back into the apartment building they had walked through while en route to this meeting. The gang banger took them up the stairs to the third floor, and let them into Royal T's apartment, where they were left to wait.

# —Chapter 26

Kalen noticed right away that the third floor he and Amy had been taken to was not like the rest of the building they had seen. For starters, it had been updated and completely remodeled. There was only the one door, whereas the other floors had several, marking the many different apartments. Since Royal T had ordered them to be taken to his own personal apartment, Kalen guessed the gang leader's was the only one on that floor.

The guide removed a key from the lanyard he had hanging around his neck, and let them in. A blast of cool air hit them in the face as the door was pushed inward. Unlike the rest of the rundown apartments in the building, this one was complete with air conditioning.

The young gang member did not say a word, but he motioned for Kalen and Amy to enter. When they did, the banger did not follow. He shut the door behind them, and hearing the sounds of footsteps going down stairs, Kalen knew the young Human had probably returned to his post on the back steps.

The gang leader's apartment had every modern comfort that one could imagine. From the large screen plasma television to the incredibly sophisticated looking stereo system that looked like it had been built by NASA, along with the huge black leather furniture, the place looked like an oasis when compared the rest of the battered excuse of an apartment complex. How Royal T could live in such luxury while people were practically living in squalor only a few feet away, angered Kalen's sensibilities.

"Kind of makes my place look like a hole, huh?" Amy snorted.

"How can he live like this while those he supposedly takes care of are living in such adverse conditions?" Kalen asked in disgusted astonishment.

"Welcome to my realm," Amy answered acrimoniously. She shook her head. "You know, I became a police officer to stop these kinds of miscarriages of justice. I never had any grand illusions about being able to save the world from people like Royal T, but I've been helpless to prevent his crimes and they've been going on in my own backyard." She sighed. "Maybe getting suspended from the force wasn't such a bad thing. Maybe it's a chance to think whether there's a better way to stop corruption."

"Corruption is not something that is confined to the Human realm," Kalen interrupted her introspection. "I have seen plenty of examples in my own realm. It is never easy to see until it is flaunted in your face in this manner."

He finished his statement by sweeping his arm around the large living room so Amy would get the idea to take in the whole picture.

She smiled lightly after hearing Kalen speak so frankly about the corruption from where he was from. She walked over to the oversized, soft leather couch, and plopped down. "I hate to admit it, but this is the most comfortable couch I've ever sat on." She shook her head. "Why would someone as hard as Royal T need such soft and delicate furniture?" She laughed at her own question. "Since we are stuck here, you might as well take a load off," she said to Kalen, patting the soft leather with her hand, indicating the Elf should have a seat as well.

Kalen walked over, and sat next to her on the couch. He shifted his weight around, and got comfortable. With a smile on his face he turned to the detective and said, "This really is nice, and though I hate to say it, quite comfortable."

The Elf's smile was contagious, and they both shared a much-needed laugh. Nothing about this case had been easy. They had been running from one end of Los Angeles to the other, scrambling for any clue or crumb of information that would help them find Drè Fao'lain. They had been attacked, and Reggie had nearly been killed, Amy had been suspended, and now they were turning to a drug lord for help who, for all intents and purposes, had them trapped in his poor man's penthouse. It felt good to just sit and relax even if it was for a short period of time.

Amy looked around the large apartment, and finally spying what she was after said, "I could use a drink. You want one?"

Kalen thought for a moment before answering. "Yes, I think a drink would be nice."

She walked over to the built-in bar that made up nearly one whole wall. It was done up in black lacquer and mirrors. On the shelves were several expensive looking bottles. She finally settled on something called

Cognac Banchereau. The bottle said it was imported from France so she figured it must be good. She grabbed two whiskey snifters and poured them half full. She carried them back over to the couch, and handed one of the glasses to Kalen.

"I hope you like cognac," she said as he took the offered drink.

He looked at the dark amber liquid. He brought the glass to his nose, and took in the rich smoky aroma before gingerly taking a sip. The flavor of the cognac exploded in his mouth. His eyes grew large and watered up as he swallowed the liquid fire. It burned all the way down his throat, and set his stomach ablaze. He coughed reflexively, and tears continued to flow from his eyes.

Amy, having taken a sip herself, let out a loud "woohoo" sound before she could finally get some words out. "Wow, that'll sure knock the point off your ears."

He was still too busy trying to regain his composure to offer up any semblance of a reply. He looked at the glass of alcohol in his hand as if it might explode at any minute before hurriedly setting the volatile liquid down on the coffee table that was in front of the couch.

"Your people actually drink that?" he asked amazed. "It is no wonder you Humans act so strangely."

Amy laughed in spite of herself. She took another quick sip of the cognac and said, "Speak for yourself Elfboy, I happen to like this stuff."

He rolled his eyes before adding, "To each their own I guess, though that explains a lot."

Amy smirked at the Elf as she also set her glass of cognac on the glass coffee table. The afternoon was starting to slip away into early evening, causing the shadows to gradually glide across the interior of the apartment. They both sat silently with their thoughts, not really knowing what else to do.

When the silence became too much for her to bear any longer, Amy turned to the Elf and asked with sincere curiosity, "Tell me about your home, Kalen. I have heard you mention things about it. Tell me what it is really like."

A small tremor of homesickness washed over Kalen when Amy asked about his realm. He sighed audibly before answering, "It is a beautiful place. My words cannot do it justice."

"Please try," she implored. "You have seen my realm, now help me try and see yours."

She watched fascinated as a sparkle shone in the Elf's blue eyes. She really did want to know what his world was like. This was the first time since they had met that she had the opportunity to inquire. The rest of their time had been spent chasing down leads.

"All right, Amy, I will do my best," he said.

He was actually fairly excited for the opportunity to talk about his home. The Human realm was so alien to him that it had been terribly hard for him to relate to Amy at times. If he could show her what it was like where he was from, then maybe it would bring them closer. It could help them understand each other, and that prospect made him feel excited as well.

He closed his eyes, and recalled his memories of the Great Ash Forest his people called home. He could almost smell the fresh evening breeze, and see the smooth bark of the sacred trees as they glistened in the moonlight. He could hear the cry of the silver eagles; the large birds nested in the trees, and they were also the symbol for the Elven Royal Family.

"If you could only see what I have seen," he said reverently when he opened his eyes.

"Tell me," she urged in a whisper.

"My people do not live in great cities with large structures. We call the forest home. We believe the Ash Trees that make up that forest are sacred. They were a gift to the world from the moon goddess Alorien. They are so tall you cannot see the tops from the ground. Their silver bark is smooth and warm to the touch. They are as alive as you or I. The Elves have a symbiotic relationship with the Great Ashes. They nurture each other, and as one goes so does the other. The Great Ashes are everything to my people."

Amy could see how emotional Kalen was about his home. The way he talked about and described the trees was almost as if he was describing a lover. The timbre of his voice reflected the deep emotional bond the Elf had with his own realm.

"The Elves also believe that the moon is where the Goddess Alorien makes her home. Alorien created the Elves by planting pieces of the full moon next to the Great Ash Trees. The trees nurtured the moon seedlings, and the Elves grew from those pieces. That is why my people have such an affinity for the land. Alorien is our sacred Mother. We hold these incredible festivals in her honor every full moon phase. It is a glorious time," he finished.

"It sounds beautiful," Amy commented when he finished. She had to wipe tears away from her eyes; hearing Kalen speak so passionately about the Elves had stirred her own emotions.

Seeing Amy so emotionally involved in his words moved him. He reached over to wipe away a stray tear from her eye, and brushed his hand along her cheek gently. He heard her sharp intake of breath, and the next thing he knew they were locked in an embrace sharing the most tender of kisses.

Her lips were soft and delicate. He could taste the cognac she had sipped, and the rich flavor only added to the excitement of the moment. He was startled when Amy's lips parted and he could feel the wetness of her tongue against his own mouth, and he followed her lead. As their tongues touched, the tenderness of the kiss turned to overwhelming passion. It was the most sensual moment he had ever experienced.

When the intensity of the moment began to slowly subside, he began to gradually pull back. They eventually separated with one last, soft, tender kiss. He had no idea what to say, and would not have been able to speak anyway. She had quite literally taken his breath away, and his head was still reeling from the sensory overload.

"Whoa, where did that come from?" Amy asked, out of breath herself. She was too surprised by her forwardness to say anything further.

"I... I... I ..." Kalen stammered, unable to find the right words to explain his own uncharacteristic behavior.

"Exactly," Amy replied, equally shocked.

They both leaned back into the plush couch. Neither wanted to be the next to speak. They could only stare ahead awkwardly, hoping the other one would find something to say that would make everything go back to normal again.

After several long moments of silence, he felt compelled to try and explain himself. He reached out and took Amy's hand in his own. The feel of her warm skin gave him the courage he needed to speak.

"Amy, I am sorry. It was not my intention to offend you. If I did, then I am truly sorry," he offered up his most sincere apology.

Amy smiled, and squeezed the Elf's hand gently. She had no idea what had come over her, but she was determined not to over think this. Deep inside, in a place she let few people ever see, she had been hoping for this moment. She had been attracted to the Elf from the first time they had met, and hearing him speak so eloquently had only increased that attraction.

She smiled playfully at Kalen before responding. "You sure don't know much about women if you think I was offended."

"You are an amazing woman, Amy Sommers," he said with the utmost sincerity. "You are correct though, I do not know much about women, but I am always willing to learn."

Amy laughed and then asked, "Was that a joke? Did the morbidly serious Kalen Or'wain just crack a funny?"

He joined in her laughter when he heard her questions. The awkwardness that had been building only moments before was now completely gone. They sat holding each other's hands in comfortable silence. The apartment had grown darker as the California sun began to set.

"Hearing you speak about your home and your people makes me want to find this Drè even more," Amy said.

"He must not be allowed to complete the ritual," Kalen responded somberly.

"Can it really turn the moon's light into poison?" she asked, her voice filled with concerned curiosity.

"That is what the legends say," he answered after a pause. "You do not fully understand what it means to be an Elf. The moon is the focal point of every aspect of our culture. Without the moonlight, the Great Ash Trees would die, and without the trees, my people would not survive. The Ritual of the Dying Moon is the most horrifying evil imaginable. I will do whatever it takes to stop Drè, no matter the cost."

"We'll find him, and we'll stop him together. I promise," she vowed, more assured than she actually felt.

He squeezed her hand in acknowledgement and appreciation. He believed Amy would do everything in her power to help him, but he was not sure if that would be enough. Drè Fao'lain was no ordinary killer. It was going to take extraordinary measures to stop him.

The sounds of footsteps approaching caught Kalen's attention. There was a rattle at the apartment door as it was unlocked, and Royal T entered.

He did not look well. Whatever had happened had left the gang leader stricken. He looked furious, like he was going to explode in a rage. Kalen would not have thought it possible, but the self-proclaimed King of the Streets had paled considerably.

Kalen and Amy stood up from the couch at the same time and met the big man's wild-eyed stare. When he saw them, he had to take a deep breath to calm himself. Whatever had occurred that had caused such a huge person that kind of distress could not be good.

"Come with me," he ordered, leaving no room for argument. "There is someone I think you two need to see."

# CHAPTER 27

The day's journey had come almost full circle as Kalen and Amy found themselves once again at Cedars Sinai Hospital. This time, however, they were not there for a social visit with Special Agent Blackburn, though they had already discussed that they would pay Reggie another visit. Instead, they were there to see one of Royal T's so-called soldiers.

After Royal T had returned to his apartment, he had quickly explained about the men he had sent out to gather information on a strange newcomer a few of his customers had complained about. Only one of the three had returned, and he was seriously injured. Once the gang leader had found out what had happened, he went straight away to pick Amy and her own strange companion up. They had wanted information, well now he just might have what they were looking for.

Royal T had driven them himself in his custom made Cadillac. He was definitely shaken by what his man had told him. So much so, that he refused to answer any of Kalen and Amy's questions. He had said it would be best for them to hear the details directly from the lone scout that had returned.

Kalen could hardly contain himself on the drive to the hospital. He was too full of nervous energy. He felt that he was still coming down from the emotional high he was on after sharing that kiss with Amy, and now he was finally headed to a source that could possibly tell him where Drè was hiding. The toughest fight he was ever going to face was looming in his very near future, yet he kept returning to the memory of the passionate kiss. He smiled in spite of the impending danger.

Kalen became aware of the silly smirk on his face as he caught Amy stealing glances at him. He did his best to hide it, but from the way she kept looking at him, he could tell that she, too, was having trouble staying focused on the task ahead. She looked toward Royal T. The massive gang leader was stoic and tight lipped about the details of what had happened to his men. True to his word though, Royal T had returned with the information she and Kalen had requested.

By the time they had pulled into the hospital parking lot, the sun had completely set. The stars were out in full as the smog that had clouded the afternoon had finally dissipated. The night was calm, yet Kalen could feel an underlying tension in the air. The time of the conflict was near; he could feel it in his bones.

Royal T led them through the hospital like he owned the place. It was really no surprise that the gang leader had a working knowledge of the interior of the hospital. He had been there countless times before, visiting other soldiers he had sent off to fight in his own private wars. Maintaining his power base had a price, and he had no problems using his soldiers as the currency to pay that price.

The person they were there to see – W-Dog, as Royal T had named him – was currently in the intensive care unit. After being brought in by ambulance, W-Dog had been taken straight into surgery to repair the damage to his severed right arm. He had lost an incredible amount of blood, and had almost died during the procedure. However, doctors had been able to stem the flow of blood and stitch up the stump of his arm just above what had once been his elbow.

Kalen and Amy found themselves in the intensive care unit. W-Dog was asleep in a hospital bed. He was still unconscious from the sedatives he had been given. He had IVs coming out of his left arm, and a large gauze bandage wrapped around the stump of his ruined right arm. His dark skin was pale and had an ashy quality to it. What struck Kalen the most was how young W-Dog was. He was barely more than a child.

He looked over at Royal T in disgust and asked, "You call this youth a soldier?"

"Do not even pretend to judge me," the large gang leader answered, offended and angry. "W-Dog joined of his own free will.

The injustice of Detective Sommers' police force provides me with all the new recruits that I could ask for."

"It does not change the fact that you sent a boy to face a possible serial killer," Amy responded, her own anger beginning to kick in. "And now your soldier is missing an arm."

W-Dog began to stir in response to the loud voices. As soon as he heard the deep baritone voice of his leader, Royal T, his head began to move from side to side, as though trying to clear the fog from his head that was a side effect of the medication he had been given. Being a loyal member of Royal T's gang, W-Dog would not want to appear weak in front of his leader. He fought to come around.

"Good, he's starting to wake up," Royal T said trying to deflect some of the sting of Amy's accusations.

Seeing that the young gang member was indeed starting to wake up, Kalen forgot about his disdain for Royal T's leadership qualities and instead focused his attention on the injured boy.

Royal T walked over to the bed and, in a not so gentle manner, grabbed W-Dog's leg and shook it. "C'mon Dog. Time to get up, soldier."

The young Human opened his eyes and asked, "T, is that you man?"

"Yeah Dog, it's me," Royal T answered. "I've got those guests here that I told you about. They want to talk to you about what happened."

W-Dog was still groggy, but ever the vigilant soldier, he tried to sit up and follow his leader's order. "Yeah, I'll do what I can, T."

Kalen walked over to the bed so he could question W-Dog about his experience. He did not like having to talk to the young Human while he was at a hospital trying to recover from a horrific wound, but this kid could be his only link to discovering Drè's whereabouts.

When W-Dog caught sight of Kalen approaching, his eyes grew so large that it appeared that they would pop out of his head. His jaw dropped and hung open in shock. He had completely frozen out of sheer terror. The beeping from the heart rate monitor came so fast that it almost sounded like he had flat-lined. He began to tremble so violently the needle in his arm from the IV began to pull out, causing the puncture area to bleed.

When Amy saw W-Dog's reaction to Kalen, she cut in front of him to block the Elf from view. Having a good idea who maimed the young gang member, she grasped W-Dog's good arm, and spoke quietly and soothingly to the terrified boy.

"W-Dog, it's okay, you're safe. No one is going to hurt you here," she tried to keep her voice even toned so as not to alarm the already-frightened young man. She tried to get W-Dog to focus on her, and draw his attention away from Kalen.

Her plan worked, and W-Dog looked at Amy when she touched his wrist. He blinked his eyes several times like he was waking from a trance. He still could not speak, however. The shock of seeing what he thought was the maniac from the warehouse that had killed his friends had been too much for his already-fragile psyche to take.

"It's all right," Amy continued to reassure.

W-Dog was finally able to get over the initial shock to his system and get himself back under control. He took several deep breaths and his trembling began to subside, signaling he had been able to calm his frayed nerves once again.

He looked at Amy intently and said, "Thank you, lady."

She gave W-Dog a friendly smile as a response to his politeness. Whatever this kid had seen, it had left far more scars than the ones he would have left over from his surgery. The scars that were going to run the deepest were the emotional kind, and she could already see that W-Dog was going to be a long time recovering, if he ever did.

Kalen cautiously stepped out from behind Amy so that W-Dog could see him. The wounded kid flinched again, but did not lose control of his senses. Kalen gritted his teeth in frustration when he saw the reaction. He was not angry with the young Human, but he was furious with Drè. This poor kid was just one more person on an ever-growing list of victims whose lives had been ruined by his former friend.

"Do I remind you of someone?" Kalen asked. He was careful to keep his voice quiet and calm, and he limited his movements so as not to throw the already fragile and emotional youth into hysterics again.

W-Dog stared at Kalen with fear mirrored in his eyes. He continued to look at Kalen uncertainly, but he relaxed some as he heard the Elf's calm voice. "You look like the guy that Taz, Bone, and I ran into," W-Dog answered shakily.

At the mention of his friend's names, W-Dog teared up. He had to pause and turn his head so he would not break down and cry. When he regained his composure, he continued. "He killed Bone. I don't know what happened to Taz, but I heard him screaming, and then he just stopped."

"How did you get away?" Royal T asked from the back of the room in a slightly accusatory voice.

"He let me go," W-Dog answered. "He could have killed me just as easily as he did Bone, but he wanted me to warn people about what happens if you mess in this guy's business."

"Tell me where you found this man," Kalen ordered a little more harshly than he intended. He did not want to scare the young Human any further, but the information W-Dog possessed was too vital to worry about niceties.

"He's at the New Getty Villa Warehouse," W-Dog answered after taking a noticeable gulp. "I don't know what he's got in there with him, but whatever killed Taz wasn't human."

"That is all I need to know," Kalen said, eerily calm. He turned to Royal T and asked, "Can you get me there?"

"Wait a minute," Amy said, interjecting her opinion. "I may be suspended, but one call from me, and I can have that place surrounded by SWAT."

"Amy, you have seen what Drè is capable of. Plus, if he catches wind that we are on to him, he may disappear again," Kalen tried to explain.

"I don't want any pigs to help anyways," Royal T butted in. "Those were my soldiers that fool killed. If anyone is going to end that fool, it's going to be my crew."

"You have no concept of what Drè can do," Kalen said.

"Look, I'll get you there, but my crew is coming, no matter what," Royal T responded.

Kalen thought for a minute, and seeing no other alternatives decided to concede the point. "Very well, let's go."

"What, right now?" Amy asked, confused. This was all happening too fast for her liking.

"Amy, he must be stopped. You know what is at stake. If I can catch him off guard then all this madness can be over," he said, hoping she would understand.

"I don't like this one bit. We don't even have a plan," she said, trying to reason with the gung ho Elf.

"We'll think of something on the way," Royal T offered as he pulled his cell phone out of his pocket. "I'll have my crew armed and ready when we get there."

"I have to do this, Amy," he said knowing that she would agree.

"I know, Kalen. Let's go," she said, surprised by how calm she was.

"I need you to go to Reggie. His organization may be able to help," he said.

Amy's mouth fell open for a moment before she answered. "I want to go with you. I can help watch your back," she pleaded.

Her face crumpled slightly as she fought to keep tears from the surface. She looked imploringly into Kalen's eyes and the Elf was reminded that they had grown very close over the past twenty-four hours. He knew she wanted to see this through to the end at his side. He searched for the right words to say.

"Please do not misunderstand me. I want you there, but I am not sure about Royal T and his men. If you can get to Reggie, his people at least know what is going on. Do you know how to find this New Getty Villa Warehouse?"

"Yeah, I think I do," she answered.

"Good, then meet me there," he said.

"You ready to go?" Royal T interrupted after he hung his cell phone up, and slipped it back into his pocket. "My guys are preparing as we speak."

Amy did not like having to stay behind, but she knew Kalen was right. Reggie could help, and it would not take her long to talk to the special agent, since he was right there at the hospital. She would feel better if Reggie could offer any kind of help. Kalen had been right about not trusting Royal T. The gang leader would more than likely make things worse. If she and Reggie could get there to watch Kalen's back, she would feel much better.

After making her decision, she walked over to Kalen and kissed the Elf hard on the lips. When she backed away, she said, "You be careful, and don't do anything rash until I get there."

Kalen nodded to her in reply. He was glad for the kiss, and said a silent prayer to Alorien that it would not be the last he and Amy would share. She had become very special to him, but right then, he had to finish the job he had been sent to do.

"I am ready," he said to Royal T.

With a final look at Amy and a tight squeeze of her hand, he and the gang leader made their way to the exit. Kalen knew his mission would come to an end one way or another that night. It was time for him to meet his destiny.

# CHAPTER 28

As the sun set, turning the evening sky from a bright reddish orange to the soothing black of night, Drè Fao'lain began to stir. Much like an unholy vampire rising from its earthy crypt, so did Drè arise from his trance.

He awoke from his slumber with a nagging buzzing sensation buried deep in his brain. It had been just a few short hours since his altercation with his unheralded intruders. The memory of the slayings brought a wicked grin of glee to the Elf's already twisted features. All he wanted to do was sleep, but something was drawing him back into a conscious state.

He could still smell the salty, copper-like aroma of blood. It had permeated the air as it dried on his discarded clothes, and filled the room with its intoxicating bouquet. Even with the glorious scent making him feel invigorated as he gradually grew more awake, he could still feel that incessant sensation that something was out of place or just plain wrong.

The prickling feeling in his head was different from the warning he had felt when those stupid Humans had wandered into the warehouse, tripping one of his many warding spells. There were no unwanted visitors this time, of that he was certain, but something was definitely calling to him. In his sleep-weary mind he was unable to ascertain what exactly it was.

Even though it had only been a few mere hours of sleep, he felt infinitely better than he had before. He was more in control of his senses, and the weariness that had caused him to ache all the way down to his bones was almost gone. He was still not one hundred percent, but if needed, he was sure he would be able to call upon the Shadowed Arts. How long he would be able to sustain its use was another question altogether.

He climbed out of bed, his bare feet hitting the cold, concrete floor, and then stepped in the cooling blood that had pooled and congealed by his bedside, making him shiver in ecstasy. He could most assuredly get used to waking to that sensation. He almost felt compelled to grab his blood-soaked garments and wrap them around his body like some sort of an evil imitation of a child's security blanket. Then he felt the pulling buzz at the center of his brain again, and all thoughts of his soiled clothes were forgotten.

The sensation was growing stronger and more intense. Standing there unclothed in his sleeping chamber, he could almost discern what the nagging buzz was. It was deeply frustrating not being able to understand what was happening. It was like having a long awaited answer to an important question be right on the tip of your tongue, but it might as well be a thousand miles away because despite your best efforts, you just cannot grasp it.

The buzzing in his head became louder and more intense. He could feel it tugging at him like he was a pet dog on a leash. He hated the feeling of being helpless and at the mercy of somebody else's whim. He was not a marionette to be toyed with by pulling his proverbial strings. At the same time, though, the feeling was familiar to him, like hearing the adult voice of a friend you had known as a child for the first time.

When his unseen master pulled the leash again, Drè followed the urging until he was out in the main area of the warehouse. The scene of the brutal afternoon carnage was played out in the brilliant glow of countless stars as their incandescent light shone through the many windows. Seeing the mutilation and havoc he had wrought, caused the Elf to pause in awe of his own handiwork. The smell of blood mingling with the other effluence that makes up the Human body was strong and thick. Mixed as it was with the fresh air blowing in off the ocean, it was more potent than any elixir he had ever sampled. If only he could have somehow bottled the effects the fragrance had on him, he would be able to experience the euphoria he felt right then, whenever he desired.

What was left of the intruder's bodies would have to be disposed of. The stench of their soon-to-be-rotting flesh would perhaps draw more unwanted attention. Though he could experience the near addictive feeling of killing for pleasure on all those that did dare intrude, he had a ritual to complete. Only when he was standing over the decayed remains of his people would he experience true happiness. When that time came, maybe then would he indulge in his dark desires, and cut a swath of evil slaughter across this pitiful race, the likes of which they had never seen.

This time the buzzing switched from a small annoyance to a painful bludgeoning inside his skull. The pain almost drove him to his knees. It took several long seconds for the shock waves to filter through his brain. Though it required nearly all the focus he could muster just to stay on his feet, he thought he caught an image flash through his mind. It was that of another Elf.

The buzzing was not just a painful tearing at his psyche that was pulling him to an unseen destination; it was something trying to communicate with him. It was guiding him to an understanding. Was this a warning of some kind?

He looked around the warehouse. All his warding spells were still in place. He could feel them just as he could feel the solid floor beneath his feet. He also felt an undercurrent of charged energy as well, and he knew instantly that the buzzing was a call from the magic of the Shadowed Arts.

He had long ago come to the realization that his body was merely a vessel for the Shadowed Arts' twisted magic to channel itself through. He was not the master of this evil form of magic, he was simply the caretaker. Unlike the other Elven Magisters, who were so proud of their limited ability to manipulate their magical powers, he was not limited in what he could achieve. The Shadowed Arts had no boundaries, no limitations to hold its users back. As long as his body could hold out and withstand the onslaught of energy, his potential for ultimate power was infinite.

Instead of fighting the buzzing feeling, he closed his eyes and surrendered himself to it. He let the magical compulsion wash over his naked body. He could once again feel the pull of imaginary strings. This time he allowed the unseen master to guide him by that magical buzzing leash to wherever it was he was meant to go.

He felt like he was having an out of body experience. He began walking in the direction he was being compelled. With his eyes closed, he felt as if he was walking on air, almost gliding. He gave in completely to the yearning call of the Shadowed Arts. The buzzing increased with every floating step he took.

He had become so used to the buzzing vibration in his mind, that when it abruptly stopped, he felt a sharp aching and a sudden sense of saddened loss. He opened his eyes and found himself standing directly before the Tree of Sacrifice. The twisted, evil-looking tree was the physical embodiment of the Shadowed Arts. Once the circle of sacrificed hearts was complete, this magical tree would grant him the power to complete the Ritual of the Dying Moon, and thus bring about the annihilation of the Elven race. Now, though, the tree needed him for something else.

Just like it had when the tree had sucked the life out of the gang banger, Drè felt a rumble from somewhere deep underneath the floor. Then one long black root tore itself free from the concrete with a sickening wet ripping sound that reminded Drè of rending flesh. The long root swayed back and forth like a King Cobra being lulled into complacency by an Indian flutist. It did not entangle Drè like it had done with the Human intruder. It slowly slithered around behind the crazed Elf, and slid methodically up his body until it was poised directly behind the base of his skull. Then like a pit viper, without hesitation, it struck.

Drè jumped like he had been electrocuted, and the current was still running through his body. Almost immediately images began flashing through his brain too fast for him to comprehend. He could not move a muscle, but he could feel them twitching due to a spasm from the strain. The Shadowed Arts had called him, and he would listen, no matter what effect it would have on him.

After the first initial pinprick, he did not feel anything. There was no pain, no pleasure only the images speeding through his psyche. He tried to concentrate on the flashes as they passed, and to his astonishment, the images began to slow down. He could see people, but if they were Human, Elf or some other race, he could not tell. He focused even harder on the pictures that were appearing in his head.

Then, after throwing all of his cognitive abilities into trying to concentrate, the images became crystal clear. What he saw both amazed and angered him. He witnessed Kalen Or'wain and the meddlesome female officer talking to the intruder that had lost his arm. There was one other Human in the picture, but Drè did not recognize him.

He watched irate as Kalen left in a hurry with the Human. He could not hear any sounds, but their intentions came through loud and clear. They were coming after him. His warning to that sniveling Human had backfired. Instead of keeping others away as he had intended, it was going to bring Kalen right to him. He continued to stare at the images, and he watched as the female conversed with the Human male he had burned with his magical fire at the scene of his last sacrifice. Had he been at full strength, that Human would have been burnt to a crisp instead of lying in a hospital plotting against him.

Drè understood why the Tree of Sacrifice was calling to him. His enemies were conspiring to stop him from the completion of his revenge. The magic was putting him on notice to be ready. If he was going to see his plans of mass devastation come to fruition, he would have to deal with Kalen and his Human cronies. That would be fine; he was actually looking forward to it.

Sensing that Drè had understood all that he was shown, the Tree of Sacrifice released the Elf from its magical clutches. The root pulled itself free from his brain stem, and returned to its place on the warehouse floor.

Drè fell to his knees once he was released. He had to gasp for air before he was able to draw enough into his lungs to be able to function. Bright white lights were exploding behind his eyes. After shaking the aftereffects away, Drè rose to his feet, took a deep breath, and smiled wickedly. He had guests to prepare for.

# CHAPTER 29

Once Kalen left with Royal T, Amy decided to leave the young gang banger, W-Dog, to his internal turmoil, and go see Reggie. The special agent's room was located two floors up from the ICU. The sooner she could get to Reggie and inform him of what was about to transpire, the quicker she could be on her way to the New Getty Villa Warehouse to watch Kalen's back.

She still did not like being left behind, especially when someone she cared deeply about was walking into potentially grave danger. She knew getting Reggie and his agency involved was the correct thing to do, but she could not shake the feeling of disappointment. She sincerely hoped Kalen was not trying to placate her by sending her off on a fool's errand. Up until that morning, she had been an LAPD homicide detective. She had been in her fair share of fights, and though this one was going to be far different from anything she had yet to see, she knew she could help.

The elevator she had boarded seemed to be taking forever. Time was not on her side as every minute that passed brought Kalen closer to facing a killer without her by his side. The nervous tension was starting to get to her. She could feel herself starting to become emotional. This was a trait that had long been a source of embarrassment for her. Whenever a situation became incredibly stressful, she tended to tear up. By the time the elevator doors slid open, she was wiping those tears from her eyes.

She walked the short distance down the brightly lit corridor until she came to the special agent's room. Reggie was sitting up on the side of his bed finishing up his evening meal. It was good to see Reggie up and out of bed. In all actuality, it was good seeing the cranky agent moving at all after the blast he had taken.

Remembering the magical fire that had nearly killed Reggie only made her worry about Kalen even more.

"How they treating you?" she asked the agent from the doorway.

"What?" Reggie uttered in confusion as he turned around to see who his visitor was. "Sommers? What are you doing here?"

"Didn't they teach you to never sit with your back to the door?" she asked as she ignored his inquiries. "I surely hope that my tax dollars are not being wasted on your training."

"Oh, Sommers, if you only knew," Reggie responded, playing along, but his brow creased as his investigative skills came into play. Amy guessed that he picked up on her trembling voice and could see her glistening cheeks. His eyes darted about, looking around Amy and out into the hall beyond the door. He frowned deeply.

"Where's Kalen?" he asked cautiously, his voice heavy with worry and full of concern.

Just hearing the Elf's name brought a fresh round of emotional tugging, and she almost lost control all together. The last thing she needed to do at this point was to end up crying on Reggie's shoulder. That would in no way help Kalen, and it would just add to the delay of getting to him.

She took a deep breath to help put her emotional state back at ease. She sniffled a couple of times, which of course was a dead give away that she was trying not to cry. She truly appreciated the fact Reggie did not acknowledge her personal struggle. The special agent just sat patiently, and waited for her to reply.

After finally regaining her composure, she was able to answer. "He found Drè. He's on his way to face him right now."

Reggie let out the breath he had not been aware he was holding. He appeared relieved by the news, and yet still worried. Kalen was not dead, but the night was still young and he was on his way to a confrontation. Reggie's worst fears might still come to pass.

After collecting himself, Reggie asked, "You let him go off alone?"

"Not exactly," was her cryptic reply. "I brought in an old contact to help us. He's a gang leader here in LA. As it turns out, Drè killed some of his members. Kalen is with him. He asked me to come to you and ask for help. He was hoping your agency would help."

Amy was surprised when Reggie snorted in a derisive manner. The special agent was acting like he was privy to a secret that only he knew. As his silence dragged on, she grew even more suspicious.

"What is it?" she finally asked.

"I'm not FBI," Reggie said, letting the cat out of the bag. "It's just a cover we use. The agency I work for has no name. Officially, we do not even exist. We are only called in for situations of an unusual sort, and we work alone. There is no help, Sommers. I am here on my own."

Amy felt as if the air had just been sucked out of the room. Things just continued to get weirder and weirder. She felt light headed, and needed to sit down. She walked over and practically fell into the only chair in the hospital room. She was so confused that she did not know what to do next.

"Then why the FBI?" she asked trying to sort everything out.

"It makes things easier," Reggie answered calmly. "You flash a badge and say you're FBI and people listen. What do you think would have happened if I had said that I work for a government agency that is so secret that it doesn't even have a name, and that I was here tracking an Elf serial killer? Sommers, you would have locked me up yourself."

She could not argue with his logic. He was definitely right about what her reaction would have been. If he would have spewed that kind of nonsense that first night at the crime scene at ChemCo, she would have had some of her fellow officers escort Reggie right off the premises. He was correct about the FBI, too. She had fallen for the ruse hook, line, and sinker. Something else Reggie had said suddenly sank in with her.

"If you work alone, that means there's no help for Kalen doesn't it?" she asked in utter despair.

"Not if I can help it. Hand me my clothes," he said, staring her right in the eyes. This was his case, and he was not about to sit idly by in a hospital while it all went down without him.

"You can barely walk, Reggie," she said, halfheartedly trying to dissuade him.

He saw right through her poor attempt to try and reason with him. He ignored her comment, and half-walked, half-staggered to the closet where the remains of his clothes were stored in a plastic hospital bag.

Amy, seeing that he was determined no matter what she said and that he was having difficulty getting his clothes, went to the closet as well and helped the faux special agent. She took the plastic bag, and removed the garments. They were completely ruined. What had not been burned by the magic fire had been cut or ripped by the ER staff when Reggie had been brought in.

"Why don't I go find you some something else to wear," she offered, seeing the ruin that was Reggie's attire.

"That's probably a good idea," Reggie said thoughtfully. "I can't go save Kalen's Elf butt if my own arse is hanging out for all to see."

Amy snorted out a laugh of her own as she headed out to find something Reggie could wear. After finding a linen closet, and pilfering some powder-blue scrub pants and matching shirt, she returned to Reggie's room. When she entered with the scrubs, she found him going through the closet to gather the remainder of his belongings.

She tossed the scrubs on the bed as Reggie grabbed his badge and shoes from the closet. It suddenly dawned on her that she did not have any transportation. She had been counting on getting help from Reggie and the FBI. Now that she had learned the truth about his affiliation, she realized they were stuck there.

"I must have lost my gun at the scene," Reggie grumbled in frustration as he tore through the closet.

"I have the gun you left at the hotel," she offered, trying to console the angered government agent. "I think we may have an even bigger problem anyways."

"Bah, you keep the Glock," he said. Then, realizing what else Amy had said, he asked, "What other problem?"

"I don't have a car. I came with Royal T and Kalen. How are we going to get to the warehouse?" she asked, a hint of desperation started to creep into her voice.

"Christ," Reggie exclaimed. "I have no weapon, no car, and no pants. I'm like the anti-boy scout."

Amy laughed at Reggie's predicament in spite of the frustration she was also feeling. There was no point in losing their cool; they would just have to think of something. Kalen's life could depend on it, and she for one was not about to let him down.

She turned her back, and thought for a moment while Reggie changed into the hospital scrubs she had procured for him. She could hear him cussing about the color, but she also knew that beggars could not be choosers.

"Hey, if you don't like the color, you can always change back into your gown. That sight alone should be enough to make Drè surrender," she said playfully.

Reggie finished tying the scrub pants tight around his waist when upon hearing her comment he stalled and said, "You know Sommers, you're a real charmer."

"I try," she responded with an overly fake smile on her face that was meant to make her look like a perfect angel.

Reggie ignored her sarcastic facial expression and finished getting dressed. He had to shake his head in disgust when he slipped on his black dress shoes. They did not quite go with the rest of his ensemble, and he knew he looked ridiculous. At this point, how he looked was not all that important, though. Finding a ride so they could go help the Elf was. In a moment of inspiration, Reggie reached over and pressed the nurse call button.

After a brief pause, a tired, static-filled voice responded, "Can I help you?"

"Yeah, this is Special Agent Blackburn, I need to see someone from security right away," Reggie said using his best authoritative voice.

"Is everything all right?" the same tired voice asked.

"It will be as soon as security gets here," Reggie complained, his voice rising in annoyance. "I need them here, stat."

The nurse did not respond, but Amy was pretty certain she would comply with Reggie's command. The nurse was tired, and did not want the added headache of trying to placate a disgruntled patient. She would pass that responsibility on to security, which is exactly what Reggie had been counting on.

"That was a nice touch with the whole 'stat' thing," Amy again teased.

She knew the situation was dire, and that Kalen could be in grave danger at that very moment, but if she did not try to keep herself loose, she also knew she would explode from the building tension she was experiencing. Besides, Reggie was such an easy target.

"You know, Sommers, I don't know if I should fall in love with you or strangle you to death with my bare hands," he joked along. "I just haven't decided which yet."

"You wish," she chuckled, "on both counts."

Reggie did not bother saying anything else. His attention had been grabbed by the young security guard that had just walked into the room. The kid could not have been much older than twenty, and from the way he shuffled his weight from foot to foot nervously, Reggie could tell he was not used to having to deal with many patient problems. This was going to play right into his hand.

Reggie stared hard at the young man, sizing him up before saying in his best cop voice, "Son, we need your help."

"Uh, okay," the guard replied nervously.

Reggie flashed the kid his FBI badge and identification. His attempt to overwhelm the young guard with his impressive hardware worked as the guard stared back at Reggie in wide-eyed awe.

"Look kid, I don't have much time," Reggie began, sounding deadly serious. "There is a national security crisis. I need a car, and I need one now."

The security guard was definitely skittish, but the thought that he could somehow help the FBI clearly appealed to him.

"Is this for real?" he asked hesitantly.

"This is as real as it gets," Reggie said, his voice becoming filled with anger. "Now you either help us, or go get someone that can."

That was good enough for the young guard. He was not about to miss out on an opportunity to help out the FBI. If he played his cards right, maybe this would earn him a promotion.

"You guys can take the security car I patrol the parking lot with," he said enthusiastically. "Come on, I'll take you to it."

They followed the guard as he quickly led them through the bowels of the hospital, and out to the back lot where a series of cars were parked. Some were lab courier vehicles, while others may have belonged to employees, but Amy really did not care. The only automobile she was interested in was the white Toyota with the red and blue stripes along the sides that had red sirens on top. The car was an oasis for Amy in the desert of a parking lot.

The guard pulled out a set of keys from his pocket, and handed them over to Reggie, "Here, sir. I hope this helps. Is there anything else I can do?"

"Your government thanks you kid," Reggie said, still playing the part of an FBI agent. "You wouldn't happen to have a weapon would you?"

"Just my taser," the guard answered, reaching to his belt and removing a safety device.

"That's better than nothing I guess, hand it over," Reggie ordered the guard around like he was a trained puppy.

Amy watched as Reggie slid the taser into his pocket. "Just don't shock yourself with that thing, and hand me the keys. You're hurt, remember?"

Reggie tossed her the keys to the car and they quickly got in. After selecting the correct key, Amy fired up the engine, and they sped off out of the parking lot. Too much time had passed, and she desperately feared that she would be too late to help Kalen. She knew what was at stake for the Elf, and she wanted so badly to be there to help. She could see by the strained look on Reggie's face he felt the same way. She scrunched her own face up in fierce determination and gunned the security car to an even faster speed.

The young security guard stood in the parking lot and watched curiously as the car sped away and disappeared. He sure hoped he had made the right decision in giving them the car. The last thing he needed was to get yelled at by his supervisor for screwing up again. His supervisor would understand, though. They were FBI agents after all.

# CHAPTER 30

Kalen held on for dear life as the Human gang leader weaved in and out of traffic at an extremely high rate of speed. He had no idea how Royal T could divide his attention between driving so fast and talking nonstop on the communication device that Amy referred to as a cell phone. Kalen could only pray to Alorien the gang leader's luck would hold out. It would not help his people if he were killed by Royal T's recklessness before he even had a chance to confront Drè.

Royal T laughed off the Elf's nervousness. He was too busy trying to round up his crew for a strike against the maniac that had killed a couple of his soldiers. His military training was the only thing he was thankful to the government for. His men would be waiting for him and his nervous passenger, equipped and ready just as he had trained them to be.

"Ease up man," Royal T said when he finally hung up his cell phone. "In a few minutes we will meet up with my crew, and you can see the most elite fighting force the streets of Los Angeles ever produced."

"I am sure your men are very brave, but you do not fully comprehend what Drè Fao'lain is capable of doing," Kalen answered in an attempt to explain who it was they would be going up against.

"I understand that this guy killed two of my men, and chopped the arm off another," Royal T fired back, his voice beginning to rise in anger. "And because of that, I also understand this psycho is going to pay. My crew and I will make sure of that by delivering this fool's retribution personally."

"Just heed my warning," Kalen implored as he held on to his seat tightly while Royal T swerved around the car in front of them.

"By the end of this night, you may be burying far more than two members of your crew."

Royal T grew livid at that point. Kalen could tell he was not afraid of anything and was the type of man who did not like unsolicited advice. Whereas Kalen did his best to remain calm, Royal T became more agitated as they approached their destination. The Elf was reminded of young recruits who long for their first battle and do not yet know the true horror or war. Having risen to a position of power without having known more than skirmishes, Kalen was certain that Royal T felt insulted by his warnings. However, it was precisely because Kalen respected Royal T that he felt compelled to speak his mind.

Kalen could see by the steely look of determination in the Human's eyes that no warning was going to be enough to make him or his men stop at that point. The Elf knew all too well what they were going through and going up against. If Royal T wanted to endanger his men's lives by placing them directly in the path of this oncoming storm, then so be it. The fate of his entire race was at stake. He simply could not spare the time to worry about Royal T and his gang. No matter how many men the Human brought to the warehouse, he knew it would never be enough. This fight was going to come down to him and Drè – one on one.

Even though the sun had gone down, and the evening had grown dark, Kalen was able to recognize the neighborhood that was home to the Crenshaw Projects that housed Royal T's base of operations. Evidently this was where they were going to meet up with the Human's self-proclaimed elite fighting force. His assumption proved correct when a few moments later they pulled into the projects, and he could see many large, black vehicles and even more young Humans that were all wearing the now-familiar red bandanas.

Royal T slammed his Cadillac to a sharp halt, and turned to Kalen with a confident and knowing look on his face. "You ready? Because I know my crew will be."

"Just get me there," Kalen replied, deadly serious.

Royal T blinked at the Elf's eerily calm response. Kalen looked forward and frowned. The gang leader's response only confirmed his earlier assessment. This was a man who had not seen true battle. Royal T inclined his head and evaluated Kalen carefully. After a moment he swallowed hard and then nodded. Kalen could tell that Royal T was finally beginning to grasp the gravity of the situation.

"You'll get there," Royal T said trying to match Kalen's intensity but coming up short, "though I can't guarantee that there will be much left."

Things were worse than Kalen had feared. In his haste to prove his strength, Royal T must have sent men on ahead. If that was the case, then not only would Drè be aware of their arrival and be ready and waiting for them, it also meant the devastation he had been hoping to avoid had more than likely already begun.

As they exited Royal T's vehicle, the gang leader was immediately met by one of his young underlings. Kalen had to admit that he was impressed with the military efficiency the young gang members adhered to. It was a reflection of Royal T's leadership skills. He just hoped the gang members were not being led to their deaths.

"Is everything ready?" Royal T asked his crony, his voice resembling that of a general addressing his troops, which was of course exactly what the gang leader fancied himself to be.

"All is how you ordered," the young gang member responded crisply. "The ten-man reconnoiter team you wanted left ten minutes ago. They should have a perimeter set up by the time you arrive."

"Excellent," Royal T said excitedly and full of pride. "Is my baby ready?"

"She is packed and awaiting your orders as well," the gang banger said with a large smile on his face. "Shazz and Spider are waiting for you at the Suburban."

Royal T turned to Kalen, and once again shook his head, amused at the Elf's odd attire.

"You want a piece to go along with that pig sticker of yours?" he asked, almost mocking the Elf.

Kalen could only assume the over-confident gang leader was referring to a gun, but after his failure with the projectile weapon Reggie had given him, he preferred to stick with what he knew best.

"My sword is all that I need," he replied, letting Royal T's mocking tone roll of him.

"Suit yourself. If you're ready let's go get this crazy mother," Royal T said with excited determination.

Kalen followed the gang leader as he made his way to a black vehicle. He was not sure if it was the same one he and Amy had ridden in, though it looked the same. The thought of Detective Sommers only made him wish she was at his side. He hoped she had been able to contact Reggie's people. If things were going to be as bad as he imagined, they were going to need all the help they could get and Kalen sensed that Reggie's people would be more seasoned warriors than Royal T's.

When they approached the large black vehicle, Kalen recognized the two gang members that had escorted him and Amy earlier. He had overheard the initial gang member that had met Royal T name them as Shazz and Spider, and it would seem they would once again be providing escort service. This time though, they would be taking him to Drè.

When Shazz and Spider saw Royal T, they quickly snapped to what was, for them, military attention. Kalen observed that they had dropped the cocky demeanor and joking attitude they had displayed earlier. In the presence of their leader, they were all business.

Royal T made a sharp waving motion with his hand, and the two gang bangers got in the Suburban and started it up. Instead of maneuvering to get in the backseat, Royal T walked to the rear of the SUV, and opened the hatch. Kalen, standing behind the behemoth of a Human had to peek around Royal T like a small child hiding behind his father yet still curious enough to try and look around his legs. He could see a long, drab, green box lying in the trunk compartment.

"Ah, my baby," Royal T said lovingly as he reached in and popped the green case open.

Kalen could see what appeared to be a long, black tubular object. Royal T seemed especially enamored of this particular device so Kalen could only guess that it must be some kind of special weapon. It would have to be if it was going to be of any use against Drè Fao'lain.

"This is my special lady," Royal T explained reverently. "This is a genuine United States Army issued rocket propelled grenade launcher. If your little friend decides to show his face, my baby and I will blow that sucker back to whatever hole he crawled out of – in pieces."

Kalen looked skeptically at the weapon in the back of the vehicle, and then glanced down at General Brandy'wine's sword that was hanging at his hip. "To each their own," he said.

Royal T let out a loud deep bellow of laughter and replied, "To each their own, indeed. You know, Kalen, I think I am starting to like you."

Kalen raised his eyebrows in an intrigued gesture. Royal T laughed again as he slammed the rear hatch of the Suburban closed. They shared one last stare before they each walked to their respective sides of the SUV and got in. Once they were inside, the two young gang members, Shazz and Spider, turned to look at Royal T expectantly.

"Let's go," the gang leader ordered.

Shazz nodded once in compliance, and the black Suburban carrying Kalen to face his destiny hastily pulled away from the Crenshaw Projects.

# CHAPTER 31

Drè knew the instant the ten Humans arrived. After the Tree of Sacrifice had shown him the initial warning, he had returned to his room to dress and gather his equipment. Instead of relying on the ridiculous Human clothing, he had dressed in his Magister's uniform and cloak. He then returned to the tree where he found himself now.

He stood with his back to his twisted altar, the ceremonial dagger secured to his belt at his back. His father's sword was sheathed at his side.

What could not be seen, however, were the two black roots that had burrowed themselves into his body. There was one root just under each of the Elf's shoulder blades. Drè Fao'lain had truly become a puppet of the Shadowed Arts he worshipped.

The Tree of Sacrifice was a conduit to the powers of the Shadowed Arts. Now that he was being fed directly from the tree, he had access to magic he could have never dreamed existed. He could feel the power coursing through his body. He had never felt so alive. The tree's roots that were attached to his back energized him to the point that he felt he would explode with its intensity.

So when the ten Humans pulled into the lot of the New Getty Villa Warehouse, he was literally crackling with the magical energy. The Tree of Sacrifice flashed the images of the Humans in his mind. They resembled the Humans he had dispatched earlier. There was no sign of Kalen yet, so these unworthy fools would just have to be the opening act.

The Down Hood Mob strike team arrived in three separate vehicles. They were armed better than the Los Angeles SWAT team. They had been trained in the same tactics their leader had learned in the Army. That mixed with their own street smarts and toughness, made this team unbeatable when matched up with any other street gang. Even by LAPD standards, they would have been considered elite.

They moved with cautious precision as per their training. They fanned out and scanned the area surrounding the warehouse. Their target was somewhere inside. Their orders had been to enter the New Getty Villa Warehouse, assess the situation, and if all looked good, they would engage and eliminate the target.

Knowing their mission parameters, and with the perimeter secured, the strike team prepared to move in on their target. They moved silently, using hand signals to communicate. Two of their fellow gang members had been slaughtered there. In street justice terms, that was the equivalent of having a family member murdered. It called for immediate retribution. That was why they were there.

Back in its day, the New Getty Villa Warehouse had been used to store any number of items including fuel and equipment for the thriving shipping business of the time. The United States Navy had even stored supplies at the warehouse from time to time.

It was a large, sprawling building with few rooms. Their assault on the warehouse would be simple. They would use a shock and awe tactic by storming through the main entrance and overrunning their intended target before he had a chance to react. The large open area that made up the main floor would not offer much cover, but with their greater numbers, the strike team believed they would not need it. They would subdue the target quickly and efficiently just as they had been trained to do.

The ten-member team gathered by the entrance, and performed a quick weapons check. All systems were go, and without any further hesitation they moved into the warehouse.

Drè could see the foolish Humans as they entered into his domain. He was so filled with the power of the Shadowed Arts that he was almost glowing. His skin was translucent and it radiated a red-orange light. The air was charged. It was time to unleash the true power of his vengeance.

He waited while the Humans entered by twos. Even though he was on the far side of the main floor, they had spotted him right away. He was so charged that he shone like a beacon in the night. They were nothing but insects to him, drawn to his magnificent light.

When the majority of the foolish insects crawled into his lair, he struck. Drawing the Shadowed Arts' magic into his core, he flung a streaming blast of the magical fire at the first Human that had dared to enter.

The red-orange fire hit the strike team member square in the chest, and lit him up like a torch. The silence of the warehouse which had been so profound just seconds before was shattered by the burning figure's almost inhuman sounding shrieks of agony. The screams did not last long however, as the fire melted the Human's flesh and superheated his organs until they exploded in sizzling ooze. The body toppled over, leaving what was left of the man to become a bonfire lighting the way for his fellow team members to see what horror was awaiting them.

The remaining nine strike team members, though they were taken by surprise by their comrade's shocking and gruesome demise, exploded into motion. They had all made their way into the warehouse by this time. There was not much cover just as they had anticipated other than a few barrels and crates scattered around the warehouse's main floor.

They moved quickly to find defensible positions where they could launch a counterattack. A couple of members squeezed off a few rounds from their automatic weapons, but this was more of a covering fire and none of the shots reached home. They were not quick enough in their efforts though, as another member of the team fell victim to the magical fire. His screams soon echoed around the warehouse as he too became a burning pile of effluence.

The euphoria of the Shadowed Arts was incredible. Watching those two Humans melt from his fire was so satisfying that it was pure joy. He had never felt so strong. As long as he was connected to the tree, he was invincible. The Tree of Sacrifice kept feeding him energy and images of the remaining Humans. It also spoke to him like a whisper deep in the darkest recesses of his mind. The tree was giving him instructions, opening his mind to new and powerful spells.

Though the strike team was well trained, seeing two of its members turned into Human candles was a contingency they had not prepared for. The only option left that seemed logical was to try and make a retreat if it was possible. Several members opened fire at the wraith-like figure of Drè standing in front of the evil looking tree with the weird blue flames. Though several hundred bullets had been fired, none of them seemed to find their mark.

Drè laughed at the Humans' poor attempt to fight back. He singled another victim out, and after whispering a few words, he watched as a large glowing blue hand appeared. He was able to control and manipulate the hand with his thoughts, and he sent it flying forth to his next intended victim.

The team members stopped firing and watched transfixed as the spectral hand appeared. It came flying at them and plucked one of the young team members up in its fist. It pulled its unfortunate victim back to the center of the warehouse where it began to squeeze its captive in its mammoth grip. The poor team member did not even have time to scream as his other two partners had.

There was a sudden loud cracking and snapping sounds as the magical hand's victim's bones were crushed. Blood and other fluids began seeping through the glowing blue fingers of the hand. When the Shadowed Arts-fueled spell had finished its work, it released what was left of the Human. The now disfigured and mangled form hit the floor with a sickening wet thud. There was nothing recognizable left of the team member, as he had been reduced to nothing more than Human pulp.

Before the remaining members could even begin to comprehend what they had just seen, Drè struck again. This time when he called on the Shadowed Arts he shot bluish white lightning bolts from his fingertips. Guided by the magic, his aim was true once again.

The bolts of magical electricity hit two team members that were trying to take cover behind several steel drums. They were fried right down to their bones. The warehouse was quickly filled with the sickening sweet smell of roasted meat. The only thing that was left of the two strike team members were two smoking skeletons.

What Drè had not anticipated was that one of the barrels was still half filled with leftover fuel. When the electrical bolts had charred the two Humans, the fuel caught fire, launching the barrel straight up through the roof of the warehouse.

Kalen had not felt right all evening. He knew this was a portent of things to come, but it was not until the sharp, stabbing pain and waves of gut-wrenching nausea hit him that he knew his hopes of catching Drè off guard had been dashed. The men Royal T had sent ahead had awoken a sleeping giant in Drè, and they were more than likely paying for it with their lives.

If he would have been standing, he would have doubled over and fallen to his knees in pain. As it was, with him sitting in the backseat of the SUV, he leaned forward and rested his head against the back of the driver's side seat. He had to bite down on his bottom lip to stop a groan of pain from escaping. He did not realize how hard he was biting until he noticed the salty taste of blood.

These attacks had occurred before, presumably when Drè was invoking the Shadowed Arts. They had all been harsh and painful. This one though was downright agonizing. It was different in its overall intensity. This could not be a good sign, and he guessed Drè had tapped into some previously unknown source and was unleashing horrors he would rather not think about.

Royal T had caught the Elf's sudden reaction out of the corner of his eye. When Kalen lurched forward into the driver's seat, he knew something out of the ordinary was up.

"Hey man, you all right?" he asked Kalen unsurely.

Kalen heard the gang leader's question, but had to take several deep painful breaths before he could give an answer.

"We must hurry. Your men are under attack," he gasped after every couple of words.

"How do you know that? What's going on?" Royal T asked, confused.

"Trust me," he groaned. "Your men are dying."

Royal T stared at Kalen hard before turning to Shazz who was driving and commanded, "Step on it."

The driver followed his order, and Kalen felt the vehicle lurch forward as it quickly accelerated. The pain and nausea had lessened somewhat but it was still debilitating. He had no idea how Drè Fao'lain had grown so powerful, but for the first time, he felt terrified.

Shazz could sense the gravity of the situation. The team was under attack. He sped up as fast as he could, and was glad to see the exit that would take them to their destination.

"We're almost there," he said, looking in the rearview mirror at Royal T.

"What the ..." Spider said from the passenger seat when he spotted a bright flash as they came down the off ramp into Venice. "Did ya'll see that?" He pointed toward something that was on fire, flying through the air.

"Yeah man, I saw it," Shazz answered. He jumped involuntarily when the flying object exploded. "It looked like it came from up ahead, where we're heading to."

Royal T looked at Kalen with wide, frightened eyes, and was startled when he saw the Elf looking right back at him knowingly.

"Move it, and I mean now," the gang leader ordered loudly.

Shazz and Spider shared a frightened look. They had never seen Royal T so unnerved. He had always been so cool and under control. This was the first time either one had ever seen their leader so close to panic.

The remaining five members of the strike team were trying to find a way to make a quick exit. They had watched their fellow members get butchered in horrifying ways, and were in a state of shock. They may have been trained in military tactics, but they were not regular Army. They were scared kids facing down a demon from their worst nightmares, and no amount of training could save them from the terrifying power that had been set loose.

The frying of the two members that had caused the steel drum to launch had also set several small fires around the warehouse. The most hazardous of these was a large pile of discarded and broken wooden pallets that had caught fire as the flaming barrel flew past on its way into orbit. The pallets were burning nicely, and began to work their way up the wall. It did not take long for the flames to burn their way through the old ceiling, and the bright orange fire could be seen shooting through the many holes in the roof.

Drè could feel the Tree of Sacrifice pumping him full of new energy. He was the superconductor for the Shadowed Arts. In all his life, he had never felt so awe-inspiringly powerful. Through the images that played out in his head, he knew Kalen was on the way. He was almost finished warming up on these worthless insects. The time for the main event was drawing near.

The motion of one of the remaining Humans trying to flee caught his attention. The Shadowed Arts-enraptured Elf hurled a fireball at the team member, catching him long before he found the salvation he had been running for.

The huge ball of burning magical energy struck the escaping team member right in the center of his back. He paused for the briefest of seconds before exploding into hundreds of flaming pieces. The burning body parts went flying all over the warehouse starting small fires whenever they landed on something flammable.

Seeing the latest horror to befall one of their friends, the remaining four strike team members went into a frenzy of shocked terror. They renewed their onslaught by opening fire with everything they had. The sound inside the warehouse was thunderous as the uninterrupted sound of automatic weapons fire and ricocheting bullets took over. Once again though, not one single bullet found its way to Drè.

Amy and Reggie were speeding their way to the warehouse in the borrowed security car. Reggie was clearly in pain from his wounds, but he just gritted his teeth and fought through it as Amy drove on.

Amy was driving well over the speed limit. She had the red spinning lights on, and most drivers were adhering to the rules of the road as they pulled over upon seeing the lights. As she drove past though, those same drivers became increasingly angry when they saw what they thought to be a police officer was, in fact, a hospital security car.

After passing one such vehicle, Amy chanced a look in the rearview mirror to see if the driver had recognized her ruse. She spotted what looked like an oversized walkie-talkie lying on the backseat.

"Hey Reggie, grab that thing from the back would you?" she asked.

If she had guessed right, that was not a walkie-talkie but a police scanner.

Reggie turned around to see what she had referred to, and spotted the black, rectangular device. He did as Amy had asked, and picked the scanner up. He turned it over several times in his hand as he inspected it.

"This is a police scanner," he said, not really understanding why Amy had been so hopeful.

"Yeah, I thought so," she said tentatively. "Turn it on. Maybe we can pick up some info."

Reggie fumbled with a few buttons before finally figuring out how to work the contraption. At first, all they were able to pick up was static, but after Reggie changed the frequency, they found what they were after.

A distorted, static-muffled voice came across the scanner. "All units in the vicinity of the Venice warehouse district, we have a code 3, I repeat a code 3. We have a confirmed code 8 and multiple reports of a code 6 George. Proceed with caution."

After hearing the codes called out, Amy floored the security car. The fight had already started without her. She was more frightened now than she could ever remember being. She felt her hands start to tremble, and she was having a hard time keeping them steady on the steering wheel.

"All right, I don't speak LA cop," Reggie said, trying to alleviate some of the tension he could see settling in on Amy's features. "You want to translate that for me?"

"Geez Reggie, you sit with your back to doors, and you don't know police codes. Just what kind of training does this agency of yours do?" she asked sarcastically.

She knew what Reggie was trying to do, and greatly appreciated the gesture, but her worry for Kalen was not going to be lessened until she was there watching his back.

"And just how much training has the LAPD given you on catching Elven serial killers?" Reggie jokingly asked.

"Point taken," Amy conceded. "A code 3 is an emergency call for all police in the area to proceed to the designated area with lights and sirens blazing. A code 8 means that a fire has been reported and a code 6 George means that shots have been fired and that it's possible gang activity. That's got to be Kalen and Royal T."

"How far away are we?" Reggie asked, the humor now lost.

"We should be there in ten to fifteen minutes," she replied, hoping it would not be too late.

Royal T and Kalen pulled into the vacant lot that housed the New Getty Villa Warehouse. The sounds of automatic weapons along with the heat and smoke of fire welcomed them. The chaotic scene was similar to war zones Royal T had spent time in while a member of the Army.

The big gang leader barely waited for the Suburban to come to a complete stop before he jumped out and went to retrieve his beloved RPG. Kalen was right on his heels. He had a good idea what was going on inside the burning warehouse.

Royal T whipped open the rear hatch and grabbed the case from inside. Shazz and Spider stood by the side of the Suburban, but were visibly shaken by the disturbing scene.

"I have to get inside. My crew needs me," Royal T said, his voice full of concern and buried just under the surface, Kalen could hear desperation as well.

Kalen could tell that the large Human was walking a tight edge between concern for his men and panic for what he might find once he did get inside.

A loud explosion rocked the vicinity of the warehouse, nearly knocking Kalen off his feet. The main entrance blew outward in a large ball of flame. What was even more disturbing was the charred Human leg that also came flying through the fiery entrance, and bounced off the SUV, landing at Royal T's feet.

Kalen could see that Royal T was shaken by what had just transpired. The big man was livid, and looked as if he was close to exploding himself. He reached out and grabbed Royal T's shoulder to draw the gang leader's attention away from the grisly visage of the burned limb.

"Come on, we have to find another way in," he said softly yet sternly.

He felt bad for the position Royal T had been put in, but Drè was in that warehouse and he simply did not have time to play wet-nurse to this large Human.

Royal T nodded in acknowledgement. He was as irate as he had ever been, but he needed to maintain control if he was going to avenge his men.

"We may be able to slip in unnoticed on the second floor," the gang leader reasoned.

He did not wait for an answer. Instead he grabbed the green case, stepped over the charred leg, and made his way to the other side of the warehouse.

Kalen chose not to follow the Human gang leader. He needed to find his own way in, and make his way to Drè. He could do nothing for the Humans that were trapped inside. The only thing he could do would be to find Drè Fao'lain and kill him.

# —Chapter 32

Seeing the Human explode in a flaming spray of crimson from the fireball had been exquisite. There were only a few of the intruders left for him to toy with, but Drè would punish them just as horrendously as the others. When he was finished with these last few insects, the deaths of the first couple of Humans would look merciful.

Right as he was about to release another killing blast, Drè froze as he was shown a disturbing new image from the Tree of Sacrifice. It was the image of Kalen Or'wain. The one Elf he wanted to kill above all others. The one Elf who had been his friend, his surrogate brother and, in his twisted maddened mind, his greatest betrayer.

All thoughts of taking his time to destroy the remaining Humans in the warehouse fled from his disturbed mind. He could only focus on Kalen. His revenge against the Elven people would start with the death of Kalen Or'wain. Once he was dispatched, there would be nothing left to stand in his way of completing the Ritual of the Dying Moon.

The sounds of the remaining four Humans' projectile weapons ceased as they ran out of ammunition. The tree protected him from their ridiculously mundane and archaic weapons, but he needed to get rid of those fools lest they interfere with his confrontation with Kalen the betrayer.

With the magical knowledge given to him from the Tree, Drè raised his hands over his head and clapped them together. They began glowing a dark red color. The air surrounding the magical tree and its Elven puppet began to hum as if it was being charged with electricity. The humming continued to grow louder until even the remaining strike team members at the other end of the warehouse could hear the annoying sound.

When the humming reached a fevered pitch, Drè brought his hands, which were still clasped together in a macabre imitation of being in prayer, in a long looping arc that resembled someone swinging an imaginary axe.

The last four members of the Down Hood Mob strike team looked on from their respective hiding place behind a pile of refuse in anticipation of whatever horror was going to befall them next. They did not have to wait long.

A bright, blood red beam of burning magical plasma came shooting out of Drè's hands as he made the swinging motion. The beam swept across the warehouse bisecting anything it came in contact with. It went through the refuse pile, and the Humans hiding behind it like a laser scythe.

It caught the first two team members right through their upper torsos. The beam cut and cauterized at the same time. It was such a quick clean cut, the unfortunate gang members' minds did not have time to register pain or process that the body was now dead. The two Humans froze in place before their bodies began separating along the cut lines, and fell to the floor. After a few more seconds, the legs toppled over as well.

A third team member had been squatting behind his two companions. The magical energy beam had sliced right through his head just under his nose. With his skull sliced open like an overripe cantaloupe, he fell, forward into the garbage pile. The top of the skull landed a few feet away from the last member of their squad causing him to lose all sense of reality, and begin screaming like a banshee.

That last member of the strike team had been the luckiest, if one could truly call him that. He had been lying flat on his stomach weeping out of shock and fright. The magical beam had slid right over the top of him leaving the gang member unharmed except for a few scorched hairs on the back of his head. The sight of his friend's half cooked brain sliding out of the sliced skull was too much for his already fragile mind to handle. Though he had not been physically injured, the damage done to his psyche would be irreparable.

From his vantage point up on the second floor, Royal T had witnessed the last scene of devastation that had finished off his crew. He could see that one was still alive, but from the sounds of the shrieks emanating from the horrified team member, Royal T knew the kid was as good as dead. He had seen mental breaks like that before, and it was never good.

He had made his way into the warehouse by stacking some crates on top of an old rusted out dumpster. He was able to climb the crates up to a busted out second floor window, which he quickly scrambled through, green case still in hand.

The air was acrid and smoky, and it initially hurt his lungs to breathe it in. He could see flashes of a fire higher up on the third floor, and he knew it was a matter of time before this old building went up like a tinderbox. That was okay though. With a quick kiss from his "baby", he would end this stand off.

The gang leader had not waited for Kalen after their brief exchange at the Suburban, and he had not been all that surprised when he realized that the Elf had also gone off alone. Detective Sommers was keeping strange bed fellows these days. He just hoped that fool knew enough to keep his head down, and stay out of the way when he decided to let his baby go to work.

His last soldier was still lying on the ground in a fetal position screaming like a lost child. He also saw the crazed figure that could only be the killer at the other end of the warehouse raise his hands in a similar gesture as before. Whatever kind of weapon that psycho had, he was about to use it again.

That was all the incentive Royal T needed. The screaming kid's mind was probably completely lost, but he was one of his soldiers, and did not deserve to die like that at the hands of some David Copperfield magician wannabe.

The RPG-7V was loaded and ready to go. He watched for a second and saw the crazed killer's hands begin to glow that same reddish hue. He knew his soldier had but mere seconds to live.

"Hey, you crazy Mother," Royal T yelled as loud as he could as he aimed the grenade launcher.

His loud baritone voice echoed throughout the warehouse. He was happy to see that he had caught the killer's attention.

"Try this on for size!" He finished squeezing the firing pin and releasing the grenade.

Kalen heard the gang leader's voice as it bounced around the warehouse in an echo. He had managed to find a rear entrance through a large sliding metal door. It had long ago been frozen into position by the elements of this realm, leaving a gap just large enough for him to lie on his stomach and slide through.

He had seen the magical attack that had killed the Humans of Royal T's crew. He was standing to the rear of Drè, and he was horrified and repulsed at the sight of the tree connected to Drè's body, feeding him power. Only through the perversion of the Shadowed Arts could something as beautiful as a tree of nature be so evilly twisted into a tool of destruction.

The nausea he had felt in the vehicle was nothing to what was raging through his system now. The whole concept of what Drè was doing was almost too much for him to comprehend. When he had first entered the Human realm, he had entertained thoughts of capturing Drè and returning him to their own realm to stand trial for his crimes and face justice for his actions. Now though, he knew that was nothing but a pipe dream. The only way for this madness to end would be for him to become the executioner and kill Drè Fao'lain for the betterment of both realms.

He unsheathed the general's sword, and prepared to make his stand when the echoing voice of Royal T caught him off guard. He watched as some sort of flaming projectile came flying at the crazed form of Drè. The next thing Kalen knew, he was being flung backwards onto his back with waves of intense heat from the backlash of the explosion washing over him.

Amy and Reggie pulled into the warehouse lot right next to the black Suburban. There were two frightened looking gang bangers sitting on the SUV's back bumper sharing a cigarette. From inside the warehouse she could hear someone screaming, and from off in the distance she could make out the sounds of approaching sirens.

"We don't have much time before the cavalry arrives," she said to Reggie as they both got out of the security car.

Reggie sniffed the air carried by the evening breeze and furrowed his brow. He had caught a faint whiff of burning plastic. He glanced at the warehouse and could see flames shooting through the roof. "We have less time than you know," said Reggie. "It's not gonna take long before this old, decrepit building goes up in smoke and collapses in on itself."

Amy pulled out the Glock pistol as she approached the two figures at the SUV. She was surprised to see they were the same two that had met her and Kalen at the hotel. This time however, they were not the brash and cocky gang members full of confidence. Instead they looked like two extremely frightened children that wanted nothing more than to go home to their mommies.

"Where's Royal T and Kalen?" she demanded as she closed the distance.

"They went inside ..." Shazz answered, but he did not get the opportunity to elaborate as a loud explosion rocked the warehouse.

Amy did not wait for any further explanation. She looked over at Reggie, and they both took off running at a full sprint to the entrance of the warehouse. The door had been blown to pieces, and the area right through the entrance had scorch marks as well. When she stepped through, Amy was welcomed by a sight straight out of Dante's vision of Hell.

Royal T was shocked at what he had just seen. The explosive he had fired hit some sort of invisible barrier. He had seen it flash briefly when the grenade detonated against it. It appeared to be a protective bubble around the killer and the strange looking tree.

He had needed to shield his eyes from the flash of the explosions, and when he was able to reopen them, he was confused and angered. The killer appeared to be completely unaffected by the missile. Whatever that barrier was, it had shielded his intended target so completely that the killer had not even felt the heat.

Royal T looked over at the green case that had housed the RPG-7V and saw he still had three grenade missiles left. He had no idea how strong the protective shell was, but he was going to try and find out.

He quickly grabbed another grenade and loaded it into the firing tube of the RPG-7V. Normally the use of this weapon worked better with two people operating it. He did not have that luxury. However, he did have experience using this weapon and it did not take him long to reload.

Once the RPG-7V was ready to go, he did not waste any time. He aimed directly for the crazed serial killer's chest, and with a slow steady exhalation of breath, he squeezed the firing mechanism once again.

There was a loud whooshing sound as the grenade was ejected from the weapon and sent hurtling towards its intended target. The breath Royal T had just let out was quickly sucked back in as he watched, awaiting the results of his second shot. He still had two grenades left, but he hoped he would not have to use them.

Drè had been rocked hard by the first explosion. He had been protected by the same magic that had saved him from the many bullets that had been fired his way, but the concussive force had left him somewhat stunned. His ears were ringing, and in the depths of his mind, he felt the power of the Tree of Sacrifice retreat ever so slightly.

The magical shield that had surrounded him and the evil Tree had absorbed the force of the blast, and then tried to disperse the energy. It had succeeded, but at a price. The link between Drè and his source of the Shadowed Arts had weakened. He could not feel the connection as strongly as before, and this set off alarms throughout the demented Elf's senses.

He was vaguely aware two new Humans had entered the warehouse. He did not know anything about them other than neither one was Kalen Or'wain. The Tree had stopped feeding him images for the time being, so it was up to him to handle this new crisis on his own.

He had been able to discern the general location from where the explosive projectile had been launched. When he turned his attention to the spot on the second floor, he saw yet another Human. That Human had now become his main target. The two other Humans would just have to wait their turns to die. In the back of his mind, he was alarmed that Kalen had yet to show himself.

He could not waste time trying to figure out Kalen's motives and movements. He needed to eliminate his immediate threat before moving on to the next. He blocked out the ringing in his pointed ears, and called up the powers of the Shadowed Arts. When the magical energy had filled his being, he opened his eyes and prepared to send it forth on a new path of destruction.

What he saw however, was not the Human with the dangerous weapon crouched on the second floor waiting to be destroyed; he saw another of the flaming missiles headed straight for him. He did not have time to unleash the magical fire like he had intended, nor did he have time to throw up any more magic to help defend his already battered shield. All he could do was close his eyes, and turn his head before the explosion hit.

Kalen had just recovered from the effects of the first grenade explosion when the second one impacted. He was actually better equipped to handle the second blast as he was already lying in a prone position in a pile of old, mildewed boxes. The heat had momentarily stolen his breath. He had taken several deep gulps of air in an attempt to refill his lungs with oxygen.

He was on the verge of trying his luck at standing back up when the second grenade detonated. Another furnace blast of super heated air struck him in the face, once again stealing his breath. He started to feel light headed from oxygen deprivation, and he knew he was seconds away from losing consciousness.

Yellow and white spots appeared in front of his eyes. He fought the effects with whatever strength he could muster, and was finally able to suck in one large intake of hot air. It sounded like a large groan, but it had done the trick, and he remained awake.

Through the dissipating smoke, he could see Drè still standing. The explosion had not reached him, but Kalen could tell that he had at least been affected by the force of the blast.

Drè looked haggard, and his skin had a pasty gray color to it. Kalen could see that he was swaying from side to side as well. The explosive missiles Royal T was using may not be causing any real physical damage, but they were definitely taking their toll. He hoped it would only be a matter of time before Drè's magical defenses failed. Once that happened, he would have the opportunity he needed to make his stand, and take his former friend out.

He was able to find his center of gravity, and get back to his feet, and he was surprised to find he still had the general's sword gripped tightly in his hand. He still felt the aftereffects of the explosions. He sheathed his sword and stumbled as he began looking for a better hiding place.

He settled on a stack of old wooden crates. He half walked and half crawled to his destination. From this vantage point, he could see Drè standing off to the right. He was facing Royal T as the gang leader was hurriedly preparing his "baby" for another shot.

Amy had seen Kalen as he staggered out from behind the killer, and limped his way to some old crates. She wanted to yell out to him, but did not want to alert Drè to Kalen's presence. She could not see up to the next floor, but she had to assume that Royal T was the one up there raining down explosives.

The two new explosions from the grenades had set off several new fires around the warehouse. The smoke was getting thicker and blacker by the second. The roof was almost completely ablaze by this time. She could hear the sirens of the approaching police and fire departments as they closed in. Whatever Kalen was going to do, he better make it quick. Once the LAPD showed up, he might lose his chance for a one-on-one confrontation with his adversary.

Royal T could not believe the psycho was still standing. The grenade had hit the barrier, and caused the same flashing effect as before, only this time not as bright. He was encouraged that whatever shield was down there, it was beginning to fade. This led to the gang leader hurriedly grabbing the next grenade in line and fitting it into the barrel of the RPG-7V.

He decided to change his strategy with this shot. Instead of aiming directly at the killer, he decided to try and place the grenade right at the killer's feet. He hoped in this manner, a least some of the explosion may be able to penetrate through the barrier and cause some damage.

Royal T once again brought the RPG-7V to bear. He carefully aimed, took one long steadying breath, and squeezed the trigger. The grenade came flying out of the tube, leaving a fiery trail as it sped towards its target. This time however, the grenade was not meant for the killer, but for the concrete floor right in front of him.

The second blast had weakened Drè's connection to the Tree of Sacrifice and his link to the Shadowed Arts considerably. It was all he could do to keep the evil magic centered within himself to try for a counterattack.

The roots were still attached to his back, but he had felt them withdraw slightly after the last explosion. The magical barrier that had been erected to protect him had almost faltered, and was now all but gone. Though he had been unharmed, this time he had felt the heat as it had seeped through gaps in the barrier.

He could tell his strength was starting to wane as well. Even though the Tree was feeding him magical energy, it was not an unlimited source. He felt weak, and he could also feel the perspiration as it began running down his face.

He was so lost in concentration that he never saw the third missile coming. His mental link to the Tree had been severed after the first blast, and so this time he had no warning.

The aim of the missile was true, and it detonated a mere three feet away from Drè. The already depleted magical barrier failed completely as it tried to absorb the explosive's energy. It had been able to deflect just enough of the grenade's explosive power away from Drè and probably saved his life, but it could not deflect it all.

With the protective shield down, and his concentration focused inward, Drè suddenly became very susceptible to what he had thought was a primitive weapon. Though not full force, the explosion blew up from the floor and straight into Drè. He was blown off his feet and thrown ten feet through the air. The tentacle-like roots were ripped from his body in the process.

He crash-landed in a heap, up against the back wall of the warehouse. The pain from the sudden separation from the Tree and the burning heat of the fiery explosion was excruciating. The shock of having his psychic link to the Shadowed Arts severed so forcibly left him briefly immobilized.

Seeing the barrier had failed, and the grenade had been able to take the killer out, Royal T let out a loud victory shout. He kissed the RPG-7V lovingly like a father would do to one of his beloved children.

The gang leader had mistakenly thought the serial killer was dead. After firing the grenade that had brought the barrier down, Royal T had quickly loaded the last of his missiles into the RPG-7V just in case. He was going to take nothing for granted, and so he had prepared for every contingency. His former drill instructor would have been proud.

Not fully understanding what had happened, but safe in the knowledge that he was still alive, Drè heard the loud whooping from his would-be assassin. He closed his eyes, and tried to find the link to the Shadowed Arts at his core. It was gone though. He had lost contact with it the second he had been separated from the Tree.

He rolled over onto his back and could see the large Human now standing in celebration of his perceived victory on the second floor. He may not have use of his magic for the time being, but he still had other weapons at his disposal. He still had the sword that had also belonged to his father, and the dagger was sheathed at his back.

He crawled back to the front of the Tree of Sacrifice. It had been untouched by the Human's archaic weapon. He used the Tree for support, and pulled himself back up to a standing position. He reached around to the small of his back, and removed the jagged dagger that had been so helpful in the removal of his victim's hearts. Then stepping out away from the Tree to better judge the distance, he threw the blade with practiced accuracy at the unaware Human gang leader.

The dagger caught Royal T in mid shout. It buried itself to the hilt in his neck. The shout was quickly turned into a gurgle as the gang leader's ruined throat filled with blood. His victory had been short lived, and Royal T knew he was dead as he fell to his knees. In his last act of defiance before his body bled out, he fired the last grenade in the vicinity of his murderer. He never saw the results as his lifeless body flipped over the handrail, and fell to the concrete floor below.

Drè realized his mistake too late. He saw the missile hurtling in his direction. He ran toward the front of the warehouse, and feeling the heat of the grenade as it flew past, he pitched himself onto the hard floor as the explosive found another target and detonated.

The ensuing explosion was far too loud, Drè noticed. He suddenly had a horrible feeling of panic followed by the worst pain he had ever known. He was completely paralyzed by the unimaginable agony. He only had strength enough to turn his head, but what he saw was more terrible than any physical pain he had endured.

The Tree of Sacrifice had suffered the brunt of the grenade's explosive force. Its already twisted trunk was scorched and cracked. He watched helplessly as the blue flames that contained the hearts began to blink and fade. The once snake-like roots were shriveled and burned. The already crazy Elf tried frantically to get to his feet, but it was too late. The now-dead Human's weapon had already done its damage.

He looked on as the blue flames went out completely and the ruined tree began to dissolve and then sink back into the depths. The ground trembled violently as if the very thought of having to accept the evil tree back into the bowels of the Earth was causing that same Earth to wretch.

The already decrepit and fire-damaged warehouse began to crumble. He was absolutely beside himself. All his hard work was crumbling before his eyes just like the warehouse. The revenge he so desperately wanted to deliver was no more, and it was all because of Kalen Or'wain. He knew the other Elf was there somewhere.

"Show yourself, Kalen the Bold," the maddened Elf shouted out as he turned in a complete circle to take in the entire building. "I know you are here."

Seeing her chance to finish this once and for all, Amy stepped out from the rubble pile she had been hiding behind. She raised the pistol, and prepared to fire. Before she was able to get off a shot though, a familiar voice stayed her hand.

"No Amy," Kalen said as he walked out to the center of the warehouse and faced Drè. "This fight is mine."

Amy lowered her weapon, and watched as the two Elves squared off. The warehouse ceiling had partially caved in from the fire and earthquake that the magical tree's destruction had caused. The whole place would be coming down before long. She could hear the sirens as they filled the vacant lot right outside.

"Come on, Reggie," she said as she walked by the faux FBI Agent on her way out of the warehouse. She desperately wanted to stay, but she knew this was Kalen's mission. She also knew that she was more valuable to the Elf outside. "We need to buy Kalen some time by running interference."

Reggie nodded, understanding. This fight was beyond their control. With a final look back at the two Elves, he and Amy walked out of the warehouse.

# CHAPTER 33

Kalen stared at his one-time friend in pity for what he had become. That pity would not stay his hand, however. He meant to kill Drè Fao'lain, and to emphasize that point, he slowly and methodically drew the sword given to him by General Brandy'wine from the scabbard at his side. He raised the sword in a two-handed grip, and prepared to attack.

Drè watched Kalen's aggressive gesture with the sword, and actually began to laugh. He pulled the only weapon he had left, his father's sword, out of its own sheath, and held it loosely at his side.

"I always knew it would come down to this," Drè said knowingly.

"I have to put you out of your misery, Drè," Kalen responded sadly.

"Oh, you can come and try, fool," Drè spat as he gritted his teeth and charged.

Kalen met the charge with one of his own. The two Elves raced towards each other, swords at the ready. Drè slowed enough to bring his sword to bear and he swung the curved blade in a wide arc towards Kalen's head.

Being the trained soldier he was, Kalen saw the move coming and was ready for it. He lifted his own sword to block the wild swing. He caught Drè's blade on his own, and for a moment, the two swords were crossed and interlocked together at their hilts.

They stared at each other through the locked hilts of their respective swords; the growing hatred in Kalen's eyes was matched only by the madness that was glowing brightly in Drè's.

"It is time for you to join your father in failure. It is time for you to die, Kalen Or'wain," the insane Elf literally spat out, as if the very taste of Kalen's name in his mouth was poison.

"You first," Kalen pushed through clenched teeth before unlocking his sword and taking a step back.

The maneuver left Drè off balanced, and he attempted to compensate by making an awkward lunge at Kalen's midsection. Kalen was able to take a step to his right, and parry the sword thrust easily.

It was then that Kalen noticed the warehouse was almost completely filled with smoke. The entire building was ablaze, and it was only a matter of time before the smoke would hinder his ability to fight. He could even hear the structure start to creak and groan as the foundation continued to weaken.

Unfortunately for Kalen, a large chunk of the burning roof fell to the floor a few feet away from him. Drè took that opportunity to press the attack anew with a wicked slash at Kalen's midsection.

His Royal Guard training saved him. Kalen was able to turn into the slice and lessen its effectiveness. He still felt the stinging bite of a cut as Drè's sword bit into the flesh at his side. The wound was not life threatening, but much to Kalen's chagrin, it was bleeding profusely.

The heat from the multiple fires was starting to become a problem. Both Elves were sweating freely. Kalen tried to wipe his sweaty hands on his leggings. He was having a hard time maintaining a decent grip on his sword, and any slip at that crucial juncture could and would prove fatal.

He took several steps back from his adversary. He slipped off his uniform coat one arm at a time; transferring his sword to each hand as he maneuvered the coat off and let it drop to the floor.

Drè laughed almost hysterically, "You always did like to do things with a flourish."

Kalen did not bother with a response. The time for games was at an end. He meant to kill Drè, and end any future threat immediately. He might die here in this inferno, but if that were to be his fate, he was going to take Drè with him.

Kalen could feel the blood still seeping from the cut at his side. He was running out of time. If he was going to stop Drè once and for all, it would have to be soon. If he became too weak from loss of blood, he might fail, and that was an option he had no intention of allowing.

It was time to put a stop to this game of insanity. Kalen knew he could not match Drè's strength with magic, but he was Kalen the Bold, Captain of the Royal Guard, and by all accounts one of the finest swordsmen in his realm. This macabre dance he and Drè were doing had run its course.

He set his weight, and moved into a fighting stance. He held his sword in both hands with the hilt even with his eyes. He shifted his weight from foot to foot in an attempt to get a feel for the terrain as he had been taught to do. Even though the warehouse was coming down around them, it was time for calm. Kalen knew how impetuous Drè was, and the crazed Elf did not wait long before he charged.

Drè was not a skilled swordsman, but his wildness and unpredictability made him dangerous. The Elf was completely mad as well, which only added to the level of danger. His failure to complete the ritual, and the sight of all his hard work and dedication, the Tree of Sacrifice – the embodiment of his power – be destroyed, had pushed the already mentally unstable Elf all the way over the edge into the abyss of insanity.

Kalen slipped into a comfortable rhythm, blocking each of Drè's clumsy slashes. Sparks ignited from the blades every time they met. The clang of Elven steel rang throughout the burning building. If one could have seen the dark silhouettes performing their deadly sword dance against the fiery backdrop of the warehouse, they might have found the scene to be incredibly beautiful, and definitely mesmerizing.

Kalen bided his time, watching for Drè to make a mistake. When that time came, he did not miss.

Drè was tiring quickly. The use of the Shadowed Arts, his burns from the explosion, and the emotional drain had begun to take their toll. He could feel his strength beginning to ebb, and he knew he could not hold out much longer.

"You cannot win, Kalen Or'wain," he warned his most hated adversary.

Kalen did not respond. He was focused solely on the other Elf's movements. He was waiting for any sign that might give away what Drè's next move would be. Kalen had returned to his balanced stance with his sword held in front of his face at eye level. His elbows were pointed straight out. When he saw Drè flinch, he knew what was coming next.

Drè faked an overhead slash meant to draw Kalen's defenses up to block before having his head cleaved in two, and then quickly brought his father's sword around in the opposite direction in an attempt to slice open Kalen's chest which had been left unguarded.

Kalen saw the ruse for what it was, and was not fooled. He motioned his sword upward to make Drè think he had fallen for his trick. When Drè began reversing his swing to bring the sword low, Kalen brought his own sword in a downward arc, and blocked the deadly slice. He then took one step backwards to release the pressure on the sword from his parry. Then, in one swift motion, Kalen brought his sword up in a circular movement all the way around, and slashed with deadly accuracy at Drè's exposed midsection. He did not stop his slice until he had brought the sword all the way through and then up to his shoulder like a baseball hitter following through with their swing.

Drè's reaction to the fatal wound was not immediate. He stood motionless before letting his own sword fall from his hand to ring solemnly as it landed on the concrete floor. He opened his mouth to protest against the unfairness of it all, but the only sound that came out was a blood filled cough that sent red spittle dribbling down the corners of his mouth. He had no magic to draw on to sustain him this time, and he slowly fell to his knees.

Kalen remembered the seemingly fatal wound that his own father had inflicted on Drè just before he succumbed to his own injuries. The disemboweling slash that Drè had received would prove fatal to anyone else, but Kalen needed to make sure. This madness could not be allowed to continue, and the threat to the Elven race needed to be stopped right there.

Kalen stepped behind the kneeling form of Drè Fao'lain. The fire was raging in fury all around him. He knew what must be done, but the memories of their shared childhood held back the killing blow. Then, remembering his duty, he gripped the sword tightly.

"Goodbye Drè," he whispered softly into the rapidly heating air of the enflamed building before swinging the sword straight across, severing Drè Fao'lain's head.

The now lifeless body of his one-time friend toppled over onto its side. The decapitated head rolled into a wall of flame that had engulfed the entire structure. Kalen stared at the headless body, and then at the blood still dripping from the sword. He wept as the warehouse began to collapse around him.

The fire had almost totally consumed the roof, and Amy watched as pieces began to fall inward. She knew Kalen was in that inferno somewhere and it took everything she had to refrain from charging into the fire, and dragging the frustrating Elf back out.

The LAPD and the fire department had arrived at the same time. Due to the size of the conflagration, she did not have to stop the police officers from bursting into the warehouse with guns blazing like she had thought. The firemen on the other hand, had set up shop quickly, and were preparing to make their way into the fire to find any possible survivors. She did not bother trying to stop them. She did not have the strength left to fight.

Reggie could see the haggard look on her face and the smears of dirt on her cheeks caused by the tears running from her eyes. He reached over and grabbed her hand, and held it tenderly in his own. She looked up and smiled.

"You big softy," she said, fighting back more tears.

"Yeah, Yeah, just don't tell anyone. I have a reputation to uphold," he said softly, trying to comfort her.

"Sommers? I should have known I'd find you here," the familiar voice of Detective Killion called from behind them.

Amy groaned audibly. He was about the last person she wanted to see. It never dawned on her this was now a major crime scene, and she, as an officer on administrative leave, could not be here.

Killion could see that the fire in Amy's eyes matched the intensity of the fire raging in the warehouse. He chose not to challenge her. Instead he asked, "Was it him? Did you stop the killer?"

Amy looked at Detective Killion sadly and answered, "It was him, and he was stopped, but not by us."

Killion did not understand her cryptic response, and was about to inquire further when Amy and Reggie rudely brushed past him. The old detective figured he already had enough to worry about this evening, and let them go.

A loud commotion near the entrance had caught Amy's and Reggie's attention. There were shouts from the firemen, and calls for medics began ringing throughout the night. Amy ignored Killion as she walked past. She began picking up the pace when she saw the firemen bringing someone out, and it was not long before she was in a full sprint.

She arrived just in time to see the firemen help carry out a disheveled looking form between them. The figure lifted his head up, and looked directly at her. The sight of those crystal blue orbs was the most beautiful thing she had ever seen. Without thinking about what she was doing, she ran to the Elf who was now standing on his own, and frantically wrapped her arms around him. She began to cry into his chest. Kalen felt the sobs, and held her tightly.

They loosened their grips enough so they could transition their relieved embrace to that of a passionate kiss. Once they were able to release their emotional distress in that kiss, Amy stepped back and looked at the Elf. She could see the blood at his side, and knew he would need medical attention.

"Is it over?" she asked, looking into Kalen's beautiful yet pained blue eyes.

Kalen stared back at her. He had to swallow down the lump of emotion forming in his throat. He thought about Drè's lifeless body lying on the floor of the warehouse. Not trusting himself to be able to speak, he nodded his head, yes.

# —Chapter 34

The gash in Kalen's side was not as serious as he first believed, but it still bought him a night in the hospital for what the Human healer had called observation. He took the opportunity to catch up on some much needed and deserved sleep. Amy did not leave his side the entire time.

After Kalen had been taken to the hospital, Reggie decided three was a crowd, and he made himself scarce. He promised to return to pick Kalen up and return him to the place where he could cross back over to his own realm in three days time.

When Kalen was discharged early the next morning, he left with Amy to spend his final two days in the Human realm recuperating with a different type of bed rest at Amy's apartment. Once again, she never left his side. In fact, the two barely left the apartment.

After the warehouse had caved in, and burned itself out, the LAPD crime lab forensics team scanned the area for any kind of relative evidence. They discovered traces of all ten members of the Down Hood Mob strike team including the one member that had remained lying on the floor screaming until he was consumed by the fire. Royal T's body was also found horribly burned with the jagged dagger still wedged in his throat. The dagger was also matched up with the evidence from the unsolved murders, and was found to be one of the murder weapons. Lastly, the forensic team discovered a headless corpse that was burnt beyond any recognition. No head was ever found nor was the body ever properly identified.

There had been no sign of Shazz and Spider. When Amy and Reggie had fled from the burning building, the two gang bangers were long gone. The screams of their comrade and the oncoming sirens of a massive police force was not something they had cared to stick around for.

Amy's phone rang repeatedly during her two-day romp with Kalen. The captain had tried countless times to get in touch with her about her being suspended and yet still on an active crime scene. Finally after never getting a response, Captain Mulligan left an angry message that said if Amy did not return his call by the end of that day, she need not bother with ever coming back. After everything she had been through, and after the time she had spent with Kalen, she no longer cared.

In the early afternoon of the third day, Reggie returned to take Kalen home. He had almost fully recovered from his own injuries suffered at the hands of Drè Fao'lain and his magical fire. He looked much as he had that first night Kalen had met him, dressed once again in a dark suit and coat. Kalen on the other hand, had gone native.

Reggie had to laugh when he saw the Elf lounging on Amy's couch dressed in Nike windpants and a white, Los Angels Raiders t-shirt. Kalen had lost his coat in the fire and his uniform shirt and leggings had been destroyed by either the fire or the wound in his side. The only belongings he had left were his boots, sword, and the enchanted medallion that would open the dimensional door to allow him to cross back over to his home.

Even though Kalen was happy to see his Human guide doing so well, the mood in Amy's apartment was still somber. This was the moment he had been dreading for the last two days, but he could not deny that it was time. He was ready to go home.

Reggie drove Kalen and Amy back to the Angeles National Forest where the Elf had first arrived. They tried to keep the mood light on the ride over, but an underlying sadness dampened everyone's spirits, and the drive was over all too fast for Amy's liking.

Reggie parked his car in almost the exact same spot as he had on that first night. The three walked through the trees with Reggie leading the way and Kalen and Amy following close behind, hand-in-hand.

It had been raining steadily that first night, but now the sun was shining brightly, and the forest was alive with its vibrant light. Kalen could not help but feel invigorated by the beautiful trees, and he began to feel homesick.

"This is the one," Reggie said, patting the trunk of a large ash tree.

Kalen walked up to the tree, and gave it a good once over. He honestly did not recognize the tree, but things had been so crazy when he had originally crossed over that his confusion was understandable.

He walked over to the wide, solidly built Human, and reached his hand out. "Thank you, Reggie, for everything. I could not have asked for a better guide and friend to help me see my mission through."

Reggie grabbed the Elf's hand in his own meaty, paw-like hand, and squeezed it tightly. Reggie had never considered himself an emotional man, but the large lump in his throat that kept him from responding would have led one to believe otherwise. He released Kalen's hand, and turned his back so his companions would not see him wipe away a tear.

Kalen then turned to Amy. She did not even bother trying to conceal her tears. They shared a tight embrace and a long tender kiss before separating.

"Will I ever see you again?" she asked sadly.

"I do not know, Amy Sommers, but I certainly hope so," he answered feeling just as sad over having to say goodbye.

Amy smiled at him, knowing that it was time. "You better get going before Reggie breaks down and starts blubbering like a school girl."

"Leave it to you, Sommers, to really capture the mood of the moment," Reggie said, trying to hold back a laugh.

At Reggie's comment, they all shared a good chuckle, and then, when the sound of their laughter quieted, Kalen walked up to the tree. He removed the pendant Luna Caer'run had given him, and read the enchantment inscribed on the back aloud.

As soon as Kalen finished the magical phrases, the dimensional door began to appear. First a crack in the trunk appeared, and then as the crack widened, white light began spilling out. The doorway grew until it was large enough for Kalen to step through. He turned one last time to look at his new Human friends. On a whim, he tossed the magical amulet to Amy who caught it easily.

"Tà cier`sierra," Kalen said in his own language as he no longer had possession of the pendant.

Had Amy slipped the amulet around her own neck, she would have heard Kalen say, "I love you."

Without any further delay, Kalen stepped into the magical doorway and went home.

As soon as Kalen stepped into the tree, the doorway disappeared without a trace of evidence that it had ever been there. Reggie and Amy were left alone with their thoughts. They stared at the tree, which was now quite ordinary, for several long minutes before deciding to return to the car.

As they began walking down the path, Reggie turned to Amy. "So, Sommers, I hear you're in the market for a new career."

"Yeah, it seems I've worn out my welcome with the LAPD," she said, not really sounding all that disappointed.

"How would you like a job?" he asked, surprising her.

"You mean with you and the Agency?" she asked back, shocked.

They had arrived back at Reggie's car as Amy asked her question. He answered by raising his eyebrows and smiling slyly. She smiled in return, and nodded her head, yes. Then they both got in the car, and drove back to Los Angeles.

# About the Author

*Shawn Oetzel* was born and raised in Central Illinois where he still lives with his wife, three kids, and their frustratingly lovable pet pooches, Hemingway and Molly. When not working or writing his next project, Shawn can be found attending his children's many extracurricular activities, or tucked away in his favorite corner at home, losing himself in the pages of another good book.

*Dying Moon* is Shawn's first novel, originally published in 2009 by LBF Books. His second novel, *The Agency*, is the sequel to *Dying Moon*, and was published by Belfire Press in 2012.

A third novel, a young adult work titled *The Adventures of Captain Kitchen*, was published by Belfire Press in 2013.

Shawn has always dreamed of being a superhero, knight, or a writer. He is ecstatic he has made good on at least one of those endeavors.